ONLY GENTLEMEN CAN PLAY

Also by Hugh McLeave

Only Gentlemen Can Play

HUGH McLEAVE

Harcourt Brace Jovanovich, Inc.
New York

Printed in the United States of America

Library of Congress Cataloging in Publication Data

McLeave, Hugh.
  Only gentlemen can play.

  I. Title.
PZ4.M16350n [PR6063.A249] 823′.9′14 73-21928
ISBN 0-15-169940-2

First edition
B C D E

McLeave

I   In the Net

The life of a secret agent is dangerous enough, but the life of the double agent is infinitely more dangerous. If anyone balances on a swinging tight-rope it is he, and a single slip must send him crashing to his doom.

SIR JOHN MASTERMAN
from *The Double-Cross System*

1 PROLOGUE

Moscow, October, 1959

Everything seemed petrified in the leaden clarity of the atmosphere. There was that special Muscovite stillness that forecast the first snow of hard winter. From the high window of the Kremlin Palace, Comrade Lora Ekaterina Trusova could discern the stumpy silhouette of Moscow University five miles away, with the gilded star that Stalin had decreed for the city's most imposing buildings. In the foreground, the garish onion cupolas of St. Basil's Cathedral appeared daubed on the livid sky with a palette knife. Across the Moskva River, in front of the British Embassy, the embankment lights flared.

Lora strained to catch the voices in the adjoining room. Her countrymen from the Ministry of Foreign Trade were still wrangling with the British delegation. In a moment or two they must begin to break up the session and that would signal her cue; quickly, she made up her face, caking the powder over her salient cheekbones thickly enough to betray the eventual tear tracks. She had rehearsed the part well, yet felt nervous, like an actress waiting for the first-night curtain.

As though her tension had somehow penetrated the thick walls, she heard shouting from the next room. Suddenly, the massive door burst open. A phalanx of Russians emerged to push straight past her with none of their usual courtesies; behind them trailed the members of the British Board of Trade mission, their heads shaking in disbelief and dismay. Spotting Patrick Holder among them, Lora crossed the room to greet him, "Which way did they go?" he asked with a grin.

She ignored the quip. Englishmen like this foppish, effete public-school product seemed to express everything in terms of inane humor. "Have you had a quarrel?" she inquired.

"Nothing serious." Holder shrugged. "We finally had to tell your compatriots that there's a limit to the amount of caviar, crab and vodka that even bloated capitalists can consume in exchange for electrical equipment, chemicals and drugs."

3

"Does this mean that you will have to go home?" she said, putting anxiety into her question.

"Because of a few impolite noises?" He shook his head. "Anyway, it's as much as our job's worth to leave without some form of trade agreement. But let's forget work. I'm looking forward to watching Ulanova and Yuri Zhdanov at the Bolshoi tonight. Have you seen *Giselle?*"

Her expression grew sad. "No, I will have to go another time."

"But I thought you wanted so badly to come with us." Holder studied her more closely; she dabbed at her eyes with a handkerchief. "You've been crying, Lora. What's wrong?"

"It's nothing . . . my brother . . . he's in trouble with the authorities."

"Serious trouble?"

"He's a student at Moscow University. . . . You know how high-spirited students are . . . he borrowed his professor's car. Now, they accuse him of stealing it. . . . For him it is the end of his career. . . . Maybe I shall lose my job, too."

"But if he explains, and the professor doesn't bring charges . . ."

"They treat such behavior very seriously in the Soviet Union," she said. "I have to go and help him."

"Can I do anything?" he said, on impulse.

"If you could come with me, I would be so grateful," she whispered. He nodded. "I have the Intourist car here in the Kremlin." As he followed her to the black ZIL by the palace door, she sighed; she had cleared the first obstacle.

The driver already knew the route. Along Kalinina, down Arbat to Smolensk Square. There, in that gray barracks, her boss, Colonel Sergei Antonovich Kudriatov, had briefed her, even showing her Holder's *zapiski* from the mammoth card index in Machovaya Street. How, she wondered, had they garnered that fat dossier on an English MP paying his first visit to the Soviet Union? They had recorded everything: his childhood in the manor house at Cheltenham; his schooling at Eton and Cambridge; his House of Commons speeches on the Suez aggression and the Hungarian counterrevolutionary movement, on the improvement of East-West relations. He had edged into Parliament in 1954 in a by-election, but had retained the Tory seat at the recent general election. He would inevitably slide,

4

fellow MP's predicted, from back to front benches and a junior ministry; his choice as deputy leader of this trade mission seemed to bear out their forecasts.

However, his personal rather than political history had first intrigued Comrade Trusova's bosses. At forty, he seemed happily married to a girl he had met at his university. They had a son and a daughter. No one these days linked Holder with the dubious Cambridge circle in which Guy Burgess and Donald Maclean had moved and begun their conversion to Communism and espionage. Now in Moscow, Burgess had contributed to Holder's *zapiski,* not only noting his Marxist ideals at Cambridge, but also his penchant for fairhaired, male undergraduates. "An AC-DC type," Burgess had written, with a footnote: "Personal experience." Lora had queried the slang expression. "A bourgeois Anglo-Saxon euphemism," Kudriatov had explained. "To put it indelicately, if you plug him into any type of circuit, he lights up." And he flashed those yellow teeth with their stainless-steel prosthesis. "You need have no fear, Lora Ekaterina, he will not even try to hold your hand." And Holder had not, during the two months she had spent, as an ostensible Intourist guide and interpreter, winning his confidence.

The ZIL crossed the river, turned down Berezhkovskaya Embankment, and went through tree-lined avenues to the Lenin Hills. At the monolithic complex of the university they bore right. "That is where my brother, Alex, lives," Lora remarked, pointing out a low block of flats on the Rublevskoe Road.

The hubbub from the ground-floor flat met them in the hall; they entered to find a couple of dozen students moving demurely through the heat and the stuffiness of cigarette smoke to rock-'n'-roll music from a record player; others were chatting and drinking champagne. Alex played his bit part well, running over to give Lora a fraternal kiss and crying, "It's all settled. Feodorov wouldn't press charges and talked the police out of reporting me. So we're celebrating." He quashed Holder's suggestion of returning to attend the ballet and dragged them into the room to introduce his student friends. Lora recognized many of them who, like herself, worked in the Lubyanka building. Kudriatov, the oldest man there, pumped Holder's hand until he winced when Alex presented him as his best friend and a lecturer in philology.

"Fine work, Lora Ekaterina," Kudriatov hissed at her. She al-

5

most felt sorry for this Englishman. Colonel Kudriatov invariably reminded her of a well-dressed bear, or someone padded up for ice hockey. His crew-cut hair, square jutting jaw, slow Siberian speech—everything suggested the muzhik in city clothes. Yet she had no illusions. To dupe, damn and destroy this bourgeois they could not have chosen better.

In rapid tempo, glasses were filling and emptying. With each new draught of sweetish Georgian champagne, Kudriatov proposed another toast: to Alex and the happy conclusion of his escapade; to the police, may they turn gangrenous and rot; to Anglo-Soviet friendship and peaceful co-operation; to the British Conservative party; to Gospodin Robert Patrick Holder, who generously tendered a hand to a Soviet friend in need.

Lora noticed that the toasts were taking effect. Liquor and the heat had flushed Holder's face; by now he appeared too drunk to observe that most of the so-called students were filtering out of the room. Kudriatov signaled to Vladimir, a fair-haired Ukrainian member of his team. The youth picked up a guitar and began strumming and singing. First, he intoned a plaintive Russian folk song, then started to chant in falsetto, lilting English:

> "Some may talk of Harrow,
> Some of Rugby, too.
> But we'll row together,
> And swear by the best of schools . . ."

Catching the garbled words, Holder lifted his head. "But that's the Eton boating song," he cried.

"Yes," said Vladimir. "I learned it from Guy Burgess."

"Guy Burgess!"

"You know him?"

"Of course. I met him at Cambridge more than twenty years ago."

Vladimir made room for him on the couch. They chatted about Burgess, who had fled to Russia with Maclean eight years before to escape arrest and trial. Kudriatov kept plying them with champagne and toasts. He gave them half an hour to get acquainted before proffering a final toast; winking at Lora, he raised his glass to the success of the trade talks. She watched Holder drain the glass. Suddenly, he mopped his brow; he ran a finger around his collar, then attempted to

6

rise. His legs took him several steps toward the door before they yielded and he pitched forward on his face at her feet.

"Lora Ekaterina, you do not have to stay," Kudriatov whispered. But even now that she had begun to understand the end of the plot, she waited; revulsion, or fascination, retained her in that living room.

Two men humped the slack figure into the bedroom to undress and dump it on the bed. Stripping off his clothes, Vladimir climbed in beside the unconscious Holder. Arc lights beamed on both men as the young Russian manipulated Holder from one obscene posture to another, holding each pose long enough to allow the two men with cameras to shoot dozens of photographs.

In the small kitchen, improvised as a darkroom, another team developed the rolls of film. Before the negatives had dried, Kudriatov was scanning them against a yellow screen, his teeth clicking with approbation. Standing at his side, Lora heard him murmur, *"V seti, v seti"* ("In the net, in the net").

"The fruits of your first assignment, Lora Ekaterina," Kudriatov said, handing her the pictures.

Mesmerized, Lora gazed at them, her mind spinning with confused ideas. She was a good Communist, with six years in the Young Communist League, nearly a year in the party; she had congratulated herself on being selected by Kudriatov for training with the Ministry of State Security, the KGB; she had passed through the school for master spies outside Kuchino with a top rating. Of course, everyone there knew of the Mokrye Delo, the so-called dirty-water division of the KGB, and its boss, Kudriatov. But did it have to operate like this? What connection did these lewd pictures have with the ideals of Marxist-Leninism? Even if the bourgeois-imperialist states were plotting to overthrow Communism, did the KGB have to resort to such thuggery and blackmail? She fought down her nausea and began to rationalize her muddled emotions. The other side, the warmongers, was behaving worse than this. And what was this man, Holder? What was one man's damnation set against the happiness of 250 million? She handed Kudriatov his pictures.

"If he knew, General Ivan Vasiliovich would be proud of you," he said.

How could she admit to Kudriatov that her father, General Trusov, would have quit the Army and the party had he seen her here. He had wished no part of her with the KGB, which he despised along with many of the Communist ideas that had induced his only child to join the party and its secret police.

"What if Holder does not agree to work for us?" she inquired.

"He will, he will."

"But if he makes a row and alleges we trapped him?"

"Such exquisite creatures are not the type to do that. This man would rather die than risk his wife's or his party chiefs' seeing such evidence as this. And when he leaves Moscow the day after tomorrow as the brilliant negotiator who maneuvered the stupid Russians into signing favorable trade concessions, he will be only too happy to run our errands in London."

"You mean," she murmured, marveling at the meticulous planning, "that the row in the conference room was also part of our scheme?"

"Of course, my dear Lora Ekaterina," Kudriatov said, placing one of his hairy hands on her shoulder. She shivered at the contact and went to pick up her coat and scarf.

They finished taking their pictures and, like a TV crew striking camp, bundled their gear into a truck and drove off. Lora watched Vladimir and the ZIL driver carry Holder into the car to take him back to his hotel. She wondered what would become of him.

She never set eyes on the English MP again. Only the announcement of the trade agreement in *Pravda* and *Izvestia* and the departure of the British mission proved to her that the trap had been sprung. She could hardly break the rules about assignments and seek confirmation from Kudriatov. But several days later, they ran into each other at the office canteen in the Lubyanka.

"You notice the statement?" He grinned, pummeling the lemon slice in his tea glass with a spoon, then popping a sugar cube into his mouth to suck the amber liquid through it with a ripping noise. "I was right, you see." He swallowed the sugar like a man choking on a fishbone. "The Director's as pleased as a bear in a beehive. He awards you full marks."

Lora acknowledged the compliment, though she could not stifle the notion that Holder, the bright young politician, had ruined his career because he had offered to help her, and she had acted as the bait in the trap. "I wonder what will happen to him," she mused aloud.

8

Kudriatov drew off another glass of tea from the huge steel samovar and sat down again. "We'll take good care of him." He chuckled. "He needs a safer seat in the English Parliament and somebody to ensure that he makes a useful career out of politics. He'll have friends, powerful friends, and money if he needs it. Don't worry about our friend Cassius. He'll be very grateful to us, very grateful."

"Cassius?" she said.

Kudriatov banged down his glass. "Damn," he muttered, then he grinned. "Did I say Cassius? A slip of the tongue." His face grew more serious. "Forget the name, Lora Ekaterina. For your own good. Only the Director and three other people in our organization have access to that *zapiski*. It shows how much I must trust you." Kudriatov sucked down the dregs of his tea, got up and strode off shaking his head.

2

Several questions intrigued Matthew Craig as he followed his boss through the dining room of the club in St. James's Street. Why choose this crowded morgue for a confidential briefing? Why had Standish singled him out for the rare honor of a club lunch? What was the assignment?

He got the first answer easily. These relics of a defunct empire obviously suffered so much from sclerosis of the tympanum that they could hardly hear themselves. Anyway, English gentlemen in High Tory clubs did *not* eavesdrop.

More difficult the second. Vernon Alveston Standish had not created his legend in Her Majesty's Secret Intelligence Service by generosity, either with his own or the Treasury purse. Subordinates had eaten as many of his lunches as they had met white crows.

Impossible the third. Even C, the SIS chief, got prickly heat trying to decipher Standish. Not only did the man encode every sentence, but he also had a personal cerebral scrambler that transposed his declarations into hints, his minor utterances into innuendoes. Standish never let his left hand know what his left hand was doing.

Waiters soft-shoed around them. Standish curled a nostril at that day's special menu of Brown Windsor, fillet of sole, shepherd's pie and bread-and-butter pudding. Tossing it aside, he picked up the more imposing list of dishes and ordered for both of them. Smoked salmon and a Chablis, roast beef and a claret, then Stilton. Craig had begun to doubt those gossips who snickered that Standish was the only man to serve in the Cairo Embassy without once being caught for baksheesh; he had, so they said, done the whole of Egypt on a smile and a handshake, leaving baffled fellahin in his wake. For a beanfeast like this, C himself must have signed an advance chit.

As he listened to Standish's chitchat, Craig fidgeted under the gaze of life-sizes of Wellington, Peel, Disraeli and Winston. From their superior look, they would have blackballed him, he was certain. He began desperately to uncode and unscramble. He would need a visa for a month. The Second World, behind the Curtain? And warm clothing. In May? Also, an unspecified foreign language. Did he already have it?

"Good at languages, the Scots," Standish remarked.

"After the Gaelic, they only find the English difficult," Craig retorted. Two could play.

"If I had it to do over again, I'd learn Chinese."

Chinese? Peking? Have we sacked the Summer Palace again? He'd need two pairs of chopsticks.

They had reached the Stilton, its moonface partially devoured by all those hard eardrums, port wine coursing through its blue veins.

"What d'you say to a bottle of Château d'Yquem with the Stilton?" Standish murmured.

The Chablis and claret had already fired Craig's blood. "I'd say yes if I knew what it was," he replied, broadening his Scots vowels. "We didn't run much to anything but red biddy in our two-up-and-two-down in Dunfermline."

Standish's boneless face wobbled with amusement. He looked the image of Oscar Wilde in his Café Royal days. He leaned over. "My dear boy, as Sir Francis Walsingham, our great predecessor, said four hundred years ago, we're all abject men in this service. But don't let's be too self-denying."

"It wasn't Walsingham. It was his private secretary. And he was right."

Standish patted him on the arm. "I like you, Craig, despite that bit of belligerence, that Caledonian bloody-mindedness, that . . ."

"Go on, say it—inferiority complex!"

"You'll get over that." Standish grinned. "But you're too honest, Craig. Such honesty will get you and us into trouble one day. If you want to make a career in this great service, for God's sake learn the art of lying convincingly." With a silver spoon, he quarried the Stilton; he troweled butter on a cracker, loaded it with cheese, took a sip of the Château d'Yquem and swilled it around in his mouth. He smacked his fleshy lips.

"Good with caviar, too, this wine," he intoned. "You should know there are two types of caviar. There's the caviar of the beluga—and all the others."

"So, I'm going to Moscow," Craig interjected.

"Didn't I tell you? Only temporarily. As a third secretary in the embassy. The Penkovsky-Wynne circus starts on May 8 and they've heaved out the man who'd have held our watching brief."

"What's the cover?"

"You're standing in for the embassy's legal eagle." Standish sauntered to the smoking room, corked himself into a leather armchair and sliced the end off his cigar with a gold cutter. He favored gold: a gold hunter in his fob pocket, gold cigarette case and lighter, gold signet ring on his little finger, gold toothpick in a gold-embossed sheath. "Don't bother about Wynne," he drawled. "We know that side of the story. We really want some notion of how much Penkovsky will have told them before . . ." He made the sign of the cross, his eyes rolling in rhythm with his index finger. "Everything has been scripted and rehearsed by our friends the KGB and the court, but you'll pick up something from the asides."

Craig realized that Standish had exaggerated when he took his seat in the Soviet Supreme Court on May 8, 1963 for the trial of Colonel Oleg Vladimirovich Penkovsky and Greville Maynard Wynne on charges of espionage. The KGB had written no asides, no ad-libbing lines for the two defendants. In any event, he could scarcely catch more than the charges and the prosecution preamble; everything else was submerged in the racket of traffic and hammering of road drills outside the Hall of Sessions, or the applause from the front rows for prosecution points.

"The play's not much good, but the stage effects are brilliant," whispered Etienne Champy, the French Embassy official who sat with him on the first day. Craig reckoned that Champy worked for the DST, the French opposite number of the SIS. At the recess on the second day, he noticed the Frenchman in the foyer, talking to a pretty girl who was taking notes. Champy beckoned him. "Lora Trusova—Matthew Craig," he said. "She wants to meet somebody from your embassy for some article she's writing," he added, winking at Craig and strolling away.

"Sorry," Craig said. "You'll have to get whatever information you want from the press attaché. I'm only a junior."

"Don't worry, I won't quote you." She wrinkled her eyes and gave her mouth an appealing twist when she smiled. "I'm writing an account of the trial for a legal periodical, *Soviet State and Law,* and I thought of comparing our system and yours."

"The legal expert at the embassy will give you that."

"They told me that you . . ."

"No. I'm only here for a day or two," Craig cut in quickly. "In any case, with rent-a-crowd in the front seats, the road drills and traffic diversions, I wouldn't be a good witness."

"It's difficult, I know. But if I gave you a spare transcript of the trial, would that help?"

Craig hesitated. *Pravda* and *Izvestia* were running long extracts from the court proceedings, but heavily peppered with dialectical materialism and censored by omission. Standish would swap his eye-teeth for a full version. What could he lose? And she did look interesting. "All right," he said finally. "I can try."

It had begun as simply as that. Lora handed him the official trial record each morning and Standish abstracted it that evening from the diplomatic bag in London. On the third day, a coded message arrived from him. "C wishes to know more about your contact. Is he worth cultivating?"

He sent a one-word answer: Yes. He was not fooling himself. Russian journalists invariably belonged to the party and most to the KGB. But hadn't Penkovsky worked all his life for the GRU, the military intelligence organization, and hadn't that only intensified his hatred and contempt for the regime and transformed him into one of the West's most valuable spies? Who could tell with this girl? All right, she attracted him. She would most men. Not only for her

12

svelte figure, those gray-green eyes and the russet hair. Lora had a special kind of innocence that shone through, especially when she defended Marxism. Standish would have failed her, as both a liar and a conspirator. None the less, Craig stepped lightly, allowing her to do all the running.

"Well, did you think the trial was a fair one?" she asked when they had heard the sentences and were having dinner in the Aragvi, a Georgian restaurant in Gorki Street.

"What little I heard of it," Craig replied. "Those microphones in the dock must be the only ones in Moscow on the blink." He stabbed a piece of shashlik and pointed his fork at the table lamp, with its glass beads. "I wonder if these are working." He grinned.

Lora side-stepped the remark. "In Britain, would such men have been found guilty?"

"That depends. They'd have been judged before a jury of twelve men and women in a civil court and the defense would have put up more of a fight."

"If they are guilty, what is the argument?"

"Ah, but the prosecution and defense don't worry unduly about truth. They play a complicated game in front of twelve jurors who merely have to say yes or no."

"In Britain everything is a game, is it not?"

"In England," he corrected, reflecting that Standish and so many of his colleagues did treat this dangerous racket as an extension of the Eton Wall Game or the Oxford-Cambridge boat race.

"But you are English?"

"As a set of bagpipes," he answered, and smiled. "One of the original northern tribes who had their patrimony stolen by Saxon cowboys and Norman landlords." Why lie in the face of his *zapiski,* held in the KGB central index two streets away?

"I don't like the English," Lora said. "They are bourgeois and snobbish."

"They are full of the cunning and hypocrisy of true peasants," Craig prompted.

"They are warmongering imperialists and neocolonialists."

"They are decadent, undemocratic and class ridden, especially the upper classes," Craig added, wondering whose tongue was in whose cheek.

13

"I should have known from the way you speak Russian that you are Scots," she said. "They are more like Russians."

"Yes," he admitted. "They're as dour as their climate, they drink hard liquor, brawl and beat their wives."

"Russians do not act like that," she countered. "This is merely one of your bourgeois misconceptions about the Soviet Union. If you had time to stay, I would correct such judgments."

"I still have a fortnight before the man I'm replacing comes back from holiday."

"Then I will show you the real Russia," she cried.

Yes, a whirl around the churches and museums of Moscow and Leningrad, a bit of canoodling, then bed to the soft whirr of the infrared cameras and the softer whirr of the tape recorder. And after the slap-and-tickle, the squeeze. Why work for the hated English? Why not for humanity and Russia? The irony of the game appealed to him. Here they were, attempting to suborn him through this girl; and Standish was sending twitches down the line from London badgering him to recruit her as their pigeon in the KGB. He glanced at the chestnut hair, burnished and highlighted in the glow of the table lamp, at the gray-green eyes which she fastened so frankly on him. He might find the ploy interesting at that.

For a solid week she walked him off his feet. He gazed at Lenin's embalmed features with the rouged cheeks; he wandered through GUM department store, whose glass vaults reminded him of a railway station or an aviary gone mad; he handled the manuscript of *Anna Karenina* in the Tolstoy Museum; he took in the Novodevichy Nunnery and the forbidding rooms of the Kremlin. Through it all, Lora talked like a tourist slot machine, spieling out the city's history from Ivan the Terrible to Stalin the Genial. He embarrassed her speechless by asking, with feigned innocence, what happened in those faceless buildings in the Lubyanka and Arbat that housed the KGB and the GRU *apparat*.

Often, he had to jolt himself into remembering that he had an assignment, that he was not enjoying some pleasure trip, that this svelte and elegant creature worked for the opposition. Why had they chosen somebody so obviously out of their top drawer, why did she look so unlike the part, and why hadn't she already knocked all his illusions by seducing him? No doubt she soon would. All the same, he caught himself wishing that the Kremlin was the Tower of London, that she lived in Mayfair or even Muswell Hill, that this was not just an affair between two pros in a devious business. He wondered when that coy and innocent disguise would dissolve. If she didn't act quickly, he would have to force her hand.

They were having their usual lunch, on the hoof in a Gastronom near the Kremlin. Craig layered his black peasant bread with butter and caviar. "Of course," he intoned, trying to get the Standish smirk into his voice, "there's nothing like the caviar of the beluga."

"But this is beluga," she said.

"That's what I said. There's this—and all the other inferior brands." You could acquire the art of lying like any other art.

He began to twist her arm gently about the system that filled the mind with propaganda and kept people queueing for staple foods; that faced tube stations with marble and mosaics and built flats that cracked in the first frost; that constructed great boulevards which seemed to transport only party chiefs, in their ZIM's and ZIL's; that shouted peace and spent billions on nuclear missiles. As he expected, she stone-walled, so he changed his line.

"I know what I'd do if I were the people's commissar for this place," he said, pointing at Red Square. "I'd cover the Kremlin Palace, the Spassky Tower and the Lenin Mausoleum with Coca-Cola, toothpaste and detergent ads in Technicolor. The Kremlin wall would make a great car-poster display. GUM would be women in bras and girdles with lots of skin showing. Women and cars—that's what drives the West. What you need here is a good, unhealthy whiff of old-fashioned capitalist decadence."

His sacrilege registered in the narrowing eyes and the pursed mouth. After a moment, she said, "You disappoint me, Mr. Craig. You must understand that we do not pander to the baser instincts of the people. We have higher ideals."

"Comrade Trusova," he said, "forgive me. I was joking. I wouldn't see a single stone of it touched." To placate her, he had to spend Standish's money on a bunch of red roses, which, after some hesitation, she accepted. "Forgiven?" he asked.

She nodded, then smiled. "I do not blame you, Mr. Craig. I

15

blame those elements in your country which have misguided you. I think you are an honest person.''

Honest! That word again. Twice in just over a week. He must watch it. But how honest was she? He decided to find out.

She suggested taking him to Zagorsk to see the monastery and the Orthodox churches. He brushed her arguments aside. "Religion, they say, is the opium of the people, and I've seen enough churches here to hook me for life. We go to the races." Reluctantly, she arranged a car and they drove to the Moscow Hippodrome, a drab course with a threadbare track where they ran a mixture of flat racing and trotting. Explaining the mysteries of the tote to Lora, he chose an outsider and sent her off with his bet while he looked around. Moscow, he knew, had its quota of scalpers and spielers, spivs and skivers, most of them working as needle men for the KGB. On these grandstand terraces, he could count off half a dozen who had not been warned about him and would try to make their name at his expense.

His first trotter won. Lora returned with a fistful of rubles and the suggestion that they should go home. He singled out the most spavined nag in the next race and sent her off with his winnings. Unlucky again; that cantered home, too. In the third race he had no better fortune with another scrubber, which passed the post lengths ahead without breaking sweat. Were the jockeys working for them, too? Or would they have to run a saliva test on *him?* All these rubles were becoming embarrassing. He placed the lot on the fourth race and nearly shouted with relief when the horse ran last. "Now we have to go," said Lora. "No, one last bet," he replied.

He was standing alone when a crop-haired youth approached, nonchalantly sucking an ice-cream cone. "English?" he hissed. Craig nodded. "If you have English pounds I'll give you twelve rubles—four times the rate." Craig produced £20 and had just taken the handful of rubles when two uniformed policemen pounced. The young man dropped his cone and vanished into the crowd, scattering the pound notes on the ground.

Lora pushed through the crowd to witness the policemen handcuffing Craig and getting ready to march him off. "You fool," she cried when she realized what had happened. She pleaded for his release. One of the policemen pushed her aside as his eye roved over her silk dress, her leather handbag, her nylon-sheathed legs. "Another *stilyagi*," he sneered. The crowd echoed the insult, flung at those wearing Western clothes.

At the police station near Smolensk Square, a lieutenant began interrogating Craig. "You know the punishment for black-market offenses," he barked. "Five years in a labor camp."

Craig shrugged. He was listening intently to Lora's voice in the next room. "That man is innocent," she was shouting. "I saw the criminal who tried to trap him into changing money. . . . All right, you don't believe me. . . . Here are my papers . . . you can also phone this number."

A policeman summoned the lieutenant, who disappeared for a quarter of an hour and returned with a sour smile. "You are fortunate, Gospodin Craig. We have a witness who can vouch that you were the victim of a young gangster. Watch your step in future."

Lora was waiting for him outside the station. "I hope you'd have visited me in Lubyanka Jail," he said with a grin.

"It is no laughing matter," she replied, and he could see that she was trembling. With anger or apprehension, he could not tell.

"I don't know how you managed to persuade them to free me, but thank you."

"I ask only one thing—that you mention this incident to no one. No one."

Craig knew that he had risked little. His diplomatic immunity would have saved him from trial, though they might have expelled him. But why hadn't the KGB followed through by using his error to blackmail and compromise him? Lora had evidently pulled strings, but these, he suspected, were with her own friends rather than her bosses. Maybe he was misjudging her.

On the Borodinsky Bridge he stopped and caught her arm. "I have a favor to ask, Comrade Trusova," he said. "I can't go on calling you Comrade Trusova."

"My name is Lora—when we are alone."

"Mine's Matt."

Her whispered repetition made it first sound like Mutt, then Maaht. "I'll try to remember that, Mr. Craig," she said aloud.

They both laughed as they walked along the embankment like two

17

conspirators. But conspiring for or against each other? Craig wondered.

3 From London, Standish was showering oblique coded signals on him, demanding progress reports; in Moscow, Lora was treating him like some schoolboy delinquent, even phoning his hotel room at night to make sure that he was not landing himself in more trouble. Sitting in this cross fire, Craig pondered whether to confess to his chief that he had achieved all the progress with this girl that he ever would. Only, his vanity as a professional agent and as a reasonably good-looking man with some success in the seduction game would not let him. He had to find out what went on under that chestnut head and behind those gray-green glacier eyes. Leningrad might give him his chance.

His personal doubts began to evaporate when they cleared him for the trip and she met him at the station to escort him to the compartment. He smirked inwardly when he realized they were sharing a first-class overnight sleeper on the Krasnya Strela. Sleep! Something he could well do without. As the train got up steam, he was already going over the heavy seduction bit in his mind. How would she do it? Leap on him like a she-wolf on the fold, before he had loosened his collar, initiating a wordless, all-in clash of arms, legs and soft flesh? Or would it start with a caress, a nibble at his eyelid or earlobe, a tongue-in-cheek kiss, then a slow, Slavonic strip tease to a whispered love commentary from Pushkin or the latest party handbook on sex? As he reclined on his bunk and the Krasnya Strela chuntered out of the station, he plumped for the number-two approach.

Lora was unpacking her night things—a filmy nylon nightdress and filigreed slippers. Would she need those? She switched on the blue night light and began to undress. Craig watched, hypnotized. She removed her stockings and her skirt, and he glimpsed the strong, slender legs and thighs, the ungirdled waist; she pulled off her sweater and blouse, and he saw the high outline of her breasts, which needed no assistance from the bra engineers. She pulled on her nightdress, and his doubts came back with a rush.

He got up, put his hands on her shoulders and turned her around. She gazed at him, a question in her eyes. He would have to reverse the situation and try the wolf-on-the-fold technique himself. He grasped her narrow waist and drew her to him, feeling the pressure of her breasts on his chest. He began to kiss her, savagely. He felt her yield, then respond to the kiss. She was cupping his face in her hands and running her fingertips over his features. Her arms went to embrace him. He was home and dry, he thought.

It happened so quickly that he could do nothing. Something like a skewer stabbed through his ribs and heart as she hit him hard with her thumbs. He dropped his hands instinctively, and Lora caught one and jerked. Craig felt his body twist and torque and fly through the air to thump, quivering, on the bed. Lora laughed as she released the hand; she turned, calmly, to finish her toilet.

Before Craig had recovered his wind or his wits, she was slipping between the sheets. "Good night, Mr. Craig," she called.

"Good night!" He groaned. "Good night! What am I supposed to do?" Somebody in the KGB had written them the wrong lines.

"Undress and get into bed. You have eleven museums to visit tomorrow, including the Hermitage."

"And my libido? What do I do about that?" He thought he heard her chuckle.

"Mr. Craig . . ." she began. At that moment, the door slid open; they both turned to confront an elderly man and woman in the corridor. Two faces like old crocodile handbags. The man made a courtly bow and asked in halting Russian if there was room to sit down. Catching a word or two that sounded like Turkish, Craig looked harder at the heavy-lidded, slit eyes. Astonished, he heard Lora reply with several words in the same Turkish dialect. "They've been traveling for five days without sleeping," she explained. "They are going to Leningrad to find their son, who ran off and joined the Navy. We can't leave them there, can we?"

"Since I'm not going to be able to sleep on my libido, they can have my berth," Craig said.

Lora shot him a grateful look. Without a word, she dressed, offered their compartment to the old couple and led Craig to the buffet car. Behind the counter, between the great steaming samovar and bottles of vodka and cognac stood a homely figure built like the

Minsk hydroelectric dam. She filled two glasses with fiery brandy, which she served with slices of lemon to let the liver down lightly. No, she would not take the comrade's rubles; the drink was for his proletarian spirit in giving up his bed. Craig downed several brandies to steady his hands. He felt peeved; his pride and ego were rattling like the bogies underneath them. The buffet attendant had discovered that he was British; she sang the praises of the wartime convoy sailors, plied him with more brandy and questions. She had watched many TV pictures of London. Why did they show only the ruling family, the aristocracy, the capitalists and the bourgeoisie?

"Because those proletarians who have TV only have the energy to switch on and look at the leisured classes squander the money they have gained by exploiting their sweat," Craig grunted. He had heard enough Marxist dialectic for one trip.

"You must not make fun of her," Lora whispered.

"It's not me, but the people who tell her these fairy tales that have the funny sense of humor," he snapped back. "What do you and she think I am? My old man was a cobbler and my old lady took in sewing. I paid my way through the university. She wouldn't think that to look at me now—a member of Her Britannic Majesty's diplomatic service. How's that for a success story?"

"You are one of the rare workers' children who triumphed despite the system."

"Oh, I know. The local boy made good after they let him into Edinburgh University as a sop to the workers, or maybe to condition the bourgeoisie to what they might have to face in the coming class struggle," he said sneeringly.

"Here, the universities are for the people, and you would not have had to pay anything," she retorted, ignoring the gibe.

"Things you pay for are cheaper in the long run," Craig replied. The warmth and the cognac were inducing a mellow, don't-give-a-damn feeling. "Wait and see what Moscow University turns out in twenty years' time. People who've gone soft with book learning, who have crazy undemocratic notions like free speech, who'll want nude pictures in *Pravda* instead of solid reading and a heavy paper they can use as winter underwear, who don't understand the socially therapeutic value of a good, sound purge."

"But Mr. Craig . . . ."

"After my seventh cognac, anybody can call me Matt."

"Mr. Craig," she insisted. "You have a completely unobjective and erroneous view of the Soviet Union and the Communist system. We have complete freedom and the era of the purges was so long ago that nobody remembers them any more."

He gave her a glazed look. Was Lora, the judo expert, so credulous, so innocent that his sledge-hammer sarcasm glanced off her Pavlovian mind?

"No more purges? Tell that to your General Ivan Serov and the East Germans and Hungarians who died in the fifties."

"We had to save the socialist democracies from their own folly."

"With tanks and guns!"

"Oh, you are impossible . . . you are like a muzhik with a head of teak," she said. He did not hear; he was already snoring, his head tilting toward her shoulder. She cradled his head gently and called for a pillow and a blanket to make him more comfortable. He might have wondered why she was smiling.

Like him, Standish had lost patience. When Craig returned from Leningrad, with eleven museums under his belt, a cable from his SIS boss ordered him home. Lora seemed full of regret. He must spend his last evening in her flat, where she would cook him a Russian meal. Before accepting, Craig had a cautionary word with the embassy security man, a former Scots Guards sergeant-major who mumbled in undertones, as though the KGB had bugged his false teeth. "Watch it, laddie," he said. "The flat will be booby-trapped, and if you go to bed with her, they'll hand you a set of pictures that wouldn't get past the Obscene Publications Act." Out of a drawer he conjured several metal buttons, passing them to Craig. "Whenever we call an electrician or a plumber, they leave these reminders behind. It's all right; we've doctored them."

Craig scrutinized the perfect, miniature listening devices that would transmit speech over a two-mile radius. "Can I keep a couple to show them in London?" he asked. The guardsman nodded.

Lora had a flat in Kirov Street. Its sitting room was Russian-Edwardian—massive carved table and chairs, a curly-legged *fin de siècle* sofa, complete with chintz, floral-patterned wallpaper and chandelier lights. She let him in, sat him down and rushed to the

21

kitchen. "I'm sorry," she shouted. "A friend is calling to borrow two of my records."

Hardly had Craig sat down when the bell rang. Lora answered it and came into the room followed by a stocky man with fair, crew-cut hair, which, Craig noticed, also grew on the fingers of the hand he proffered. Lora introduced him as Sergei Antonovich Kudriatov, one of her old lecturers at Moscow University.

One name jumped into Craig's mind: spy master. Why, he asked himself, could spies smell each other? The way they sized one another up, like boxers in the first three minutes? The phrases they let drop, or those they didn't? Maybe they exuded some odor created by suspicion, as animals did fear or pleasure. This granite man, Kudriatov, reminded Craig of the party worker on the propaganda poster, astride a tractor, plowing the virgin lands of the Uzbek and Kazakh, reclaiming wildernesses of steppe and tundra. He wore a disguise of pullover, slacks and sandals and a copy of *Time;* he might as well have emblazoned KGB on his low brow. He small-talked pleasantly about London, which he apparently knew well. (Craig later discovered that he had helped to spirit Eugeny Ivanov, the Soviet attaché, out of Britain when the Profumo-Keeler scandal broke and undermined the Macmillan government.) Kudriatov made no attempt to pump or proselytize him; he had merely come to meet him and take his measure. Craig had no doubt that his *zapiski* would migrate from the normal files to those cataloged "potential KGB informer." After several minutes, Kudriatov picked up his Prokofiev and Shostakovich records and took his leave.

Lora had kept her promise and prepared a Russian meal. Pancakes of buckwheat flour, bedded in caviar and capped with sour cream; chicken Kiev, from which the butter jetted when he pierced it with his fork; a charlotte russe. "That makes me feel sorry that I'm flying out tomorrow," he said, pushing the dessert plate away.

"You could always stay," she suggested. "You speak fluent Russian and there are many jobs you could do."

"Hmmm. That would count as a defection. 'Embassy Official Chooses Freedom.' No, I'll just hang on to my memories of Mother Russia. I'll often wonder what will happen to you when the Kremlin finally gets you."

"The Kremlin?"

22

"The way I see it, some party bigwig will snap you up, marry you and spend the rest of his life regretting his mistake."

"You are teasing me again."

"No, I'm deadly serious. You've seen those Kremlin wives, twice as broad as they're high. They'll slit him up for marrying somebody too pretty for them, then scratch your eyes out for good measure."

"What an imagination you have! I wonder what will become of you."

"I'll ascend slowly from third to second to first secretary and wind up as consul in Lichtenstein or Luxemburg."

"No. You will go farther than that," she said with emphasis. "I will always be glad I knew you."

"I'm glad I met you," he said. "Who else would have known how the Kremlin bell got that crack, that Peter the Great slept in his caftan and that the Moscow University elevators go up 3.2 meters a second and come down at 3.5 meters? I'm only sorry for one thing."

"What?"

"You didn't give me the most interesting facts."

"But I did."

"I mean about yourself—you've told me nothing."

"I'm no secret." She smiled. She came from Kiev, where she had attended the university, studying English and German and taking a degree that allowed her to study French and the Slavonic languages at Moscow University. Her mother was dead, but her father still lived in the Ukrainian capital. Her ambition was, not to become a Kremlin wife, but to break into journalism and work abroad, preferably in London. This was hard without party membership. However, Kudriatov might pull strings for her.

"I must apologize for being so wrong about you," Craig commented when she had finished the recital.

"What *did* you think?"

"Just a crazy notion." He paused. "I don't know where I got it, but I had the idea that you worked for the KGB." For an instant her expression did not alter; then she choked on laughter, which crinkled the flesh around her full cheekbones and gray-green eyes; she stifled her giggling with a napkin. An impressive performance, Craig conceded. How would he have reacted had someone sprung a similar suggestion on him?

23

"What made you think that?" she gasped.

So he told her. The trial transcript, the fact that she had bailed him out of the police station. And her personal story, which he did not believe. That profile and those eyes did not belong to the Ukraine, but to somewhere beyond the Kazakh steppes, probably to the Kirghiz, where the old couple on the train had hailed from. Those clothes had never hung in GUM or any other Moscow emporium, but in some couture salon in the Avenue Matignon; the shoes were from the Via Veneto, the gold watch from the Rue Mont Blanc in Geneva. Oh yes, he knew party members all had friends—like poor Penkovsky—who brought them back the baubles of bourgeois decadence; but they didn't flaunt them in Gorki Street, dining out with someone from the British Embassy staff.

Lora gazed at him with amazement. "Yes," she admitted. "It is true, my mother came from the Kirghiz, but my father is Ukrainian. He is a Red Army general and he does live in Kiev." She paused. "But this fantastic theory of yours about the KGB! You are taunting me again."

Craig shook his head. During dinner he had noticed that the wooden chandelier above him had a threaded base. Standing on a chair, he unscrewed the knob and turned to Lora, triumphantly holding out one of the small transmitters the security officer had given him. She twisted it distractedly in her fingers, staring incredulously at him. "You don't think that I . . ." she cried. Craig shrugged. He picked up the telephone base, undid the finger screws and palmed the induction microphone. "Another present for you," he muttered. "You should have told your bosses that I didn't even know your phone number."

"I know nothing of this," she stammered.

"Oh, no," he shouted. "What did they want you to do tonight— climb into bed with me and let the people from your dirty-postcard outfit amuse themselves?" He flung open the bedroom door and made a pretense of searching for hidden cameras. Lora followed him. She was on the brink of tears. "You must believe me," she muttered. "It was nothing like that. Kudriatov would never have asked me to do that. Please believe me, Matt."

He hesitated at the first sound of his Christian name on her lips. "Well," he said, "what did Comrade Kudriatov think?"

"He was sure you were from the Intelligence Service. . . ."

"And I might defect or, with your help, get myself into trouble and turn traitor. Was that it?"

"You know I risked my own job to save you from trouble," she said. "They only wanted me to watch you."

"So you *were* spying on me all the time," he exclaimed with exaggerated bitterness.

"Try to understand, please," she sobbed.

"I think I understand only too well," he threw at her as he strode toward the door, where he turned. "Anyway, thanks for the dinner. That was excellent."

"Matt," she shouted. "Wait, please, Matt." He heard her still calling his name as he took the stairs at a run, not trusting himself to walk until he had gone beyond earshot. As he marched along Kirov Street, past the Bolshoi Theater to his hotel, he reflected that Standish would have patted him on the arm for his Old Vic performance. *"Good lying, dear boy. But you should have caught her on the rebound. A cuckoo like that in the Kremlin nest, what!"* His own scruples slowed his tread; he felt like running back to confess that he had just played an unfunny British joke. After all, hadn't he left her with the impression that his own people were keeping her under surveillance? But he walked on. Hadn't he, equally, done her a favor by erasing her name from British intelligence books? In his room, he pulled out a bottle of vodka and drank enough to douse the bad conscience that should never have troubled an abject man like him.

Next morning, when the embassy car dropped him at Sheremetyevo Airport, Lora was standing waiting for him in the steady drizzle, hands thrust deep into her mackintosh pockets, her shoulders hunched; her face, framed in a silk foulard, seemed smaller. She held out a huge tin of beluga caviar, and insisted that he accept it. He quickstepped to the plane with her tripping beside him. She whispered, "What do I do about last night? What do I say? Matt, please tell me."

"You say and do nothing." As an SIS man, he should have seized the moment to plant Standish's seed in her mind, to initiate her recruitment. But he could not. She trusted him.

"But you know about Kudriatov. If they knew that I had . . ."

"They won't know. I won't say anything. You have my word."

As the plane swung out of the parking bay he saw her waving. Through the blast of jet exhaust, it looked as though her face and her whole body were trembling violently.

He went straight to Standish's flat in Belgravia, but found that the great man had left for his country house, where he normally spent his weekends. His housekeeper had a message for him. Would Mr. Craig care to take his work to Mr. Standish's place at Malvern? Craig drove the hundred-odd miles into Worcestershire, conscious of the honor, since Vernon Alveston Standish kept his private and professional lives rigidly separate.

Standish's house in the Severn valley, overlooking the river, had a bit of everything: Tudor beams protruded from Georgian and Victorian stonemasonry like compound fractures; the stables housed a Jaguar, a Triumph sports and a Mini. Standish lived in some style. He was waiting in the driveway for Craig. "Know anything about insurance assessing?" he said. "There's only Marjory to fool. The two girls are at some point-to-point."

Marjory Standish showed him his room, fussed around him, then took him down to lunch. Fine-boned and fragile as a piece of Wedgwood, she chatted through lunch but fortunately asked no pointed questions about the insurance business. Did she know? Or did she think that her husband was also broking (was that the word?) a few stocks in the City during the week? "You must show Mr. Craig your fish, dear," she remarked as they were finishing lunch. "Pity Bob isn't coming over." Standish gave a twitch of regret at her comment and rose from the table. The mention of fish reminded Craig that he still had Lora's tin of caviar in his car; he fetched it and presented it to Standish. "From the opposition," he said. "Beluga." His boss accepted it with a grin.

He conducted Craig to the edge of the river that ran through his property. A brick-and-timber structure stood on the bank. Inside, fish of every shape and hue swam in tanks or in the tiny tributary, bled from the river, that ran through the building under armored glass. Standish's face glowed with pride. "I watch them for hours," he said. "They keep me sane in this rotten racket of ours." He pointed to a tankful of tiny fish, like sawn-off minnows. "Know what they are?"

26

"Fish fingers for the frozen-food market," Craig suggested.

Standish snorted. "They're guppies. Marvelous little chaps, or girls. Never know which is which." Magnanimously, he tossed them a pinch of meal. As they toured the aquarium, he attached Latin and English names to the exotic and home-grown species. Neither meant anything to Craig. "I see them like people," Standish said. "The sharks, the scavengers, the eels, the bait, even the hippies in their bright gear. You can learn a lot about life from watching them."

He drew Craig down to the river's edge, where, beneath the alders and willows, he had constructed a small hatchery. Tiny silvery fish darted between the frames.

"Salmo salar," he intoned. "The greatest of them all." He caught Craig's puzzled expression. "Salmon to you," he said. "Smolts, or young ones."

"I only recognize the middle cut in a tin."

Standish ignored him. "I'd like to see this river full of them. In a year these fellows will leave here and travel to the fringes of the Arctic to fatten up. The next year they make their run home to spawn and die. They'll stop at nothing to get here. If I put a steel net across this river, they'd get through somehow."

"What brings them back?"

"Who knows? A blend of instinct and memory, or maybe something deeper. It's where they were born and bred, where they want to do their courtship, where they want to die. Some people are like that, don't you think?"

"Nobody I know."

Standish had finished his tour; he spread his bulky frame on the riverbank and squinted in the sunlight at Craig. "You did a fine job, Matt," he said, leaning on the last word, which he was using for the first time. "Your stuff was in the Cabinet office long before the translators had gutted *Pravda*. And it was better." He paused to look sharply at Craig.

"She must be something special, this girl friend of yours. She could be a useful contact in Moscow or wherever. Can we do something more permanent with her?"

Craig was grateful that Wellington, Peel, Disraeli and Churchill weren't there. "Sorry," he muttered. "It was a one-off job. She had a friend at court, but she was so naïve that she'd have blabbed if I'd tried to recruit her.''

"Is she pretty?" Standish queried.

"Soso. Some would say she was, but she's not my type."

The story seemed to satisfy Standish, for he let the subject go. Craig drew a deep breath. He had passed the lie test. But he himself knew that he had lied only with his tongue. Not with his heart. That suspected the truth.

4 He guessed that something big was happening when two men from the Circus and two MI 5 agents flew out to settle into a huddle for hours with Standish in his office at the Olympic Stadium building beside the great arena Hitler had built for the 1936 Olympic games. That afternoon he had a summons from Standish, who was now SIS chief in Berlin. His two colleagues, Craig already knew; they introduced the rod-backed, whisky-faced pair from Military Intelligence as Fred and Bob. "Matt held our brief at the Penkovsky-Wynne show in Moscow this time last year," Standish explained. "We'd like him at the exchange point to see if he spots any old acquaintances."

"Who're they swapping?" he asked.

"Lonsdale for Wynne," Standish said. Craig whistled. "I know, dear boy, we're getting a sprat for a whale, but it's Whitehall policy and we can't argue."

To camouflage the swap they had chosen first light on April 22 and the quiet Heerstrasse checkpoint on Berlin's western boundary with East Germany. Before dawn, Craig drove along Heerstrasse, through the Grunewald forest, smoking in rain and mist, across the Havel lakes, until he hit the barbed wire and pole across the British sector. He installed himself in the checkpoint shed to assemble his Leica with telephoto lens. Resting it on the window ledge, he focused on the lean-to fifty meters distant on the other side of Bergstrasse.

Fred and Bob arrived with a squat, crop-haired figure in a white mac: Lonsdale, looking sleek and smug. A master spy for Wynne, whom the Russians admitted to being no more than a courier. How had they done it? He saw part of the answer when Wynne arrived fifteen minutes later, escorted by two KGB men. He looked sick and exhausted after a year in Vladimir Prison. Now, half a dozen men were milling around Wynne on the Russian side. Craig kept the camera to his eye, firing off dozens of shots, then reloading. A face framed in the graticule suddenly halted him: Kudriatov! The peaked cap and greatcoat had fooled him for a moment, but here stood the man who had vetted him in Lora's Moscow flat. It appeared, too, that he was directing the operation, from the way the KGB crew scurried around him. Both sides identified their men. Lonsdale smirked toward Wynne; then, like duelists, the two men and their seconds slow-marched toward the barrier poles. Kudriatov bundled Lonsdale into a yellow Wartburg and sped off. Craig drove back to the Arena, as they called it, and handed the film to a darkroom technician with instructions to blow up his seventy-odd negatives.

In the projection room, Standish sat with him as they scanned the faces flashing across the ten-foot screen. Three of them he recognized as KGB men who had attended the Penkovsky-Wynne trial.

"And this fellow?" Kudriatov's face filled the screen. The color slide had turned his eyes cobalt blue, Craig noticed. But for the jug ears, the steel teeth, the muzhik scowl and the snub nose, he might have been handsome.

"I told you about meeting him in the girl's flat. His name's Kudriatov."

"We know, old horse," Standish murmured. "Sergei Antonovich Kudriatov. Age forty-two. Born Sverdlovsk. Munitions commissar during the war. Brought in by Lavrenti Beria in 1950. Helped to purge the deviationists in East Germany in 1953 and the Hungarians three years later. Instructor in the Smersh school at Kuchino. Friend of Ivanov, the attaché in the Profumo scandal. Top man in the KGB subversion section in 1959. Now head of the KGB in East Germany."

"Why so much homework on him?"

"Because in another five years, or maybe ten, he'll be sitting in one of the really plush offices in the Lubyanka—unless somebody in the organization trips him up. And that's unlikely."

Craig might have skated over the few remaining shots and missed their significance. Not Standish. "Ah, I see they've brought along a lady," he remarked, nudging Craig, who sat up when he noted the fine line of the nose, the russet hair falling in wisps over the salient cheekbones, the clean curve of the chin. Lora! He had inadvertently caught her in half profile as she turned to enter the lean-to. "That's the girl who gave me the trial transcript," he muttered, suddenly feeling squeamish.

"She hoodwinked you, Matt."

"Fine, she hoodwinked me, but she gave us what you wanted."

"I wonder why. Couldn't have been because she was bewitched by something in that decadent, bourgeois, neocolonialist face of yours—something that few other women have witnessed."

"She's probably only covering the story for one of the Russian papers," Craig growled.

"No girl gives somebody a two-kilo tin of caviar unless she's serious," Standish went on, blandly ignoring Craig's remark.

"It's a nonstarter," Craig shouted as he picked up the tortuous track of Standish's hints. He got up, blundering through the projector beam, and left.

Standish caught up with him, falling into step and still musing. "Let's see. You're working for the Control Commission on the diplomatic side. Your CD plates will take you through the Wall without question. You could start by making your number with the East Germans, then the Soviet Embassy staff, and play it by ear from there on."

Craig turned and gripped Standish's arm viciously. "I told you I want no part of it. Get somebody else. I'm due three weeks' leave, and anyway I've had it way over my head with this capitalist stockade and its petty rackets."

Standish patted him on the shoulder. "Come, come, Craig. You're a spy and a damned good one. Why? Because you don't work for money or phony ideals. Because you're a loner and this is a lonely game. Because you hate being yourself and you couldn't be anything else. Just drive through the Wall and see what she's up to. That's all I ask."

So Craig shuttled between West and East Berlin with officials of the four-power Control Commission, sitting through its tedious sessions about the government and status of the divided city. He felt schizoid about the whole scheme and his part in it. His emotional half longed to see Lora again; his reason whispered that nothing good could come of their meeting.

On May 9, the Russians opened their embassy on Unter den Linden to celebrate victory in the Great Patriotic War. Craig had to join the scrum from sixty nations to put down his quota of sweet Georgian champagne and pickled sturgeon's roe. A hand grasped his shoulder. He turned to confront those curious, gray-green eyes. "Beluga." She smiled, raising her caviar canapé. "Beluga," he replied, following her to a quiet corner.

"I hoped I might see you. They told me you were on the commission."

"Nobody can keep secrets in this place," he said, with an edge to his voice. "What are you doing here?"

"I have a new job—working in the East Berlin office of *Trud.*"

"The Soviet trade-union paper?"

She nodded. "If I do well, I may persuade *Pravda* to send me to Paris or London."

"Still hankering to see life on the other side? Why don't you start on West Berlin, the original stolen apple? You have a press pass and your friend Kudriatov will smooth things with the East Berlin authorities."

"Then you heard he was working in the embassy?"

Craig nodded.

"His wife is here tonight."

"Don't tell me which one." He glanced around until his eyes lighted on a lady weightlifter in a strident floral frock and flat shoes. He jerked a thumb toward her. "He's chosen well. She'll go down big in the Kremlin."

Lora laughed. "But Kudriatov is only assistant commercial attaché," she said.

Yes, Craig reflected. The Ambassador probably licks his boots and he's only outranked by the doorman, who works for the GRU. "Funny side step from Moscow University," he remarked. "Is it a promotion?"

"He prefers to keep his academic background secret," Lora said, suddenly serious. "You know why."

31

"I forgot that."

"Thank you, Matt, for keeping my secret."

"I owe it to you that I was stopped from making a fool of myself three times over."

"Three times?"

"At the races, in the train when I tried to rape you, and in your flat when I accused you of working for the secret police."

"If some idiot had not imagined you were working for the intelligence service it might have been different," she said. "But then we might never have met," she added, putting out a hand to press his.

Craig rose. If he did not stop double-talking, he would vomit all over the ornate Kazakh carpet. "Sorry," he said with a wry grin. "It's curfew time in the West and I've got to get back."

"I shall see you again?" she asked anxiously.

"I'm over this side twice a week. We'll probably bump into each other." Privately, he hoped they would draft her to Moscow, or London, or anywhere except Berlin.

Standish rebuked him for not seizing his second chance to suborn her. "Bring her over and show her the sights. Buy her a few good dinners at the Bonne Auberge or Le Paris in the French sector. You can charge it. I'll even get London to give you a dress and flower allowance." Heady stuff from skinflint Standish.

"You know what they are. They won't lift the East Berlin pole for her, in case she bolts."

Standish shook his head. "Moscow tells me that her beloved father, General Ivan Trusov, has said some nasty things behind Khrushchev's back about the state of the Red Army. No, the KGB has made sure she won't defect."

He was right. They supplied her with a permanent pass and Craig drove her through the Wall, wondering what impact she and West Berlin would make on each other.

The city bewildered her. For a good half hour she stood anchored in the middle of the Ku'dam, with traffic swirling around her, looking like a child on a roundabout. She rubbernecked everything—the blunted, blitzed spire of the Gedächtniskirche, the monoliths of the Hilton and the Europa-Center, the office blocks, the colorful crowds on the terraces of Kranzlers and the Kempinski. She clung to Craig as though the noise and the gaudy images intoxicated her. She acted, he imagined, like someone who had recovered her vision, or had been cured of color blindness. She gawked at shops, with their jewels and furs, Paris dresses and Italian shoes, luxury furniture and kitchen equipment; at the restaurants, with their gourmet menus; at opulent women in smart cars.

No, she would not, could not, believe it. A capitalist confidence trick to convince good East German Communists that Marxist-Leninism did not work. "I am glad they put the Wall around it," she exclaimed.

"So am I," said Craig. "There isn't enough of it to go around, and it can be contagious."

She looked scornfully at him. "Who can afford to stay in such hotels as these?"

"That's why they built the subway—to hide the proletarians."

"And those cars! Such a waste of socially necessary labor. There should be one model, or two," she commented.

"And one standard boiler suit for male and female comrades," he said, fixing his eye blatantly on her expensive silk dress and high-heeled shoes.

"Are all bourgeois cities like this?"

"Some better, others worse—all dedicated to the art of consuming."

"What they do is consume people," she remarked.

"Societies are all much the same. They punch your card when you're born. They compute how much you'll earn and how much they can squeeze out of you, how many wives and children you'll have, whether you'll stay out of jail, what illnesses you'll collect and which one'll finish you. They bury you and balance the books. Here, it's all done neatly and painlessly so that nobody notices."

"And you can live in such an environment!"

"Me? I beat the computer men. I don't consume. Well, maybe just a scrap of food and a few drinks. Women? I'm not hard on them. And my taxes wouldn't paint the periscope of the latest nuclear submarine, so I have a clear conscience. What have I got to complain about?"

"Poor Matt! You are wasting your talent and your life, and you don't complain because you do not know any better."

She meant every word, he realized. She really did pity him!

33

"Where else do I go?" he asked. "Across the Wall, where they work to the party rule book and those that don't conform dig salt or try to talk their way out of a state nut house? My talents would land me slap in the Lubyanka." He stopped the protest on her lips. "I know—an erroneous and unobjective view of life in utopia."

"For once you are right."

He despaired of converting a girl like Lora. She applied undiluted dialectical materialism to everything, ignoring the sarcasm he used to blunt her judgments. He could see that she was searching hard for something. Finally, she found it in the street behind the Europa-Center, where street artists sold their paintings. Two hippies with shoulder-length hair and bleached jeans had chalked a slogan on the pavement. "Americans Go Home—Stay out of Vietnam." Lora appeared to view it as the germ of a new revolution that might take hold of this perverse city and overturn its crazy system. She talked to them and was crestfallen. "They only write that to sell their paintings," she muttered.

"They can still write it. Now if somebody daubed 'Russians Go Home' in Marx-Engels Platz . . ."

"You are as bad as they are," she snapped.

"*Petchalnya,*" he said. "The sad-faced one. That's what I'll call you."

She did, however, enjoy meeting his best friends, Johnny Mottram, a free-lance journalist, and his wife, Lisa, who lived below him in a Westend block of flats. Lisa took to her instantly, but whispered, "She's after you, Matt." Johnny, who had served as a wartime intelligence officer, uttered a warning: "Run for it. She's too good to be true."

At her insistence, he showed her his flat, where she carried out a room-by-room inspection like the Arena duty officer.

"No microphones, no cameras?" Craig asked. "You didn't think I was going to compromise you?"

"I would not be here if I did not trust you. I was looking for pictures."

"Of what?"

"Your wife."

"I haven't got one."

"Why?"

34

"One reason is that I'm not married. Don't ask me why. Ask the chap who punched my card and left out that hole."

"But you are attractive to women."

"To some women," he corrected. "Others have tossed me like a drunk bullfighter."

"That was because you thought I was an easy conquest."

"True," Craig admitted. "But you have my word of honor that I won't touch you again."

"Oh," she said, regret in her voice. "So you do not find me attractive."

In the gloom of the bedroom, she approached him, lifting up her face to gaze at his. Her hand reached out to stroke the nape of his neck; she balanced on tiptoe to caress his cheek with her lips; her breasts brushed against his chest, which tingled at their touch. He felt their firm points yielding, as was his resolution. In a moment his will would founder; animal instinct would overpower his reason. Johnny's cautionary whisper boomed through his head. This way lay the Urals, and beyond them the labor camp and the salt mines.

He thrust her away, almost viciously.

"If at first you don't succeed, it's not worth the bother," he grunted. "That's my motto."

"Please, Matt, you don't mean that." She was pleading.

"Maybe not." He grasped her arm. "Look, Lora, it's no good. You and I live in different worlds, and life is tricky enough as it is. We haven't got a chance of doing more than stealing a few moments."

"That is enough for me."

"Not for me. Anyway, I may be out of Berlin in a week or two."

He picked up her coat, draped it over her shoulders and led the way to his car. All the way to the Wall, they sat silent. When the barrier pole on the East Berlin side was lifted, Lora looked behind her at the Wall, which a month before she had approved. "That Wall," she muttered. "I hate it."

Standish tut-tutted about his expenses and demanded more results. He countered by declaring that the scheme was doomed from the outset. Comrade Trusova had been brainwashed too long in Marxist dogma to consider working for them. "Her father has nothing to do with it. They'd never let her past Checkpoint Charlie if she weren't a one-hundred-per-cent tovarish.''

With a crooked forefinger, Standish hooked his gold collar stud free of his Adam's apple. "Have you . . . er? . . .'' He obviously felt more at home discussing the spawning habits of *Salmo salar* than those of his agents.

"No, I haven't,'' Craig snapped.

"Hmm. What's the matter? Don't you fancy the idea?''

"No.''

The chief picked up Craig's expense account. "Not much to show, is there? London's bound to query all this high living.'' He snapped open his gold case, took out and lit one of his special cigarettes. "Craig, you look a trifle jaded. You could do with a bit of leave. Why not pop off for a fortnight?''

"Fine. I'll clear my desk and leave in a couple of days.''

"Tonight would be better,'' Standish drawled. He gazed out the window at the outline of the great sports stadium. "Come to think, you'd better drop the girl. No contact from this moment on. No calls, no letters. Nothing.''

When he returned from England in the third week of June, his secretary informed him that Miss Trusova had called every day. "Mr. Standish told me that as far as she was concerned you were very ill and had gone home on sick leave.''

"Oh! What was wrong with me?''

"He said anything but cancer or a coronary.''

"That was good of him.''

"I decided on overwork—nervous depression. It's fashionable.''

That evening, Lora rang his flat. She sounded distraught. She had been worried about him. Was he all right? He reassured her. Then could they meet that evening? He pleaded that he was working and asked her to call the next day. He put it to Standish, taxing him at the same time with the story of his illness. "A little white lie, dear boy. Of course you must go and see the girl if she seems that anxious. Oh, by the way, they didn't balk about those expenses. So, don't be too penny wise.''

As he passed under the pole at Zimmerstrasse into East Berlin, he reflected that Vernon Alveston Standish was playing an altogether too-intricate chess game with the other side. But Standish was an old

36

fox; he had bluffed the Nazis during the war by turning around their own captured radio operators; he had planted several double agents in the Wehrmacht HQ and even in Hitler's entourage. All the same, the way he was playing this game, he and Lora could wind up as sacrificial pawns.

He picked up Lora at her flat in Karl-Marx Allee. She directed him to one of the smaller Europa restaurants, near the Frankfurter Tor, and dragged him, conspiratorially, inside.

"I couldn't come to West Berlin. Kudriatov has taken away my pass and my press card."

"What for? Does he think you're going to defect?"

"They know I could not do that—even if I wanted to."

"They have a hostage?"

"My father. He has made several ideological errors, and they could imprison him even though he is an old revolutionary."

"But I thought Kudriatov trusted you."

"He did, but now he suspects me of passing information to you."

Craig guffawed. "That's absurd. He must have another reason." Already, from the way Lora was glancing at him, with a curious shy smile, he could guess.

"He thinks that we are . . . we are lovers."

"I hope you set his mind at rest about that," Craig said, though he had the impression that he and Lora were mouthing lines in some sinister drama written by Standish and Kudriatov in collaboration. Her interview seemed to have mirrored his talk with the chief.

"Perhaps I was not very convincing," Lora said.

"But you were telling the truth!"

"Kudriatov is clever at guessing what is in people's minds almost before they know themselves. He discovered my secret—the one that you know."

"I don't know—and I don't want to know," Craig said.

"But, Matt, you know I love you."

Was it true? Or was this some complicated fork with Kudriatov's black knight that would pin both him and Standish before he played checkmate? With his own emotions tricking him, would he ever discover? He paid the bill and escorted Lora out of the restaurant. He marched so quickly toward his car that she had to run to keep pace. "Matt," she cried, "what have I done wrong? Say something."

He turned and gripped her arms until she winced. "Get out of here," he said. "Get on the first plane back to Moscow and stay there. Marry a shop steward or a commissar in the Ordzhonikidze Machine Tool Factory, or anybody else, and let the decadent West go to hell its own way."

"Does it mean nothing that I love you?"

"Who wrote that line for you—Kudriatov?" he said bitterly.

"No—not this time," she stammered, and Craig realized she was sobbing. She wrenched free and turned to blunder back along the street. He hurried after her and caught her by the shoulder. "Lora, darling, I'm sorry. Forgive me." She buried her face on his shoulder, and he felt her body convulse. "Come on, I'll take you home," he whispered.

As he spun the car around and headed toward Karl-Marx Allee, she said, "No, not to my flat. I have friends who have a flat in Leuchtenburg-gasse." He followed her directions, which took them across Lenin Allee to a narrow street flanked by terraced houses showing blitz holes like rotten teeth. Halfway down she stopped him. She drew him after her through a dark hall and up complaining stairs into an apartment as sleazy as the street outside. Carpet trodden down to the jute, musty velour curtains, a primitive set of chairs around a rickety table. Beyond, the bedroom, into which Lora led him. "We are safe here," she whispered, standing on tiptoe to kiss him.

"Lora, we're both mad," he said, breaking away.

She paid no heed. In the amber light from the feeble bulb, he noticed two bright patches like fever glowing on her cheeks; her eyes seemed to flame, their wide pupils wavering; the hard points of her breasts pressed against him and he felt her body tremble. She slipped her hands inside his shirt to run her fingernails over his chest, sending small shocks of emotional current through his body. She whispered, "Matt, *dushka,* darling, is it true or am I still dreaming about it?" She was kissing him, darting her tongue inside his mouth. He could no longer wrench himself free. She seemed to have sucked the will power out of him. His heart pounded and hammered inside his head; he was surfing along on his passion, which was submerging his caution, his fears, even his reason.

He heard the scuff of her shoes as she kicked her feet out of them, the hiss of silk against silk as her dress slid over her legs. The lithe, tawny body exuded some odor—resin and honey? He was groping after her toward the double bed, everything forgotten: the sordid room in the sordid district, the sordid and dangerous racket that had ensnared both of them. And now he was drowning in his own pleasure, aware only that whatever deceit they had practiced on each other was dissolving in these frenzied movements.

She made love as no one who was playing a role could make love, giving everything of herself as though his body and these moments were the last things on earth she would sense. And yet, he felt himself possessed.

As they lay, slack and spent, he knew why she had spurned him at first and why he had resisted so long.

They had both crossed the wall that separated their two worlds, that defined their loyalties. Cross it a few more times and he might begin to confuse, to doubt, his loyalties.

She lay watching him as he dressed. "We've broken the rules, Lora," he said.

"The rules?"

"Peaceful coexistence—no encroachment on the other's territory. No fratting."

She laughed. "I knew I would break them. Can you guess when?" He shook his head. "That night on the Leningrad train, when we argued and you fell asleep and snored on my shoulder. I never thought a British diplomat would snore."

"Only third secretaries." He grinned. "That's why I'll never make ambassador."

"But you will, Matt. Only . . ." Those tilted eyes, which held the light of snow and green mountain torrents and dark firs, gazed at him, suddenly pensive. "Only, you must watch Kudriatov and do not listen to what he might propose."

He drove along the deserted boulevards, with their forbidding apartment blocks, through Checkpoint Charlie and into his own world. He stopped in the Ku'dam to drink a beer and watch the midnight patrol of lovers and leather-booted prostitutes moving from one fluorescent pool to another. No wall separated them. Abruptly, he wished it twice as broad and as high as the Europa-Center—strong enough to keep him on his own side. He had a presentiment about that stolen hour. Had she caught him as surely as if Kudriatov had ordered her to compromise him? He would talk to Standish and get out before he compounded the act.

But he said nothing. And, despite himself, he returned the next night and every night that he could. Hadn't he had women like this before? It started, as they said, with a bang and finished with a whimper. They would soon tire of each other. But no. Even against the bleak backdrop of East Berlin, against the grubby charade their masters and organizations were playing, their love grew. He realized that whoever kept the books would debit him in some way for his first real love, but he did not appreciate how much. He understood something of Standish's ploy; the chief was obviously maneuvering him face to face with Kudriatov, either to enlist him or to discover some aspects of the game from his side of the board.

And, inevitably, he met Kudriatov. First at an embassy cocktail party, then in Lora's flat, and several times after that in restaurants and hotel lounges. The KGB man used the classic gambit: the future was Communism; mathematically and morally, the proletariat should decide its own fate; the East had adopted the Marxist system, soon the West would reject decadent and extinct capitalism. As Craig had imagined, he spoke with the poetic fervor of a man in love, about the flourishing steppe and tundra, about steel plants and five-year plans.

He probed for Craig's weak spots, flattering him by talking culture. Russian culture. The great heritage: Pushkin, Gogol, Lermontov, Dostoevsky, Tolstoy.

"Is there anything in the West like *War and Peace?*" he asked with unconscious irony.

"I don't know," Craig replied with a straight face. "I haven't read it, but I'm hoping one of these days someone will pass me the typescript when they've finished."

"Typescript!" echoed Kudriatov. "You can find it in every bookshop—even in English translation."

"I'm like the Russians. I won't read it unless it's in *samizdat.*"

"*Samizdat,*" Kudriatov growled, as though he had never heard the word for Russian underground literature. Suddenly, he snorted through his broad nose. "I like your wit, Mr. Craig. It is true, many young Russians will not read anything unless they think it is clandestine."

40

Craig wondered when the humor would turn sour. But Kudriatov, the patient and skilled spy master, bided his time; he dropped subtle suggestions, then broader hints. Finally, he made his proposition.

5 Once Kudriatov had made contact with him, officially he kept clear of the Arena. He and Standish met like conspirators in any one of a dozen beer cellars and, of course, at the vast Berlin aquarium, in front of his chief's favorite life form. "A beauty, Craig. Hooked and netted on Tayside in 'thirty-five by the gillie, Laurie Campbell. Fifty-three pounds, uh!'' And with *Salmo salar*'s embalmed eyes fixed on them, he would issue his instructions. To Craig's amusement, he appeared in different disguises, which would not have fooled a man with a white stick. For the French Zone, a beret, turtle-neck sweater and Pierre Cardin pants; for Charlottenburg, a German suit, which looked as though spun from synthetic sauerkraut, and woven plastic shoes. At their first meeting, he mumbled, with a beer glass before his mouth, "They teach these KGB men to lip-read.''

"Kudriatov didn't mention it,'' Craig grunted. "But he made me a better offer than I have from you—£200 a month and expenses. Unless London ups the ante, I might accept.''

Standish shuddered visibly at the vulgar turn of phrase, or perhaps the mention of money, but steadied himself with a sip of beer. "Civil service grades, you know. . . . We might . . . er . . . manage a small augmentation.''

"It's a joke,'' Craig retorted. "Do you think I'd even give it a thought?''

Forgetting the sordid corner of the *Bierstube* and his native costume, Standish produced his gold case and lighter, his tailored cigarettes. "It's not a joke,'' he whispered. "Kudriatov's your man. I've pointed you toward him.''

"And what do I give him for his money?''

"We'll feed you—stuff he already knows, and harmless bits and pieces he doesn't.''

"He's tricky. He'll guess I'm working for you.''

41

"Then admit it if he asks, and let him believe he's turned you around."

"Kudriatov's brighter than forty watts."

"I know, but he thinks you've fallen for the Trusova girl. It's true, isn't it?"

"None of your bloody business if it is," Craig cried. "But if it means involving her, I tell Kudriatov that the deal is off."

"Now, now. She won't come into it." Standish paid the bill, smiled and patted the *Kellner*'s arm in lieu of a tip. He was rising to go when Craig stopped him. "What do I do with the money?"

"You'll earn it, so buy a Merc or a Porsche and have a good time." He retrieved his straw hat (made of pressurized biscuit?) and ambled off.

Craig sat on, wondering why he had let this double trap spring around him without saying anything. However, neither Standish nor Kudriatov had put the screws on him; it was his own decision, like all the previous ones. He needn't have listened to that lecturer at Edinburgh University who hinted that the foreign service could use his gift for Slavic and Teutonic languages; or to the retired brigadier who'd handed him Russian and German Bibles and asked him to translate from Job. Job, of all people! He could have escaped after the interview with the London colonel whose pink-gin complexion chimed with the red and pink areas spreading over his world map and who discoursed on the Communist menace in Eastern Europe and the Far East. They were using every means—propaganda, economic sabotage, political muckraking, spying—to ensure world conquest. "For these people, spying and sabotage are a continuation of the war." And alone, fighting this subversion, were the agents. Craig hardly listened, except when the colonel shot a finger at him. "No fire brigade if you burn yourself. No official acknowledgment if you're picked up dead in a dark alley. But you'll know that the PM reads your reports and Her Majesty's Government acts on them." What could an abject man like him do with his Russian, Czech and German but get a job teaching or translating? He shied away from the system that had broken his old man at his last, and his mother at her sewing table. Her Majesty's foreign service sounded like the way out for him. He had no ideological fervor, no yen to become a pulp-fiction hero, using a pistol sheathed with silencer like some Freudian symbol. Nonetheless, he emerged from the GYM in Sussex with top rating in shooting, unarmed combat, forging (authentication, they called it) and the art of the double cross. He would need that last faculty now.

He waited three weeks before accepting Kudriatov's proposition. The Russian demanded a written outline of his career, then cross-examined him on it, revealing that the KGB dossier on Gospodin Craig stretched back nearly ten years.

"Interesting," Kudriatov murmured. "I wonder the intelligence service has not used your talents."

"But they did—a couple of times," Craig murmured. This would be his supreme lie test.

"Where was this?"

Craig thought desperately. It could have been Warsaw, Belgrade or Budapest; he had a one-in-three chance. "Budapest in 1956," he replied.

"Da, da," Kudriatov exclaimed, rubbing a hand over his bristly hair. "And of course during the trial of the traitor Penkovsky."

"Just a watching brief. We thought there might have been a leak on Penkovsky from London."

"Oh." That one had stuck in Kudriatov's throat. "Where in London?"

"We never found out."

The Russian drew a deep lungful of papirosa smoke and sent it spiraling. He looked relieved. "Of course, we could put you in a position to be of great assistance to your former masters." Craig raised his eyebrows, appealing for enlightenment. "Let us imagine you approach them, saying you have been contacted by the Soviet State Security organization to gather intelligence about your job with the Control Commission."

"I don't get the point," said Craig. "I could land up without a job and lose everything."

Kudriatov gave him a pitying look. "They will supply you with the information they want us to have—but you would be able to penetrate their organization and produce what we really need. Its names, locations and plans."

"That might take time."

43

"Time is what *they* don't have," Kudriatov said.

"I need a cutout between us," Craig suggested, adding that he could not come to the embassy or Kudriatov's flat.

"Do you have someone in mind?"

"Miss Trusova—she knows both halves of the city and, as a woman, is less likely to create suspicion."

He expected the Russian to reject the proposal outright, knowing his protective feeling for Lora. Instead, he hesitated before saying, "*Harasho.*"

It seemed to Craig that whatever personal emotions Kudriatov had were sublimated in his KGB work. But later he discovered how wrong this impression had been.

How would Lora take the news when Kudriatov told her? Craig sat on his apprehensions for a week before calling her at the *Trud* office. "At my flat," she said. When he arrived at Karl-Marx Allee, she was pacing the floor. "Matt, *dushka,* why did you do it when I warned you about Kudriatov?"

"It was a good offer," he replied.

"Money, money! Is that all people in your bourgeois society can think about?"

"Lora, darling, I didn't do it for the money."

"Then why? You do not believe in the Communist system, so you must have some other reason."

"You know the reason," he said.

"For me," she stammered, her temper suddenly abating. She came into his arms. He sensed her body convulse and heard her sobs. Lora, the strong, resolute comrade—crying! He tried to hush her, but she was mumbling, "Matt, *dushka* . . . you fool . . . you fool . . . is it true?"

"Yes, it's true." For once he did not have to lie. Maybe he had not probed and analyzed the instinct that had caused him to listen to Standish and Kudriatov; maybe he had acted like the great majority, after all, the people whose emotions won every tussle with their intellect. When he reflected then—and much later, when they stuck him in a prison cell and he had nothing to do but reflect and remember—he felt that his answer to Lora was perhaps the only shred of truth in the whole dubious exploit.

"I never meant it to end this way," she said, still crying. "He did

44

not order me to trap you . . . but he knew I would. . . . I could not help it."

He placed a hand over her mouth to stop her self-accusations. Standish had willed it, too. And he himself. "It's not your fault, Lora," he muttered.

She broke away and went to the window to stare silently out at the wide boulevard, the Marxist showpiece of East Berlin. Though sunlight slanted into the room, she tugged viciously at the heavy curtains in order to shut out the glare, the impersonal flats and the city. And the Kudriatovs, as well, perhaps. She snapped on all the lights, then, turning to him, began to undress slowly; her sweater and skirt, her slip fell to the floor. Craig watched her face, still tear-stained, but its expression now frozen into a hard mask. Standing naked before him, she said, "I am the price you paid . . . go on, take me . . . you have the right." He did not budge. "What are you waiting for, Matt? I am what you thought I was the first time. A whore." She advanced toward him, arms outstretched, her face still like marble.

His control snapped. He swung hard at that face, catching it with the flat of his hand. He shouldered past her and strode to the door.

Lora ran after him, gripping the hand on the doorknob. "Matt, don't go. Please stay. Say you forgive me."

"I shouldn't have lost my temper and hit you," he muttered.

"I deserved it," she said. "And I know why you struck me."

"You were making a fool of yourself."

She shook her head, then cupped his face in her hands and began to kiss him. "A lover's slap says more than a thousand sweet words," she whispered in Russian.

"What's that—one of your quaint Kirghiz proverbs?"

"No, this is my own."

He let her draw him toward the couch and pull him to her. This time, their love was no collision of flesh and will, but something infinitely tender in which each surrendered everything to the other. Lora's mask had dropped; through her half-closed lids, the gray-green eyes seemed to film over, and her lips parted slightly. Her face had the innocence of a Giotto saint's. He felt shame as he began to understand that she had debased herself with no thought of humiliating him, that she had offered herself like a whore to cancel the debt she considered she owed him.

"Stay with me tonight, Matt," she said as he rose to leave.

45

They stayed in each other's arms until the night was leaking away and their passion had burned out and only their love remained. She breathed her confession to him. Yes, he had guessed correctly the first time they met. She did work for the KGB. Kudriatov had recruited her against her father's wishes. She had believed everything he told her about the threats to Russia and Communism from the West and the necessity for countering them by operating as a secret agent. "I still trust in our system," she said. "But I no longer have faith in such . . . in such people. You must not work for Kudriatov."

"Lora, darling, I know what I am doing and why I'm doing it." But even at that moment he had doubts. Standish and Kudriatov had made it sound too simple.

And it seemed so easy. Standish provided him with SIS names that the KGB would already have in its files in Moscow; he processed details of Control Commission meetings and snippets about the military structure. So grateful did Kudriatov prove that he handed Craig a bonus of £300. However, he pressed for more facts and more names, and Craig had to parry this demand by stating that his one SIS contact dealt mainly with his German opposite numbers. "Ah, that swine Gehlen," Kudriatov growled.

General Reinhard Gehlen was the man the Russians hated most. One of Hitler's espionage chiefs on the Russian front, he had bartered his secret files to the CIA, and won not only his freedom but also money to finance his spy network in Germany and its infiltrations in the Eastern bloc. Kudriatov blamed him for every security leak from East Germany; he detested him above all for employing former SS men. Now, the West German government had incorporated the Gehlen organization into its state security service and it had some contact with the SIS. "Matthew," said Kudriatov, "we must lay hands on several of Gehlen's men." Craig shrugged aside the idea, but the KGB chief persisted until finally he had to raise the matter with Standish.

"Nothing would suit us better, old man," Standish said, beaming. "Gehlen's people will put a couple of men over the frontier who know they'll be caught. They'll confess everything and offer to work for the East Germans, who'll jump at the chance."

46

"Why don't they do it on their own?"

"Coming from them it would be suspect. But if they get the names from you . . . They trust you, Craig."

"And if the East Germans don't fall for their story?"

"They're not that sottish. A dead spy is worth nothing, a live one is an open book."

Why did he listen to the man? Was it, he wondered, because spies like him had to confide in somebody, and if not their spy master, who? Nobody else shared the secret game, with all its hazards, its frustrations and its petty rewards. Standish was his confessor. But he had another reason. He admired and respected the man, despite the lofty posturing, the social climbing, the status seeking. He had one of the most brilliant minds in the SIS. As part of Craig's training, Standish had once handed him the Nazi files on the Cicero case. The British ambassador's valet had rifled the embassy safe in Ankara at night, photographed top-secret documents, including the official minutes of the Teheran Conference and the D day code name, and handed them over to the German Embassy. The Nazis could not doubt the truth of the classified information, so they paid Cicero (in phony currency); but those documents worried Ribbentrop, for they pointed to the ultimate doom of Nazi Germany. He drew one conclusion, not shared by the Gestapo: Cicero was a British plant.

"Well, who was he working for—us or the Nazis?" Standish asked when he had read the files.

"Working for them and helping us."

"You're learning, Craig. Who did he think he was working for?"

"If you were running him, he probably didn't know."

Standish had chuckled. "Some of the best spies have never understood the value of their secrets, or even who their masters were."

Therefore he might well wonder what lay behind Standish's plot— whether he was trying to turn Kudriatov around to operate for them, or whether he merely wanted to know precisely what the KGB man wanted him to know. Craig knew better than to ask silly questions, to do anything but soldier and wonder on.

Within several weeks, Standish came to him with two names: Horst Stölcker and Franz Dieringer. He indicated the point on the Baltic coast where they would cross the frontier and outlined their cover stories. He had the full co-operation of the Nachtrichtendienst.

Craig passed them to Kudriatov and heard no more—not that he expected to keep track of them. In the shifty atmosphere of Berlin in 1965, who noticed two "blown" agents who had disappeared into some limbo of the secret battleground? He considered he had done the West Germans a favor.

In the following months, on half a dozen occasions he handed more names to Kudriatov. "I'm taking my life in my hands," he muttered.

The Russian smiled. "We never forget those who work for us, Matthew. We have ways and means to do what the Americans call 'horse-trading,' and the British call 'springing,' if anything unforeseen happens. You are one of us, remember."

Sometimes he had to remind himself where he stood. But for Lora, he could never have practiced the deception for a week, let alone the three years he acted as a double (or was it a triple?) agent. She seemed to share his feeling of walking that high, slack wire with no safety net underneath. Yet somehow, moving around as part of the sinister masquerade in which both sides hid their real faces heightened their love for one another. It made every moment they spent together sweeter.

Though Kudriatov had lifted the ban on her visits to West Berlin, she refused to pass the Wall. "I might be tempted," she said.

"By the bright lights?"

"They mean nothing to me."

They both had the same longing, to stay with each other; but they were captives of one system or the other. Over Lora hung the threat to her father, whom she loved; Craig had to play the game through to the end. Only in the dingy apartment which the elderly Seilers rented them in the Leuchtenburg-gasse could they forget for a few hours what they were doing. Each night they spent there, Lora would walk with him to the public park where he left his car. They would embrace as though this might prove their last kiss, their last whispered good-byes.

"Don't take any chances, Matt," she murmured one evening.

"Who, me? A respected member of the diplomatic community?"

"Others have been caught. One day they'll suspect you and arrest you, and I shall never see you again."

"If I am, Kudriatov has ways and means of getting me out. He told me so."

"He means Cassius," she remarked absently.

"Cassius?" It was the first time he had heard the name. "Who's Cassius?"

He felt her go tense in his arms. "I don't know his name," she lied.

"Well, I can always ask Kudriatov," he said jokingly.

"No, Matt." She gripped his arm. "If you do that, we shall all be lost."

"He must be something very big, this Cassius."

She hesitated. "I should not know about him, and I should not tell you, but he works for us in London. I think he has helped to arrange the exchange of spies between our countries. You must not mention him."

He did. To Standish, who appeared intrigued enough to demand more information. But Craig soon forgot Cassius. Other things drove the name out of his mind.

6 On the face of things, he had nothing to worry about. He merely had to shuttle between the old privileged class in the West and the new privileged class in the East, to hand over a few bits of paper, to memorize and vocalize a few names. And he had Lora. If it sometimes crossed his mind that one day they would have to part, that wouldn't be tomorrow. Yet he remained puzzled about who was gaining from these devious double entries he was making in the ledgers of the KGB and the SIS. Both his spy masters expressed satisfaction—Standish, the cunning peasant with the Eton and Oxford gloss; and Kudriatov, the learned muzhik from the tundra.

Only their character and behavior differed. Standish doled out for him beer and bockwurst like a man with no pockets, while Kudriatov showed his gratitude by throwing him bonuses as though he were tossing buns to a bear. Compared with Standish, the KGB man seemed lavish to the point of ostentation. Through his posh flat in the Karl-Marx Allee, vodka and caviar avalanched. There, Craig rubbed shoulders with the right people—Russian and Eastern-bloc secret policemen thinly camouflaged as embassy attachés or trade dele-

49

gates. He had no doubt about the value of the gossip and the names he picked up—priceless information for Standish and the SIS. Craig disliked both the company and the parties. If only the proletariat in the gloomy barracks sectors beyond could lift a chink of this curtain to see how the new society really lived . . .

It was at one of these parties a year after he had begun work as a double agent that he had his first shock, his first real glimpse of the abyss below, his first realization of how high and slack was the wire he was walking. He and Lora were drinking with some Czech and Russian security men when they started arguing about the current chess congress in East Berlin. To settle the dispute, someone flourished a copy of *Neues Deutschland*, the official East German newspaper. The front-page headline bludgeoned Craig between the eyes. TWO GEHLEN SPIES CONFESS, it ran. He grabbed the flimsy sheet. Stölcker and Dieringer! He skimmed over the account of their trial. They must have spent months vivisecting them to squeeze such material out of them. And the verdict! Sentenced to death by shooting! The words wriggled before his eyes like a can of fishing bait. He felt suddenly queasy.

"Matt, what's wrong? You look as though you are going to faint." Lora linked her arms through his to support him.

"It's nothing," he stammered. He was standing in the middle of a carousel; everything reeled around him—the room, the ceiling, the champagne glasses, the grotesque faces. All except one. Kudriatov's. He grabbed the KGB man by the arm, pulling him into a corner. Above the din and his own pounding head, he shouted, "You've got to save these men." He thrust the paper with the headlines and the picture into the Russian's face.

Kudriatov glanced at it. "Bah! Two of Gehlen's men. I would like to see another hundred go like that."

"What about me? I gave you their names."

"Gave! Gave!" Kudriatov sneered at him. "You sold them to me. You got your thirty pieces of silver and more. So they are no longer any concern of yours."

Craig caught the flash of his steel teeth as he scowled; his big arm swept in an arc to scythe him down. Something exploded in Craig's head. He parried Kudriatov's lunging movement and stepped aside. He aimed at the center of Kudriatov's jaw, bringing his fist up from waist level and punching through. He heard the crunch of bone on bone and the crack as the Russian's teeth snapped shut. Kudriatov toppled like an oak in the gale, all arms and legs. He lay where he had fallen.

Everything froze around the two men. No one moved, until Craig seized a champagne bucket and hurled water and crushed ice over Kudriatov's face. Three KGB men rushed him, pinioning his arms while their boss opened his eyes and shook his head as though he had water in his ears. From his gimlet look, Craig wondered when he himself would join the two Germans at the execution wall. But suddenly, Kudriatov grinned. "He has had too much vodka. These Englishmen can't take it. Go home and sober up, Craig." Heavy hands pushed him toward the door.

He stumbled into the broad boulevard, glad to escape from the vodka-and-caviar binge, to give his sick stomach some air and straighten out his thoughts. He walked along the canyon of monolithic flats, all blueprinted in Moscow by some *apparat* architect as faceless as the company he had quit. He thought: Standish provided those names—and the assurance that no harm would come to the men. But was it his fault? He, Judas, had taken the money, and two men had died. How much were two murdered men worth? More than all Kudriatov's bribes and Standish's bent sense of fun. He could walk on, through the Wall, and quit. He began to march toward his car. Behind him, he heard her voice calling his name. Lora? He would lose her. She was right. They had trapped him. Well, he would take their money, but now he would unload it before it scarred his hands; he would invest it in personal insurance for both of them; he would act as nobody's carrier pigeon, would memorize and vocalize no more.

"Dushka, wait for me." Lora was running down the boulevard behind him. She came up, gasping. "Matt, I will come with you."

"Where to?"

"Wherever you say."

"You're forgetting they have a hostage."

"No, I am not."

Would she really sacrifice the old General for him? He shook his head. "I'm not going anywhere," he said.

"But Kudriatov will kill you. You humiliated him. I wonder why he didn't kill you in the flat."

Craig had posed the same question. Maybe Standish had the

51

squeeze on him. Or maybe he himself figured more prominently in the KGB books than he had imagined. "He still needs an errand boy," he said.

"What did you quarrel about?"

He told her about the two spies. She listened quietly, then put her arms around him. "Matt, I am afraid for us," she murmured.

"You've got nothing to worry about."

"What would I have if anything happened to you?"

"Nothing is going to happen to me," he said. But already the safety net had gone. One slip now, and . . .

"I told you that man was evil."

"No, it's the racket that's evil."

"What does that make those who work for it?" she asked. "I wish . . . I wish I had never met him."

In her voice he heard the echo of his own doubts, his own confused loyalties. "I'll walk you home," he said.

"No," she replied. "Let's go to our own flat."

From that moment he lived with the presentiment that something would one day trip him. It took another couple of years and, ironically, it was two other lovers who caused the crisis.

At several of Kudriatov's parties, he and Lora had met Igor Pavlovich Strutchkov, one of the KGB chief's brightest operators in East Berlin. Invariably, he came with his girl friend, a slender, sad-faced Fräulein who worked in the Ministry of Culture. No one who met them doubted their love for each other.

Craig soon discovered that the girl, Heidi Schultz, had a problem, shared by thousands of Berliners. Her parents lived in West Berlin, having managed to cross the sector boundary a day or two ahead of the Wall builders. For nearly six years, the girl had fretted about seeing them again. From her behavior, she seemed determined to make a bid to rejoin them permanently.

Kudriatov should have weighed this situation. It amazed Craig that he did not nip his lieutenant's romance in the bud. Did he think that, in a tussle, Marxist-Leninism would triumph over love? Or that love was simple biochemistry, overlaid by yet another bourgeois myth got up to sell double beds or promote the consumption of refrigerators and washing machines?

52

Craig observed the pair, as any trained agent would have done, taking stock of the whispered conspiracies, the lovers' tiffs and other signs of a coming storm. Long before Lora came to whisper what Heidi had confided to her, he had guessed that Strutchkov had decided to leap the Wall with the girl.

"They'll never get away with it," he told Lora. "Advise them to rent a flat somewhere and forget defection or marriage. She can see her folks through Balkantourist on the Black Sea coast like thousands of other Germans."

"But they're in love," Lora expostulated.

"So are we, and what can we do about it?"

"You have many friends on the other side. You could help them."

"Are you mad?" Craig demanded. "Pushing a prominent KGB official over the Wall! They'd shoot us both."

She persisted, giving Craig the impression that she identified herself with Heidi and him with Strutchkov. Finally, he had to meet the KGB man, a floppy, fair-haired example of the new breed from Moscow University and the International Languages Institute. Strutchkov certainly had pluck, risking his skin to outline a defection plan to someone he knew worked for his boss. Craig blew cold on the idea of escaping. The agent countered by fishing a small package of microfilm out of his pocket. "My passport," he explained. "The filmed records of the head office here for the past four years."

Craig stared at the cassette of microfilm. Not even the Berlin tunnel which tapped the Kremlin wires for months, not even the West's network of agents in the Eastern bloc could have yielded as much information as these bits of film. Standish would let him drink and eat his weight in beer and bockwurst for that.

Strutchkov noted his hesitation. "If you think this is a trap, keep this file as—what do you say, collateral?—until I am safely in West Berlin."

"I'll have words with my contacts," Craig said.

Standish went into raptures about Strutchkov and his dossier. "Think of it, old chum, he has everything—the inside story on those spy-trading operations which have worried us for years. Maybe even the name of our friend Cassius. Let's get him over before he freezes up. Tell him we'll have him, his girl and her parents in London two hours after he crosses the Wall.''

Standish left the escape plan to him. Since Strutchkov refused to budge before Heidi had reached West Berlin, Craig arranged to move her in the morning and the Russian in the late afternoon. With Heidi, he had no bother. He was rarely halted on either side of the frontier, so he stowed her away in the trunk of his Mercedes and drove across.

For the KGB man, he had to evolve a more elaborate scheme. He and Standish chose an SIS man from London who resembled Strutchkov; they equipped him with a chauffeur's uniform and two passports. He would drive through the Wall in a Control Commission car. Once in East Berlin he would change into an ordinary suit and hand his uniform and one passport to the Russian. Strutchkov would then drive back into West Berlin.

Craig supervised the swap, which they made in the flat at Leuchtenburg-gasse at twilight. Dusk and fine rain were dropping over the city as he fell in behind Strutchkov's car and followed it along Lenin Allee. He reckoned the Vopos on Checkpoint Charlie would not look too hard; in half an hour they would change shifts after a long day. Around Alexander Platz and along Rathaus-strasse traffic impeded them, but nothing was tailing them as they sped around Marx's bust and up Unter den Linden. Turning into Friedrichstrasse, he groaned on noting the queue up to the checkpoint. Topaz clouds, shot through with the lights of West Berlin, lay before him, and heavy rain was tumbling out of them like water from a giant sponge. He positioned himself three cars behind Strutchkov and edged toward the frontier.

The CD car had reached the red-and-white pole at Zimmerstrasse. Only another hundred yards. A Grepo took the Russian's passport and returned it. The pole swung up like a howitzer. "He's through," Craig exulted. As the car passed underneath the pole, two men stepped from the checkpoint hut to bracket both front doors. Even had Craig not seen them in Kudriatov's flat, he would have identified them as KGB men—Strutchkov's own colleagues. One of them put his hand on the door handle. At that instant a shot rang out. The man pitched forward on his face. Strutchkov had flung open the door and was sprinting for the other side, jinking as he ran to make a difficult target for the Vopos. He got no more than thirty yards when two volleys sounded from the checkpoint hut and the Vopo tower on the right. Strutchkov's back arched and his arms flailed outward before he sank quietly to the ground, his blood pooling on the tarmac.

Four Vopos were already doubling across no man's land to retrieve the fallen figure. As Craig watched them bear back the slack bundle, he prayed that the Russian had died. For everybody's sake.

He had to think of himself, and Lora. Strutchkov's film still lay in his pocket. To cross the barrier with that was inviting the KGB man's fate. He spun the car around and into Schutzenstrasse, drove into a back street and dumped it. He walked back to the checkpoint, slipped into Zimmerstrasse to the block of flats overlooking the frontier. From the third landing of the circular stairs he could watch everything. They had shut the frontier and were turning the queue of cars back into East Berlin. Behind him, he heard an ambulance siren honking down Friedrichstrasse. Coming from the Charité, probably. He trained his glasses on the stretchers as they carried them out. Damn them for covering both faces and bodies! Slipping downstairs, he ran back to the car, and had reached the main street when the ambulance passed. He dropped in behind it, but could not follow it into the Charité complex. Instead, he strolled through the gates and into the main reception area. He glanced at the duty list: Casualty officers Herr Doktors Siebert and Geissler. He asked the receptionist to put him through to Geissler on the intercom phone.

"Dr. Geissler, there has been a shooting incident on the Wall."

"Who are you?"

"Kühnicke from Administration. They have just phoned."

"You are too late. We already have the men."

"Ach so! They are in good hands."

"One of them is. The other is dead."

"You have his name for the records?"

"Neither had any papers. Ask the police."

Craig put down the phone. He regained the car and drove toward Alex Platz until he spotted a café in a back street. He parked the car a quarter of a mile away, walked back and ordered a beer. In the toilet, he wrapped plastic sacking around the microfilm and dropped it into the cistern. Now, he must fix his alibi with Lora. He drove to her flat and let himself in with his key.

The flat was empty. He noted, too, that Lora's suitcases had disappeared. Had she heard about the shooting and tried to get through the Wall? Did that mean Strutchkov was still alive? He was sieving those questions when the door opened. Kudriatov walked in.

"Ah, Craig, I wondered if you would come. How long have you been here?"

"Couple of minutes. They turned me back at the Wall. There's been some incident—a shooting, I heard."

"That is not important," Kudriatov grunted.

He had answered Craig's question. Strutchkov was dead; otherwise, Kudriatov would have grabbed a bedside seat at the Charité to get his confession. Standish would have played him more cleverly.

"I came looking for Miss Trusova," he said.

"Did they forget to tell you? Comrade Trusova's father was taken suddenly ill. She had to return to Moscow."

"For how long?"

"One never knows with these old soldiers."

"What does that mean—that he's in one of your psychiatric units with bars?"

"Let us say he is under observation."

"So, you've ordered Miss Trusova back, haven't you?"

"For her own good. She needed to have certain ideas and confused emotions corrected."

"Where? In one of your labor camps?"

"Never mind where," Kudriatov growled. "The less said about Comrade Trusova, the better for you and everybody else."

"If she's gone, you'd better get yourself another messenger boy. I won't work with anybody else."

"Oh, no! You will operate for us when and where we need you."

"And if I don't?"

"I can post your dossier to certain addresses and you will never work for anybody."

"You forget, Kudriatov, that I told them everything in the SIS and they were using me, too. How could they accuse me without compromising themselves?"

"Just force me to act and we'll see how brilliant you really are, Craig."

"What do you want me to do?"

56

"Get your masters to post you back to London and await instructions. Do nothing until we contact you."

"You owe me some money."

Kudriatov sneered. From his pocket he produced a bundle of dollars and scattered them on the floor. "Get down on your knees and pick these up, then get out of here," he shouted.

Craig collected the money and left. For an hour, he drove aimlessly around the boulevards, hoping that Kudriatov was bluffing, hoping to catch a glimpse of russet hair and a quick, tripping step. But she had gone. Of that he was convinced. Somebody had blabbed, and if Kudriatov had made no mention of it, he nevertheless suspected them both of planning Strutchkov's flight. He had not needed to phone the Charité Hospital; he already knew what had happened at the checkpoint. But why had he pushed Lora out of Berlin so brusquely? Because proof of her betrayal might be laid at his own door? Because of his own protective feelings for her?

And he, Matthew Craig, bounced from the KGB. He didn't think they sacked people from the chain gang. Kudriatov had let him down lightly. He wondered about that, too.

He turned the car around and headed for the checkpoint. There, he realized that whoever had tipped Kudriatov off about Strutchkov also knew about the file. For two hours they went over him, probing every orifice in his body and leaving his suit without a stitch of lining. His car looked as though it had been rejected by the knackers.

Standish commiserated with him that evening. "Jolly good try, Matt. We can't win them all."

"The KGB has handed me my cards," he said.

"You can't crib. You had a good run and earned a bit of pin money. What about the file Strutchkov was going to give us?"

"He had that on him when he was shot," Craig lied.

He had to recover that film. But how? Everywhere he went in East Berlin he had company—two cars and a posse of half a dozen men on foot filling his steps. How had they deduced that he had cached the file on their side of the Wall? It took five days of maneuvering before he shook them off and retrieved the microfilm. For several minutes, he considered burning the filmed documents; if they caught him with this evidence, Standish would pick him up from the Spree.

But no, a man had died for this flimsy bit of film. Somehow, he would conjure it into West Berlin.

He made a packet of the cassette and thrust it into an American cigarette package, gumming back the cellophane paper. He marched through a maze of back streets until he hit Marx-Engels Platz. As he had envisaged, the usual afternoon procession of American matrons gawping at the cathedral. He waited until they straggled toward the Pergamon Museum and made his choice: a stumpy lady with fluorescent hair and plangent Brooklyn accent who carried a camera and straw handbag and stubbed out her cigarette before entering the museum. He applied smarm, and when they reached the Babylon room she was preening like a peahen. Politely, he held her bag to allow her to take some forbidden snapshots. What a curious coincidence! He, too, was staying at the Kempinski. Would she have a drink with him that evening?

Later, he wondered if she had crossed the checkpoint or was languishing in Karlshorst insisting that she had never smoked that brand. But that evening she turned up in the hotel lounge. To anaesthetize her, he put up four quick martinis, then murmured in a mid-Atlantic drawl, "You certainly did the U.S. intelligence service quite a favor today, ma'am."

Her flush nearly melted her eyeliner. "For heaven's sake, how was that?"

Craig was suitably abject. "I'm afraid I had to resort to a small subterfuge and put a pack of cigarettes in your handbag. The pack contained top-secret material which could save many American lives."

The martinis held her together, though she huffed and puffed as though she had water in her tubes. Rattling around in her bag, she produced the pack, handling it like snake venom. "Gee, if I'd of known . . ."

"Forgive me, ma'am, but I thought it better not to tell you. I may say, however, that the CIA and the Pentagon will be extremely obligated." He changed down an octave and whispered, "But not a word to anybody, not even your nearest and dearest. Not a word. If the other side knew . . ."

Her imagination completed the threat. For once her vocal apparatus failed; she could hardly croak a good-bye.

Standish arranged his new posting and flew back with him to London, saying that he, too, needed a break. In his flat, Craig blew up the Strutchkov film. The dead KGB man had not exaggerated. He could have sold that file anywhere for his freedom and a life pension. And the man must have carried much more in his head. No wonder they had shot him.

Craig kept his own counsel about the microfilm, figuring that one of these days he might have to use it as his personal passport if the Russians contacted him again.

7 Like everybody else in the Circus, he had followed the reports from their embassy and SIS field agents in Prague that spring and summer of 1968. If nothing else, the build-up of KGB staff made it obvious that the Russians intended to intervene in force to stifle both the Dubček government and socialism with a human face. Each diplomatic bag listed the new KGB arrivals. Craig was poring over the latest names when his eye halted:

Lora Ekaterina Trusova, age about twenty-eight, KGB operative working from the Russian diplomatic quarter, Zàtorka, under Soviet Resident-Director, Sergei Antonovich Kudriatov.

He immediately sought out Standish. "We'll need a few more hands in Prague," he said.

"What for? The whole thing has been carved up already. For all we know, Brezhnev and Johnson have made a secret deal to allow the Russians to go in."

"But you know they'll purge everybody who has uttered a single heresy. And some of those men in the Dubček movement were working for us. What about them?"

Standish looked at him, then turned his fleshy face to gaze out over St. James's Park. By the lake, among the planes and willows, couples lay spread-eagled, fondling one another; groups of hippies, bare to the waist, were performing a ritual song and dance. "It's the season." Standish sighed. "You can't stop people rutting any more than you can prevent salmon spawning."

"If you think it's because of her . . ." Craig retorted.

"Whom?" Standish asked. He pointed to a girl whose breasts were hidden only by her long tresses and who lay in a crucifix position as though she were inviting sexual violation. "You know, they get prettier every year," he drawled. "But I sometimes wonder if they're worth saving, or even bothering about."

"Do I or don't I go?"

Standish ceased contemplating the park. "No," he said. "And you know why. You're blown, Matt. Blown both ways. Why do you think they haven't contacted you in nine months, since Berlin?"

"We've done it before with blown agents."

"They weren't involved to the same extent as you. I've been watching you since you came back from Berlin. You've got this girl in your blood. And that's dangerous for you and all of us."

"Who pushed us together?"

"All right, I'm guilty. But if I sent you to Prague you'd be honey for the bears. Anyway, it'll all fizzle out in two or three weeks. Take a fortnight's leave and forget it."

"And go salmon fishing, I suppose."

"That's the best notion you've had. It'd do you no end of good." Standish seized a pad and wrote a name and address on it. "Jameson Garvie, the best gillie on Speyside. He'll teach you the wrinkles. Bring one back that we can smoke for the club, old chum."

Craig cleared his desk and took a taxi to his Knightsbridge flat. He opened the plumber's hatch under the bath and fished for the Strutchkov microfilm and his private envelope; he then phoned to book himself on the next flight to Prague.

He chose the Praha-Palace Hotel in the Old Town. In its Kafka corridors and salons he collided with dozens of improbable tourists like himself—East Germans, Poles, Bulgarians—spectators of the retreat from Moscow.

He could not attempt to contact Lora directly. Instead, he took a café seat across the square from the Wenceslas statue, gathering point for the Dubček supporters, and the KGB. Among the crowds he must have spotted a hundred young Russian agents, got up in

60

sweat shirts, bleached jeans and gym shoes. Where did they get the student kits? he asked himself. From CIA surplus?

On the third day, he glimpsed the girl walking down the steps of the National Museum behind the square; he had to look twice before identifying her as Lora. She had bubble-cut her chestnut hair, which emphasized her high cheekbones and the tilt of her head; she was wearing blue jeans and a stars-and-stripes sweater which was becoming on her. He elbowed through the crowd and tapped her shoulder. She spun around. "Matt," she cried, her eyes lighting up and just as quickly showing apprehension. "What are you doing here?"

"You won't believe it, but I'm on holiday."

"Turn your back and whisper where you are staying."

He gave her the hotel name and his room number; when he looked around she had disappeared. He returned to the café and ordered a drink. A man had sat down at an adjoining table and was firing off dozens of shots with a hand camera as though recording faces for somebody else's picture album; he might have passed for any American tourist. Broad well-fed face, blond crew-cut hair, fine-spun polyester suit and ever-shine plastic shoes. As he lowered the camera, his face seemed familiar. Then Craig remembered. As their glances crossed, he nodded at the man. "Berlin . . . the Control Commission?" he said.

"You're Matt Craig, aren't you?"

"Middleton, isn't it? Dick Middleton?"

The American nodded. "I'm standing in for the trade attaché at the embassy for several weeks," he said.

"I'm on holiday."

"I might have guessed. But don't ruin it by talking to the girl I saw you with over there."

"I thought she was Czech."

"Russian," Middleton amended. "Just preparing for the moment her bosses step in to break up these shenanigans."

"Unless the CIA does something to stop them . . ."

"Or the SIS," Middleton countered, grinning. "Like you, we're chickening out of this one."

They had several drinks, then walked to Národni Street to eat a snack and swap notes about the situation in Czechoslovakia. Craig was sizing up Middleton. He might need a friend if the Russians took

61

over. How much could he reveal? How would Vernon Alveston rate this agent? He could hear the Oxford drawl: *A fair operator but lacks the quintessential dishonesty and untrustworthiness which characterizes the really gifted field man.*

"How long until the shooting starts and they shut the frontiers?" he asked.

"Hard to tell. Two weeks? Three at the most. But you won't be staying for the whole performance?"

Craig hesitated. Finally, he said, "I knew about the girl. She's KGB, but I may have to smuggle her out."

Middleton raised his eyebrows. "I hope you make it."

"It'll be tricky."

"If I can help, let me know."

"I might, at that."

He was listening to the midnight news when he heard a rap at the door. Lora stood outside. Her hair and face glistened with rain and she was breathing heavily as though she had run across the city. "Matt, *dushka,*" she whispered. He drew her inside, but as he made to kiss her she broke free and put a finger to her lips. "It's all right." He laughed. "I've debugged the room and put all the microphones around the Eastern-bloc tables in the dining room." Her glance went to the bed. "I searched that, too, in case you would come."

"Nothing would have kept me away," she said, standing on tiptoe to kiss him. A soft, moist light played over her eyes and she explored the contours of his face with her curiously blunt fingers. "It was my fault you were betrayed," she said.

"I'm still here."

"I had no way of knowing. I had nothing of you . . . no photograph . . . no letter. Nothing. And I thought, 'I shall never see him again.' And when I saw you in the square, I tried to be brave and stay away in case I betrayed you again. And I had to come." She was crying.

"Hush, darling," he said. He drew her down onto the bed and they lay close together, murmuring words of love in Russian and English and holding each other with a tenderness that was a language of its own.

She woke him before dawn as she was dressing to leave. "Matt, who knows you are here?"

"Nobody, I hope. I'm traveling under the name of Robert Martin, a British tourist."

"But they might have spotted you in the street or at the airport. Kudriatov will have you killed. He would have done it in Berlin if he had had the chance."

"Why didn't he?"

"I don't know. He knew you helped Strutchkov plan his escape. He thinks you stole the microfilm."

Craig produced the cigarette package. "He's right. I brought it back as a token of good faith. Only, I want something in return for it." He noticed her quizzical look. "It's hardly a fair exchange, but I'll swap it for you and your father. Safe-conduct out of the Soviet Union."

"Matt, you know I love you. . . ."

"But not as much as Mother Russia and the party?"

"They are all I know," she said simply. "Anyway, they don't let our kind resign."

"Then we both quit," he said. "We go somewhere that nobody can find us. There must be some backward, nonaligned island that has no secrets to keep because it hasn't discovered fire or the wheel, that hand-washes what clothes and dishes it possesses and where the Deepfreeze and the fish finger haven't made their mark."

"It wouldn't work, Matt."

"You may change your mind when the Russian tanks come in."

She stared incredulously at him. The KGB evidently kept its trade secrets well.

"Tanks!" she repeated in an undertone. "That is just more capitalist propaganda."

Craig shook his head. "Oh, they'll shout that the Czechs asked for help to crush the counterrevolutionary elements, revisionists, imperialist reactionaries, the fascist avengers of Bonn and so on." He cupped her face in his hands. "Lora, listen, we have time to run now before they seal off the frontiers."

"No, Matt, I cannot do it. But you should go."

"Not this time. Not without you."

"You'll be caught, and . . ." Her voice faltered.

"I'll take that risk."

She gazed at him for a moment before walking to the window and scanning the street. Without a word she began to pack his clothes

63

into the small valise. When she had finished, she said, "The night porter will be working for us. I shall walk to the fifth floor and ring him to say that I am sick and need brandy. When the elevator goes up you can go out through the front door. I will join you in the street."

"And I thought I knew all the dodges." He grinned. "It pays to go to the right school."

Her trick worked. They marched through the light, tepid rain, keeping to the back streets but emerging on Wenceslas Boulevard several hundred yards below the square. Lora opened the main door of an old block of flats and climbed the spiral staircase to a second-floor flat. Once inside, she whispered, "It belongs to a friend of mine, an air hostess with Aeroflot. She is on internal flights for a month, so we are safe here. But you must not go into the streets. I will bring you food at night."

"All right, I'll lock myself in—but on one condition. You share my exercise periods and give me breakfast in bed."

"I can slip out of my hotel room after midnight," she said. She kissed him and he watched her hurrying along the deserted street.

He did not need to venture beyond those two rooms, tiny kitchen and bathroom. Lora stocked the flat with provisions that she must have wheedled or purloined from the KGB quartermaster: tins of borscht, beef and stew (army type), caviar, bitter Russian chocolate and a choice of papirosa or the Cuban cigarettes that even the Czechs spurned, preferring smuggled Western brands. That week, the Czech radio grew even more vehement in denouncing Russian interference with the Dubček reforms; it attacked especially the KGB, listing its headquarters and offices in Prague and naming several Russians, including Kudriatov, who were directing their own and the Czech secret police. "They do not realize that we have come to help them," Lora expostulated.

The propaganda had its effect; now Wenceslas Square seethed with crowds night and day. Craig and Lora were watching the scene one night from their balcony window when he suddenly felt he had been caged long enough; he grabbed her coat and threw it over her shoulders. "Come on, sweetheart, we'll take a look." She protested, but followed him into the boulevard. The square had the air of a fete; whole families had turned out to listen to the speakers shouting for freedom, or to batten on the latest copies of *Literarni Listi* and *Lidovà Demokracie* and read about the new democracy.

64

Craig and Lora had just arrived when a scuffle broke out among the youths in jeans and T shirts; they had pulled a man and a youth from a passing car and were spraying them with red and blue ink. "What have they done?" Craig inquired. "They are traitors who are working for the Russians," one of the youths shouted. At the head of the street, students were ranting in front of a building labeled Czecho-Soviet Cultural Institute; one of them was writing GESTAPO in tar across its walls. "Is that where you work?" Craig asked. Lora nodded and turned away without speaking. She drew him back to their flat. "Matt, perhaps I had better not stay tonight," she said. "It is too dangerous for both of us." He insisted that she might run into trouble from the mob and finally she agreed to stay.

He had been asleep for hours before he awoke suddenly. Someone was tugging at his ear. Lora hissed, "Matt, the file? Where have you put it?" She ran to the window and shouted, "Hurry—there are two cars." Heavy boots were thudding on the stairs. Craig rummaged for the file and an envelope he had brought with him from London; winding plastic wrapping around them, he ran to the toilet to push the package under the ball valve of the cistern. "Get back into bed," he ordered. They had just drawn the sheets over themselves when two uniformed policemen burst into the room, their guns drawn. "Get dressed," one of them said in Czech.

"Not until you tell us what you're here for," Craig said. One of the policemen grabbed him and cuffed him across the face. "Now get dressed or we take you as you are," he bellowed.

They handcuffed both and marched them downstairs. Craig saw them manhandle Lora into the first car before they thrust him into the second. He wondered which KGB cell he would find himself in.

8 He guessed where they were heading when the car turned south along the Vltava and then southeast through the back streets. As they drew up before the bleak walls of Pancrac Prison, he noted that the second car was pulling up behind them. He had no chance to speak to Lora; they hustled him through the gates and across the prison yard to a barred room. There they forced him to strip while they searched his clothing. A pug-faced police captain was studying his passport. "These rats are coming up from every sewer," he muttered to the two lieutenants who had arrested him.

"Can I ask what the charges are?" Craig said.

The captain glared at him and slapped him twice across the face with his passport. "No," he growled.

"As a British citizen I have the right to know."

"You know already. Spying against the People's Republic of Czechoslovakia."

"I have nothing to do with spying. I am a British tourist on holiday."

"Who speaks fluent Czech and is found in the company of an identified member of the Russian counterespionage service," the captain replied. "You still maintain you are a simple tourist?"

All at once, it dawned on Craig. "But," he stammered, "you don't think I am spying for the KGB?"

"I don't think anything. I know. But you will be given the chance to refute the evidence in a free court." He thrust a paper in front of Craig. "Now, you will make a statement."

"I will say and write nothing before I have seen the British Consul."

The captain jerked a thumb at the others, who grasped Craig's arms and ran him down a flight of stone steps to a cell which contained nothing: no bed, no chair, no blanket. It stank of urine and the ordure which covered the stone-flagged floor. They had kept his clothes and he stood shivering, wondering if they had treated Lora in the same humiliating manner. How ironic could things get? One Communist country accusing him of spying for another! He could always call Standish and Kudriatov as witnesses. He hammered on the door; the peephole opened. "Give me my clothes," he shouted.

"When you have decided to make a confession," the guard said.

For three days they kept him in that cell. Every few hours they dragged him upstairs to submit to a perpetual series of questions by the police captain. He denied everything; he had picked up this girl who had a flat. All right, he had had a bit of fun with her. But he assumed she was Czech since she spoke that language and he did not understand Russian. He had never had anything to do with the British or Russian intelligence organizations. He demanded, as was his right, to see the British Consul.

Downstairs, they had begun to give him the treatment. No food or water until midnight and then only enough to keep his tongue moving. When he had exhausted himself with exercises to keep the cold out of his bones and lay down, the peephole opened and the guard woke him with a bucket of cold water. The filth no longer bothered him; he contributed to it himself, for they would not allow him to leave the cell and gave him no bucket. On the fourth day, he hardly knew where he was; his head was spinning and he felt too weak to rise when the cold douche hit him. All right, he thought, let them take their evidence. He would sign anything.

They pulled him from the cell and handed him his clothing. A guard prodded him into the prison yard; the light trembled before his eyes and the ground yielded beneath his feet; he stumbled over to a bare room with a trestle table and two stools. In the glass partition, he caught sight of himself. Matted hair, four days of beard and his eyes like two cigarette burns on a bed sheet. The portrait of the spy as an abject man.

Behind him the door opened. He looked at his visitor; he had a moonface, terra-cotta complexion and wore a regulation pin-striped suit. "Jenkins," he announced. "I'm second secretary at the embassy." He did not offer his hand.

"So they finally got around to telling you," Craig muttered.

"No, old chap," Jenkins said with a shrug. He held out a copy of one of the underground newspapers which circulated in Prague, indicating some paragraphs. Craig's mind absorbed the words slowly. The headline read: RUSSIANS NOW USING FOREIGN AGENTS. Under this, the story stated that Robert Martin, purporting to be a British citizen, had been arrested with a known KGB agent. Both were working against the interests of the Czech people and the Dubček regime. Both had been arraigned and would be tried and sentenced. They had not named Lora; for that he was thankful.

"Do they know in London?" he asked.

"Do they know! They're hopping, barking mad. Your boss has more or less told us to let you rot where you are."

Yes, Standish would take that line. He hardly blamed him. "Can you get me off this hook?" he said.

"Not a glimmer, old fellow. As much as I could do to have this word with you. The Czechs are a bit rabid about the Russians and have a bad case of spy mania. Your only chance will be the confusion that follows punitive action."

"You mean when the Russians take over?" Jenkins nodded. "So, what do I do—make a run for it?" Craig asked with heavy sarcasm.

"They'll have to release a lot of people. We'll cross our fingers and hope that you're among them."

Yes, he would get his release. He'd step out of Pancrac into the Lubyanka. Kudriatov would be delighted to open this door and close the other one.

"You'll certainly have a lot of explaining to do when you get back to London," Jenkins said.

"If I go back." Craig watched Moonface's eyes expand and the unspoken question in them.

"We'll do what we can for you," he said, rising and filtering out of the room as quietly as he had come.

For another day Craig suffered the cold, the hunger, the douches of cold water. But, thank God, no questions. Was it the captain's day off? Early the following morning he was squatting on the floor when he heard the noise; at first he thought he had gone light-headed with lack of food and sleep. But the rumble continued. He sensed a slight tremor in the floor. Those were tanks! Outside the cell he heard the thump of running feet; the prison suddenly filled with shouts. Someone screamed in Czech, "The Russians are invading." What did it mean to him? He might even regret Pancrac when Kudriatov showed his face.

In the afternoon, feet scuffed outside his cell door. It opened. Lora stood outside with a guard. "Is this the prisoner?" she demanded, the authority in her voice weakening when she caught sight of his naked and filthy body. She recovered her poise. "You," she ordered, "get dressed and follow me." They handed him his clothes; he put them on and stumbled behind her to the gate, where she flashed her KGB pass. "Get into the car," she said.

She drove toward the Vltava and turned into a back street. She stopped and looked at him. He saw tears in her eyes. "Matt," she cried, "what have they done to you?" She kissed him, drew his head down on her breast and ran her fingers through his matted hair. "They might have killed you," she said.

"A bath and a can of borscht and I'll be all right," he croaked. "I was worried about you."

"They did not dare touch me," she said.

At that moment, two tanks clattered past; they heard several explosions and a burst of machine-gun fire not far away; overhead, a flight of pigeons scattered like shrapnel at the noise. Rain was spattering on the windshield, misting it over, isolating them.

"I didn't mean the Czech Gestapo," Craig said. "I meant those." He pointed to the tanks.

"You were right," she said in a low voice. "I cannot believe it." Now she was crying openly.

"Lora—*dushka*—don't cry." He put his arm around her, but she pushed him away.

"No, Matt, I can't bear it." She wiped her eyes on her sleeve. "Do you have money?" When he shook his head, she thrust a handful of crowns at him. "There are trains through Pilsen to the West German border. I will drive you to the station."

"I only go if you come with me."

She hesitated, her hand resting on the gear lever. She gave a toss of her head. "No. It would kill him. I cannot do it." She was talking, he knew, about her father, the general who still had faith in Russia and the party.

"Give me the flat key. I'll wait there for you." As though too weak to argue, she found the key and passed it to him. He kissed her and climbed out.

"Where will it end?" he heard her cry as she put the car in gear and drove off.

To reach the flat took him two tiring hours. Russian tanks and armored cars had barricaded the main streets into the center of Prague; Czech crowds had blocked others by overturning trams and buses or setting the army vehicles ablaze. He did not need the key; the door swung open. Inside, the flat seemed intact. His package had survived, too. He washed and shaved, then waited for dusk before taking to the streets again. At the end of Národni Street he crossed the Vltava bridge and cut through back streets to Trziste Street. They seemed to have left the embassy quarter alone. He bluffed his way past the guards at the gates of the American Embassy. The courtyard looked like an army vehicle depot and, inside, the old building had a wartime atmosphere of action stations; pungent fumes filtered upward from the cellars as the staff burned everything marked "classified."

He located Dick Middleton emptying his desk and filling a briefcase. "I heard about your spot of trouble." He grinned. "Glad you got out with a whole skin."

"When are you leaving?"

"Tomorrow—before they lower the boom and keep it down. Do you want a lift?"

Craig shook his head. He produced his package and prayed he had read Middleton's face right. "I'd like you to take these out for me and hand or mail them to Johnny Mottram, a friend of mine in Berlin." He wrote down the address. "It's personal stuff, but it might be better to go in the bag." The American pocketed the material without questioning him.

"Sure you don't want a lift?"

"No, I have to see this through."

"If you get into trouble and I can help . . ."

"I'll remember that again," Craig answered.

He had to walk down the Vltava past three bridges before finding one with no guards. Now, the Warsaw Pact troops had invested the city and it lay under self-imposed curfew; he had to dodge tanks and foot patrols and circle the flat three times before daring to enter. From his window he observed the chaos in Wenceslas Square. Flames enveloped two tanks; he saw students leap on the tracks of another to drop lighted matches into its gas reservoir; crowds of Czechs had hemmed in bewildered Russian soldiers, shouting and shaking fists at them. Above him, jet fighters rasped low over the town center and the castle on Hradčany Hill. Scattered gunfire and the boom of an occasional shell came from the direction of the TV and radio building behind the square.

He had seen the pattern twelve years before in Budapest. He had got out then by the skin of his teeth. This time he wasn't running.

Lora slipped into the flat late that night and they barricaded the door. She would eat nothing and say nothing, but sat with her head in her hands listening to the Czech underground radio advising the citizens of Prague to give the Russians no help, to do everything to impede them. Not a glass of water or a slice of bread for the invaders. Tear down street names and efface door numbers to prevent the KGB from arresting patriots. Kiss and cuddle in front of these barbarians to show them what freedom really means. The announcers listed the men who had died that day, shot by the Russians and their allies.

Lora snapped the radio off; she swung around suddenly and said, "Matt, you were in Hungary. Tell me about it."

So, without embroidery, he described his first assignment during those four murderous days in November, 1956 when the tanks entered Budapest and blood flowed in its streets, when thousands of people died fighting, thousands more perished before firing squads and tens of thousands fled across the Austrian frontier.

"And they were men like these?" she said, pointing to the troops in the square. He nodded. She sat, silent, for several minutes. "I never believed those stories. None of us could. They were lies, we said. Bourgeois lies. Capitalist and fascist propaganda."

"We had Suez about that time. The Americans have Vietnam now. All just causes—if you read the right paper."

"I read the wrong paper," she exclaimed. "But those who still read it will believe the lies we shall tell to cover what we have done. Now I have seen it and I am finished with lies and deceit. I am not going back."

"It's a bit late," Craig remarked, thinking that he had given their passport to Middleton. "They don't like people quitting your game any more than a gangster will let one of his thugs quit the mob."

"But you said . . ."

"That was before the frontiers were shut."

She pondered for a moment. "You have contacts with the British intelligence. They can help us in exchange for what I can tell them."

"Yes, and after you'd sold your soul to them you'd hate yourself for the rest of your life. And you'd hate me for acting as the middleman." Why was he playing devil's advocate? He hardly understood that himself. He could only mutter, "There's nothing to choose between your side and theirs, and I should know."

Nevertheless, Lora insisted that he contact the British Embassy. When he eventually cornered him on the phone, Moonface Jenkins sounded more frosty than ever. "You might have informed us when

71

they released you," he said. No, it was impossible. The embassy had too much to do for him to keep clandestine engagements with . . . was he going to say "jailbirds"? If Craig wanted to see him he could come to the embassy.

At dusk the next evening, they slipped out to walk to the embassy. Several times, Lora had to talk them past Russian patrols; at the medieval tower guarding Charles Bridge, she had to show her KGB papers. Craig had that prickly sensation of being followed all the way to Thunouska Street and the embassy gate. He had never felt so relieved to see the Union Jack and the royal coat of arms.

Jenkins was waiting, pacing up and down. He refused even to talk to Lora, and ushered her into a waiting room. He then rounded on Craig. "You should be back in London," he snapped. Patiently, Craig explained what he wanted. When he had finished, the embassy official exploded. "What do you think you're playing at? Are you trying to compromise the embassy more than you have already? You know the situation here is ticklish, very ticklish. Now, my advice to you is to get that . . . that friend of yours out of here and get back to London."

"For Christ's sake, man, stop acting like a Sunday-school teacher. I've brought us one of the KGB's top agents who wants to defect and you're treating her like a smallpox case. Be a good chap and give us a CD car to cross the frontier while the Russians are busy with the Czechs."

The moonface froze. "I've told you, we want nothing to do with this woman and my orders from your own people are to put you on the first available flight for London."

Craig grabbed his pin-striped lapels, hoisted him several inches off the ground and shook him. "Tell them this—they can stuff their job but I won't go back without this girl."

Jenkins retreated behind his mock Chippendale desk. "Look, Craig, let's be reasonable. She's chosen the wrong moment. London doesn't want her. It would embarrass us here and poison what relations we enjoy with the Eastern-bloc countries at this moment. Now, I'm exceedingly hard pressed, so take your Miss Whatever-her-name-is away and, if you know what's good for you, report to the embassy tomorrow."

"Go to hell."

72

"Nobody wants us, Lora," he muttered as they began to back-track toward the flat. Rain was still falling but the city lay quiet, its streets deserted, their windows shuttered or curtained. Lora appeared to have shrunk into her mackintosh. She clung to his arm. "There is a farm on the Mělník road," she whispered. "It is run by a Czech called Maček who has helped many people to cross the frontier."

"We'll try it tomorrow," Craig replied. He had vaguely heard of Maček and the escape line; but at that moment he felt too close to despair to consider the suggestion.

In a narrow alley near the Old Town Square he brushed against a man coming out of a basement; through the doorway, he noticed several men and women sitting around tables drinking. "I could do with a drink," he said.

"No, Matt, it is too dangerous during the curfew."

Disregarding her protests, he pushed downstairs and through the cigarette stuffiness to a corner table. A dozen pairs of eyes followed him as he walked to the counter and brought back a bottle of slivovitz and two glasses. Somebody boosted the volume of the radio, broadcasting from a Prague station controlled by the Russians. They did not like strange faces, he thought.

They sat with their backs to the wall. Lora sipped the fiery brandy while Craig swallowed several glasses in quick succession to stifle his resentment, to blot out the faces of Jenkins and Standish. He would straighten out everything tomorrow. Tonight, he would get drunk. Lora was studying him anxiously. "Matt," she whispered. "Take the bottle and let's go home."

"Home? Home? We've got no home. Didn't I tell you?—nobody wants us. Your home's in Moscow and mine's in London. Different worlds." He was speaking thickly, slurring his words.

Lora rose to leave, but he pulled her down beside him. "Sit down, sweetheart, *dushka,* and I'll tell you a funny story. It's old . . . I should've told you five years ago . . . but it'll still keep you laughing all the way back to Lubyanka."

"Shut up, Matt. You don't know what you're saying or who is listening."

"I know what I'm saying all right. Listen, remember the first time we met? You and old Sergei Antonovich thought I was working for

73

the SIS. You were right. Thirteen years, boy and man. I fooled you and I fooled him. I'm not sorry about him, but I'm sorry I had to fool you."

He looked at her, expecting her to show astonishment or wrath. She did neither. Slowly, she lifted the water carafe from the table, tugged back his coat and shirt collars and poured the cold liquid down his back. As he spluttered at the shock, Lora seized his wrist and screwed it hard; the pain shot Craig out of his seat and she thrust him through the bar and upstairs into the street. Only when she had marched him fifty yards did she release his arm.

"I'm sorry I had to do that, Matt."

Craig groaned. "I gather you didn't think my story was funny."

"No, but other people down there might have."

"Ah, but you didn't hear the end. Good ending. I didn't fool anybody . . . anybody but myself. Lora, I don't know where I'm going or what I'm doing any longer. You're not angry, are you?"

"No," she said. "I knew."

They heard the rhythmic thud of boots on the cobblestones. Lora pulled him into a doorway as a patrol passed within yards of them, half a dozen Russians with submachine guns and a portable radio.

"You knew!" Craig muttered. "When?"

"I had an idea from the time we met in Berlin, but I knew that night you hit Kudriatov."

"And you never told anybody?"

"You know why," she said.

"I'll never begin to figure you out, *dushka*. Tell me, what have you in mind now for a drunken member of Her Majesty's Secret Intelligence Service?"

"We take him home and put him to bed."

"We?"

"You and I."

"But only he, Matthew Craig, has the privilege of being tucked in. Promise?"

"I promise."

"And tomorrow?"

"He and I begin to look for that island he talked about."

"Where I invent the wheel and you wash up our banana-leaf plates."

They skirted the radio building, ringed with troops, and crossed

74

Wenceslas Boulevard below the square. No crowds, no echo of Dubček and freedom. Just a circle of tanks guarding nothing but the
bronze king on his bronze horse and the blown and sodden roses and
lilies and wreaths at their feet.

A few hundred yards more and they would reach the flat and
safety. Lora had linked arms with him to support him. He felt secure
and warm; he had lost the sensation of being tailed. Had he not drunk
nearly a bottle of slivovitz, had Lora not been guiding his steps, they
might have noticed the two humpbacked Tatras cruising aimlessly up
and down the street. A third lay parked fifty yards from their flat.

The men had closed on them before he realized the danger. "Run,
Lora," he cried. "No," she shouted back. Three came from the
front, three behind. Craig pushed Lora into a doorway and backed up
against her. He met the first man with a knee in the groin and a fist
that sent him spinning into two others; he had to turn and ward off a
couple of thugs who rushed at him swinging truncheons. Two of the
men had grabbed Lora and were carrying her, kicking and yelling,
toward their car. Craig broke free and stumbled after them. He did
not hear the running feet behind him. Nor did he feel the stick thud
on his temple. He caught a faint voice calling his name before he
dropped on the pavement, senseless.

He came to with the salt taste of blood in his mouth and his head
going like a rivet gun. The dripping street, the doorway into which
they had bundled him fell gradually into shape. He was not on the
road to Lubyanka. They had only wanted Lora. Perhaps he had
proved just as embarrassing to the Russians as she to the SIS. He
pulled himself up only to topple over on his numb legs, his wet
clothes squelching. He managed to crawl the hundred yards to the
flat and collapse on the bed. Through his pain, one obsessive thought
throbbed: she had gone, this time for good. They thought they would
beat the system; they had come so close. But by tomorrow they
would have Lora back in Moscow to face charges of subversion or
even treason. This time he could not hope to follow her or even contact her.

Something else nagged at his mind: why had Kudriatov, who had
obviously issued the order to abduct Lora, left him alive and free?
After a while, he gave up trying to plumb that mystery.

It took him two days to recover. For another two days he hung around, telling himself that she might manage to escape and rejoin him. When he finally reported to the embassy, Jenkins greeted him with offhand courtesy. "They've instructed me to travel back with you to receive fresh orders and to make sure there's no trouble at the airport," he said.

In the airport, they merely glanced at their passports and hurried them through. They still had to fly to East Berlin and cross the Wall to Tempelhof. In the lounge, as they waited for their flight call, Craig noticed that Jenkins shuffled from one foot to another like a man who had eaten too many prunes; he steered them across the Tarmac with evident relief. When they had loosened their seat straps and the Lufthansa hostess handed around that day's papers, Craig saw the reason for the embassy man's uneasiness.

ENGLISH TRAITOR BETRAYED GERMAN INTELLIGENCE MEN TO RUSSIANS ran the flaring headline in *Bild-Zeitung*.

Whoever had documented the story had applied to the right source. He had dug up everything. The English traitor and double agent, Matthew Templeton Craig, had informed the Russians about the agents Stölcker and Dieringer, who had been executed; he had given the names of half a dozen other agents who had crossed the Wall to vanish without a trace. He had tipped off the KGB and the Vopos about the defection of Igor Strutchkov, the biggest potential catch Western intelligence had made in a decade. Strutchkov had died. *Bild* even had the dates and locations where Craig had passed information about Western diplomacy and defense organizations to his Russian contacts in East Berlin. Over a five-year period Craig had received more than £10,000 for his dubious services. He had been spotted in Prague, helping the Russians to stage their counter-coup. Had it not been for a Czech VKR (Military Intelligence) agent who had fled across the West German frontier during the invasion of Prague, the English spy would still be selling secrets to the KGB.

Now Craig understood why Kudriatov's gorillas had merely hit him on the head and left him lying in the street. Sergei Antonovich had planted that defector with all his information and no doubt plenty of documents to support his story. To pay him out for his betrayal nine months before, to damn him in Lora's eyes, he had thought up a sweet revenge. Better than death.

He caught Jenkins looking furtively at him as he threw down the newspapers. "It seems pretty bad for you, old chap," he murmured, a cloud crossing his moonface.

Bad enough for two Special Branch men to be waiting at London Airport to escort him to a cell in Bow Street. Bad enough for C, the supreme SIS chief, to cancel his annual holiday and return to supervise his interrogation and give him the worst two days of his life. Bad enough for Vernon Alveston Standish to slip off to Scotland for an unseasonal fishing trip with his trusted gillie, Jameson Garvie.

9 Two days after his return, he appeared at Bow Street Police Court. There they charged him on three counts under the Official Secrets Act for communicating information prejudicial to the safety of the state and of use to a potential enemy. He pleaded Not Guilty and his trial was fixed for September 22. Not until he had spent a week on remand did Standish visit him in his cell at Wandsworth Prison. He apologized for his absence.

"I'd have come sooner, but you've given us a lot of headaches in the department with this senseless escapade of yours."

"Stop hedging, Standish. You'd still be chasing salmon if C hadn't asked you to persuade me to change my plea. It stays Not Guilty. I'm damned if I'm going to rot in a cell because you were trying to be too clever by half."

"If you'd listened to my advice and kept out of Prague, you wouldn't be sitting here."

"All right, I made an idiot of myself, but you could have bailed me out."

"I pulled every string, Matt—believe me. I've even been to Number Ten. But it was too late. The press here and in Germany are shouting for your head. You know the rules. If we're found dead they don't know us. If we're caught, we take what's coming and say nothing."

"I'm playing my own rules from now on. I'm going into the witness box to blow the whole dirty racket."

Standish rose from the prison bunk and began to quarter the four-by-two cell. He lit a cigarette, dragged twice on it, squashed it with his foot and lit another. He seemed agitated. Finally, he sat down and placed a hand on Craig's shoulder.

"Think of it, Matt. Five years' work gone. All the information you gathered that the other side knows nothing about. Spill that in court and we'll never untangle the mess. And a few of your friends and our agents will pay with their heads." He paused to fix Craig with his eyes. "We can't let you do it."

"Who's to stop me?"

"Nobody, if you're witless enough. If you don't change your plea they'll merely put up the shutters in court and Lord Chief Justice will have to send you away for life to stop you talking out of turn."

"Maybe I'll take you with me for company in the long evenings."

"An SIS chief testifying in open court or even in secret session!" Standish slowly rotated his head. "If the defense forced me, I'd lie in my teeth and deny everything. On orders."

"Right! If I'm getting all the stick I'll at least give them their money's worth."

"Who? The public? They've condemned you sight unseen. The SIS? We know the score already. The only people who'll laugh are the KGB."

"The KGB?"

"One way or another, they'll steal a copy of your testimony. And then they'll know the lot."

In every dialogue he had ever held with Standish there came the point where the famous cerebral scrambler and encoder faltered, and a word or a sentence escaped clearly. Deliberately or unwittingly—Craig could not be sure. KGB was that word. Standish was scrutinizing him. Waiting to see how well he could decode and unscramble?

"They know it all by heart," he muttered, wondering where Standish was heading.

"She might have told them about Strutchkov and about Prague. But I doubt it."

Standish had finally got there; he had thrown his spinner, or his spade-ended fly hook, at him. Lora! How would she fare if he unloaded everything? No one would ever discover. The KGB did not stage its inquisitions in the Supreme Court; nor did they publish anything, even the names of the deceased. Doubt filled his mind. "But Kudriatov knows," he stammered.

78

"I hardly think it would be in his interest to mention such facts," Standish said. "But if the Attorney General had to bring her name into evidence . . ." He chopped off the end of that thought and shrugged.

"Kudriatov saved her once. He'd do it again."

"I hear that one of his good friends, Kyrill Gregoriev, is sharpening the knives for him. No, Kudriatov would be put against the wall with her."

"He should have thought of that before sending his pigeon across the German frontier."

"You asked for it, Matt. We all make one slip."

"You made it. I'm paying."

"No, you're paying for your fortnight in bed with your tovarish in Prague. But they may let you down lightly."

"How lightly?"

"That depends how you plead. Not Guilty and they'll heave everything at you. Guilty and you'll do five years—just over three with remission. And nobody need whisper Comrade Trusova's name. I have C's word on that."

"His word? What's that worth?" Craig turned to Standish. "Go back and say I'll plead the way I choose." He seized Standish's rolled umbrella and rattled its yellow ferrule along the bars of the cell to signify that he had listened to more than enough double talk.

Nothing seemed real. Not the Lord Chief Justice, a scarlet-and-white splash framed against a high-backed chair like some eighteenth-century portrait of himself; not the phalanx of lawyers in wigs and gowns, wedged in their amber pews; not the pressmen, reading their day-old stories; not even the two familiar SIS faces in the public gallery. Through the glass dome of Number One Court at the Old Bailey milky light spilled, transfiguring and transfixing everything, bleaching hands and faces, torturing his eyes. He had the impression of blundering into some theater where they were playing out some macabre costume piece with himself as the sole spectator. Yet they were trying him for the nearest thing to treason and he had already made their decisions for them. Only the legal charade remained.

He hardly heeded the court clerk's wintry soliloquy delineating the charges.

79

"Matthew Templeton Craig," the clerk said. "How do you plead? Guilty or Not Guilty?"

He hesitated. He could still change his mind. He would have liked to let a snake loose in this frigid assembly. The bleached faces all converged on him. "Guilty," he said quietly. They had given him three syllables for his walking-on part; he had uttered two of them. He sat down. As the court stirred, he remembered quipping to Lora that British justice was an intricate game of offense and defense where truth often finished as the real casualty; he never envisaged then that he would be caught in a tangle like this.

The Attorney General, Sir Gwyn Lynton-Morgan, had risen to state the Crown case. A friend of Standish's, a heavy-paunched Establishment Tory, he had a tombstone voice and a port-wine, pimpled face, which he mopped from time to time with a matching red polka-dot handkerchief. He took it slowly, dwelling on Craig's background as the boy from a poor home who had won scholarships to schools and universities, who had a brilliant gift for languages, who had chosen his own career in Her Majesty's Intelligence Service.

Yes, they'd have to go for the money motive. The indigent, penny-grubbing Scot dazzled by handfuls of Russian rubles. Where had he heard the echo of that one? The Penkovsky trial, of course. Poor Penkovsky, he'd been accused of selling his soul for champagne-filled slippers and a barrowful of treasury bills.

"As your lordship is aware, Craig has made a complete avowal of his crime and his document has been submitted as the main evidence for the prosecution. However, we are dealing with such a grave breach of the law that I can only touch on the broad aspects of his confession. If the accused or his counsel wish to bring other details from this document into evidence I shall have to request that these proceedings be conducted *in camera.*"

His silk polka dot fluttered over his face. "I can say that, in the course of his intelligence duties, Craig was contacted during 1964 by members of the Soviet secret service who offered him payment to work for them. To do him justice, Craig reported this offer to his superiors. But what he did not divulge was that under the guise of operating as one of our own intelligence men he was still acting as a Soviet agent. This man handed over documents and information about British and allied policies which did unaccountable damage to

80

the cause of this and other countries. He betrayed two men who died, and imperiled the lives of many others whose fate we do not yet know. For nearly five years he was able to carry out his treachery. Unfortunately, because of the grave nature of the offense, I cannot instance to this court, or disclose in any way, the information which Craig sold to the Soviet Union. . . ."

No, nor can you say that it was handed to me by my boss and your friend, Standish, and it didn't matter a damn to us or them. Tell them about the information I got for us.

"There are traitors who change their allegiance because of their politics, their moral or ideological views. Craig was none of these. It must be acknowledged and admitted that he belongs to the worst type of traitor, the man who sells his soul for money, the venal spy."

Go on, say it: the abject man.

The Attorney General was stuffing his handkerchief into his breast pocket; he looked at Craig, then at the Lord Chief Justice. "This closes the prosecution's case insofar as it can be presented. I must crave the court's indulgence for my brevity. I will leave it to your lordship and the defense counsel to decide if we can continue in open court."

Standish had urged him to choose Sir Ralph Corry, a Queen's Counsel, to defend him. ("One of the most able barristers in the country, Matt. But don't tell him everything. If they clear the court and he drops a name or a hint or two, *they* might pick it up.") So he had given Corry an edited version of the facts; and, as he had done in his confession, he omitted all mention of Lora.

Corry was on his feet. "I must request your lordship to clear the court and hear my plea in mitigation behind closed doors," he said.

"Hmm. Is it necessary in this case? I have a strong repugnance for *in camera* hearings."

"I must insist, m'lud," Corry snapped back. "What we have heard so far in this court has been in the interests of state security. I would now like to be free to say something in the interests of my client and of justice."

"I have no objection; indeed, I support the plea," Lynton-Morgan interjected.

Ushers began to escort people from the public gallery and the well of the court. Even the senior and junior barristers assisting the prosecution and the defense had to leave. So did the newspaper reporters. Craig spotted four Special Branch men searching the public gallery and the pews for the tape recorder or the hidden microphone. It took half an hour before Corry could resume his plea before the Lord Chief Justice, the Attorney General, the clerk and one shorthand writer.

He did brilliantly. Had he been pleading Not Guilty before a jury, the trial might have taken a different turn. But the barrister's eloquence appeared to bounce off the flinty face on the judge's bench.

"We have been forced to listen to my learned colleague's abbreviated and highly censored version of this tragic case," he said. "As I listened, it occurred to me that perhaps the sorriest victims of the secrets game that goes on between countries are the men we call spies.

"Matthew Craig was a spy. That was his business. We trained him for it. We paid him to do it. You have his record in front of you, m'lud, and you can appreciate that this man had great talent for what is, we must own, a sordid profession."

The Lord Chief Justice raised a hand. "What point are you trying to make, Sir Ralph?"

"Just this simple but vital point. When you select and hire men for this dangerous job, you cannot expect them to conform to the general run of people. They are not men of honor, motivated by high principles or the good of humanity. Neither are they the heroes nor the villains of popular mythology fighting some secret war for good or evil."

"What are they then?" The voice from the dais breathed boredom and sarcasm.

"They are spies, men whose jobs and whose lives often depend on their ability to practice deceit, to trick and hoodwink their fellow men; they are men whose methods we would condemn if we met them in the ordinary course of business. But our state fashions and manipulates these men, like Craig here. We may fancy that our spies are different from the spies of other countries. They are not. They have the same morals, the same code of behavior, the same scruples . . ."

". . . Or, do you mean, the lack of them?"

"As you infer, m'lud—or lack of them." What might have been

82

blood flushed to the Lord Chief Justice's face. Corry had paused to turn to Craig, sitting between two jailers in the dock.

"What the Attorney General could not reveal in open court was that we asked this man not to play the part of one spy—but two spies. We asked him to become a double agent, to spy for us while ostensibly spying for the Russians. We encouraged him to undertake this role, to accept the Russian offer, to pocket the bribes they handed him. It served the purposes of the state to use him this way, and he carried out our orders. How successfully, I will not rely on him to tell us. We have the sworn statement by a senior member of the SIS who was Craig's immediate superior. I shall read it."

"Don't bother. We have the document in evidence."

Corry read it, despite the Lord Chief Justice's protest. Standish had praised him fulsomely; Craig would never have known had the barrister not produced the affidavit. The SIS man had described him as the most brilliant of all his agents and one who had never flinched at the most dangerous tasks. He had a long record of loyal service and had been under no suspicion until just over four years ago. His last assignment, as a double agent, had doubtless imposed a very severe strain on his mind and personality and this had almost certainly contributed to his shift of loyalties. Standish had said more than Craig ever hoped for.

Corry was pointing to the paper he had just read. "There, you have the nub of this case," he said. "It is clear from what his controlling officer suggests that it is not so rare for men like my client to be placed in just such a situation where their allegiance, their personalities, their very minds become confused. The double agent constantly faces the danger of exposure, he has to submit to extortionate demands, his life is often under threat. Is it any wonder that they cede to such pressures? Is it any wonder that Craig began to doubt his loyalty? He is less a victim of his own weakness than of the system that created and abused him."

Altogether, Corry had spoken for just over forty minutes. The moment he sat down, the clerk summoned the ushers, who removed the wooden shutters from the swing doors to admit the lawyers, the press and the public. When the Lord Chief Justice was ready, the two jailers pushed Craig to his feet.

"You stand convicted of a felony," the clerk said. "Have you anything to say on your behalf before you are sentenced according to the law?''

"No," Craig replied. He could only feel relief that no one had mentioned Berlin, Prague and Lora.

The Lord Chief Justice took exactly nine minutes, addressing himself to Craig, who stood in the dock.

"I have already indicated my regret that the national interest obliged us to exclude much of the essential evidence of this case from the public domain. However, your own confession leaves this court in no doubt about your guilt and the damage you have done to the interest of this country and its allies. Against this, I have weighed the written testimony by your senior colleague and the very able if somewhat emotive plea by your counsel. I accept that men like you are often subjected to intolerable pressures, but you knew this when you chose your profession. You undertook positions of great public trust and committed what I consider a treasonable offense.

"Public interest unfortunately makes it possible for me to divulge only a part of your treachery. But I have to make it clear that your motives for betraying your country and others were of the basest. You sold yourself, you sold other men's lives for your own personal gain. Such despicable conduct merits heavy punishment. On the three counts to which you have pleaded guilty, this court therefore imposes on you a sentence of twenty years' imprisonment.''

Craig caught the gasp from the public gallery; he noticed even the press benches stir before the guards nudged him downstairs to his cell below the Old Bailey.

He was sitting waiting for the prison truck when the key turned in the lock. Standish soft-footed in. "Matt, old chum, what can I say? I *am* sorry.''

Craig glowered at him. "What do they give you for murder?''

"But we can appeal against the sentence. We can do something for you.''

"You can right now. Get out of here before I take you apart, bone by bone.''

"Give it a year or two, Matt, and I'll think of something. I won't let you molder away in jail." He sounded sincere, but Craig had long ago passed the point where he lent credence to anything Standish said.

"Just close the door behind you and leave me alone."

"The least we can do for the moment is to keep an eye on your girl in Moscow."

"Leave her alone, do you hear? If you as much as try to contact her, I shall kill you," Craig roared.

Standish beckoned toward the guard and put a finger to his lips. "If you need anything, Matt . . ." But he did not finish. Craig grabbed him by the jacket and banged him hard against the cell bars until the guard opened the door. "Keep away from me," he shouted as he thrust Standish into the corridor.

In the truck that took him the short ride through London to Wormwood Scrubs, he sat thinking of Lora. Odd, how their story had begun with one trial and ended with another.

II An Abject Man

Spying is such a dirty game that only gentlemen can play it well.

GENERAL REINHARD GEHLEN

1

Craig had finished folding the army blanket on his iron bunk and was cleaning out his cell on the fourth floor of D block when the guard rattled his keys on the bars. "Couple of gents to see you if you've slopped out, Jacko," he said. This screw called everybody Jacko, his way of emphasizing that crime was crime whether it entailed pinching a library book, poisoning your mother-in-law or selling state secrets. Craig dropped his slop pail and ambled at prison gait along the gallery and down the iron stairs. The screw's truncheon jabbed into his spine, for he never allowed even a trusty prisoner to walk behind him. He propelled Craig through the exercise yard toward the governor's office in the admin block and indicated a room at the end of the corridor. As he pushed Craig inside, two men rose from the armchairs; the taller man held out his hand, but Craig ignored the gesture.

"You can leave us alone, officer," Standish murmured.

"Against prison rules, you know," Jacko the Screw replied. "No maximum-security prisoner is permitted to have visitors except in the presence of a prison officer."

Standish thrust a piece of paper at him. "What we have to say is private. Here's our authority. I'll call you when we've finished."

When the guard had gone, he turned to Craig with a bland grin. "Nice to see you again, Matt," he said.

"If I'd known you were here I'd have had them double-lock my cell."

"Oh, come now! Cigarette?" He conjured his gold case into his hand and offered his gold-tipped Bond Street brand. Craig knocked the case and his own temptation away; he ferreted in the lining of his denims and produced a hand-rolled cigarette no thicker than a match. "We smoke our own snout here," he said. Refusing the flame from the gold lighter, he fished once more for a pin-sized match and a strip of abrasive. In four years a handy man could acquire the art of splitting a single match into ten lights and rolling one fag into five pass-

89

able smokes. He lit the cigarette and, through the blue smoke curling in the sunlight, glanced at his visitor.

He had not set eyes on Vernon Alveston Standish since the gates of Wormwood Scrubs had closed behind him nearly four years before. He noted that those years had added a notch or two to the waistcoat belt and a few new fleshy contours to his gills. Life still sat easily on him, even if he did look more than ever like Oscar Wilde in his more desperate days and had those dead-fish eyes. Craig saw the patrician nostril curl at the odor of carbolic, stale sweat and prison hash which permeated everything, even the governor's wing, where they sat. What had brought Vernon Alveston to the Scrubs before eight o'clock on a fine morning? He would probably never answer that question.

"Perhaps I'd better introduce you," Standish said. "This is Superintendent Cyril Ross of Scotland Yard."

"The Special Branch?"

"You could . . . er . . . you could say so," Standish drawled.

"Then why don't you? I can keep my mouth shut."

"Still the same old Matt. You know, Ross, he was one of the best of us. Indeed, I'd venture to say *the* best."

"Ross has read the whole story, and he knows they said the same about Lucifer and Judas, don't you, Ross?"

"I always cared for your sense of humor, Matt, that barb of cynicism. We had some good laughs."

"We did that. Could hardly keep our faces straight when they sentenced me to twenty years on evidence that you helped to provide."

"That was policy from on high, old chum. You know I did what I could."

"Yes, to screw me."

"Why would I do that?"

"Because you want to be the top man in the SIS. What are you now—number three, number two or number one?"

Standish smiled, rose and walked to the barred window and gazed at the courtyard and the high wall beyond. "The old place has changed since I did my stint here." He turned to Craig. "It was before your time, but we ran part of MI 5 from here during the war until a bomb hit us. In a way, it was the best billet we ever had."

"We try to live it down," Craig said, aware that Standish had veered away from the subject of his trial and condemnation.

Standish turned. "How would you like to get out—oh, not this minute, but in a year or two?"

"How would you like to tell me how?"

"We want a bit of help from you."

Craig shook his head slowly. "You know where you can stuff that one."

"He's Scottish and bloody-minded," Standish remarked to Ross.

"He's been had too many times before," Craig put in.

"If you'll listen and co-operate, Matt, I might be able to get you a parole or at least several years' remission."

"I'm not interested, I tell you."

"You mean you don't want an earlier release?"

"I mean that I don't trust you and whatever you promise I'll still have to keep a clean nose and do ten years in the mailbag shop. But I'm not bellyaching. The people here are straighter than some I used to work with."

"It's a good offer, Matt."

Craig did not answer. He marched to the door and hammered on it until Jacko appeared. "We've finished," he said, about to step out of the door. Standish ran after him to grip his arm.

"Matt, old horse. Before you go, take a good look at this."

He was holding out a crumpled leaf from a notebook. Craig gave one glance and stopped in his tracks; he slammed the door in the guard's face and stared at Standish.

"So she's alive," he shouted. "Where is she? Where?"

"That's what we'd like you to tell us."

Craig grabbed the fragment of ruled paper with its scribbled message in Russian. The Cyrillic characters with their backward slope and peculiar tails stamped the writer's identity as surely as her fingerprint. She had also thickened the Russian N's and G's—their personal code. Anyway, the content would have convinced him.

I hope you remembered our anniversary. I drank to yours on July 28. I shall probably visit the Lighthills on August 6 and stay a few days. I had thought of looking up our friends in the country on August 14 or 24. Much love, dushka, darling, Lora.

"Where did you get this?"

"In Warsaw on July 29. She came to the embassy but was very unlucky. Half the staff were on leave and she ran into a junior press

91

attaché who didn't know who she was or what she was talking about. She scribbled this note. By the time we got back to the embassy with instructions she had vanished.''

"She probably knew what happened to Volkov when he knocked on our consulate door in Istanbul.''

"Ah, but there's no Philby in London these days to tip off the Russians.''

"Maybe Lora has a better idea about that than you,'' Craig said dryly.

Standish lit another cigarette. Had his tobacco craving increased? "Of course, we would have granted her political asylum had she asked only for that.''

"What did she want?''

"Something we couldn't have given her even if she had waited for the answer.'' Standish sucked in smoke and studied Craig. "She wanted you, Matt. Free. Delivered to a neutral country. We thought at first that this might be another variation of what one of our wags dubs Russian chesspionage—swapping their pawns for our kings, queens and rooks. But we know that your Russian friends intend to let you rot here during Her Majesty's pleasure. And Comrade Trusova seems too scared of her own countrymen to be playing a double game.''

"So if there's no swap I can get back to the mailbag shop,'' Craig said, rising from his seat.

"Hold on a second. Don't you want to know what she was trying to swap?''

Craig shook his head. "If it was important enough to bring you out here at sparrow fart to see a poor bloke in stir you're not going to tell me, are you?''

Standish curled his other nostril at Craig's prison slang. "Did you know she was working in the KGB Central Index?'' he asked. Craig shrugged. "She stole a file from there.''

"The file she mentioned in the other half of the message—the bit you kept.''

"It had the highest classification or I'd have shown it to you.''

"Then they've got copies in the Index.''

"We don't think so. Only a handful of the top KGB men knew about it. Comrade Trusova has probably taken the only copy or destroyed the others.''

92

"She didn't tell you that," Craig said suddenly.

"Perhaps not." Standish stubbed out his cigarette, flicking a glance at Craig. He was still sharp, he thought. He had done— what?—four years in this hole. They had changed him. Prison diet and lack of exercise had fined down his features, given him that candle-grease skin and a neck twitch; he spoke with the frozen mouth of prisoners who had learned to whisper "across the gap" without falling foul of the guards. What had he expected would happen to an intelligent introvert deprived of social and intellectual challenge? Matt showed all the symptoms of stir fever. Yet he could still ram home points like those last two. Watch it, Standish, he said to himself.

"Let's say we have good contacts in Moscow." He grinned.

"Did your Moscow nark tell you what was in the file, too?"

"All I can disclose is that it concerns a matter of state security of the highest importance."

"British or Soviet?"

"That depends which school of thought you belong to."

"So both sides need it," Craig said. "Good for Lora, picking the right one. I hope she gets away with it."

"She won't—unless you tell us where she'll be on those dates in her message."

"Sorry, I don't know."

"But surely you can work out the code! Being picked up by us is her only chance."

"Her only chance?"

"Your old chum Kudriatov has been given a small army to track her down and recover that *zapiski.* You know what that means."

"So does she, and she's prepared to risk it rather than deal with you."

"A big risk, Matt. They've put the *istrebeteli* on her trail."

Craig hesitated at the sound of that word. The *istrebeteli,* the executioners of the KGB ninth section, would hunt Lora down as they had others who had defected. They would have orders to kill her if they could not bring her back to Moscow to face summary sentence and execution. Not even Kudriatov could protect her this time. But no, he would make no more bargains with Standish. He looked at the SIS man and Ross. What was a Special Branch superintendent doing here? Did they imagine he would carry out his threat to strangle his

93

old boss? Or did Lora's file concern some politician? Whatever the answer, he would keep his own counsel this time.

"I'm sorry, Standish. I've brought you all this way for nothing. I wouldn't know where to start looking."

"Like a copy of the message?" Craig shook his head. "Well, if you change your mind, the governor will put you in touch immediately."

"I won't change my mind."

The two men watched the guard eclipse the tall figure in the doorway. Standish strolled to the window to follow them as they crossed the exercise yard. "I wasn't joking, Ross, when I told you he was the best man we ever had. He had only one weakness."

"Women." The superintendent grunted as though, in his policeman's ethic, the word summed up every male fault.

"No." Standish emphasized the word by shaking his head. "Just that one woman. She destroyed him."

"He seems to have got over her now."

Standish drummed on the windowpane with his fingernails. "You don't know Matt as I do. We used to play chess together in the old days. We were both good, but Matt always had the edge on me. He could play both black and white pieces, the other man's game, as well, if not better, than his own. I've made my move. Now it's up to him."

2   So Lora was alive, and free! For more than four years he had run a mental permutation on her fate from the moment, that August evening in Prague, they had both decided to flee. He remembered how they had walked down the main boulevard past the dripping Wenceslas statue in the square with the sodden roses and lilies, with memorial plaques to dead Czechs at its base, with Russian tanks hemming in the handful of students who still sat on the wet cobblestones. Lora had wrapped a foulard around her head, peasant style, though an errant lock of russet hair had escaped. Hands thrust deep into her raincoat pockets, collar turned up, she seemed to have

94

shrunk in the rain like the crowds around the statue who had shouted for freedom, a freedom as fugitive as their own. They had almost beaten the system. Another day, another hour perhaps. But she was alive when he had once thought she would have perished in some Siberian labor camp. Kudriatov must have played the devil's advocate to get her a job in the Central Index of the KGB. And, of course, there was his own trial and conviction. That would have helped exonerate her.

But alive and free for how long? She had stolen a state secret and they would find and silence her somehow. No Kudriatov to bail her out this time. Craig mentally figured the game from the Russian's and Standish's viewpoints. The KGB chief knew every assignment Lora had ever undertaken: Berlin, Warsaw, Belgrade, Prague and others. He would split his force, concentrate on those cities, enlisting KGB resident directors in each to check every address she had frequented. And Standish, who wanted not Lora but the *zapiski* she had taken? He would concentrate on Warsaw, Berlin and perhaps Prague; he had the advantage of those dates on the message, which he would rightly assume to indicate meeting places. Standish had revealed only half the message, for Lora would have begun the note with the words *"Dushka* Matt." In the half he had seen, she had cleverly omitted the dates that only he could guess. The missing bit of paper probably contained the key to the file she had stolen. What did the note say? . . .

"You going somewhere special today, Jacko?" Craig felt the screw's stick rattle off his collarbone; he realized that he had unconsciously discarded four years of prison slouch and was quick-stepping across the exercise yard. For four years he had not bothered to count the minutes, the days, the weeks; he had more than ten years to do, and where to go when they let him out? Now, the days, the minutes, even seconds seemed important. For the first time since he had donned prison uniform his brain had focused on something tangible and was alert.

"What would you say, Jacko the Screw, if I told you I was going to escape?" he muttered beneath his breath. Funny, he had made that resolve, instinctively, the moment he had heard of Lora's bid to free him. She had pitted herself against the KGB; he could surely find a way over this high wall. How? He had no friends outside. But there was Frank, here in the Scrubs.

As they reached the gallery leading to his cell, he suddenly halted, doubled up and clutched at his stomach. "Come on, Jacko. On your feet." The truncheon bit into his back. Craig grimaced, pointing to his stomach. "Move on. No lead swinging on my block," the screw growled, hustling him forward. Craig stumbled and fell. Tensing himself, he sank his teeth into the soft flesh of his cheek, sucked in the blood and coughed it into his palm. While Jacko stared hard at the blood the gallery erupted with noise; spoons rattled along cell bars and boots thumped on the floors. "Go on, Jacko," Craig's friends shouted. "Put the boot in. Finish him off." The guard pulled Craig to his feet, turned him around and prodded him back down the stairs. "You'll walk to casualty," he ordered. Craig tottered on, doubled up, with the whole block yelling encouragement at him.

Frank Lucas was working in the dispensary when they arrived. Craig winked at him, letting the guard explain what had happened. Lucas, who wore the blue band of a trusty prisoner, shoved a thermometer into Craig's mouth and felt his pulse. "Fast," he muttered. "Pain in the stomach and around the back?" With the glass tube in his mouth, Craig could only take the hint and nod. "Comes on when—just before you eat?" Again, Craig nodded. Lucas pulled out the thermometer, scanning it. "It's high—102." He rounded on the guard. "Four years of nosh in this place would give anybody an ulcer. Good thing you brought him along. He'd better wait for the quack."

"When he's through get him back to D block," the guard snapped and walked off.

"Frank, I've got to get out, and quick," Craig whispered.

"Take it easy, Matt. The doc will give you a fistful of pills and a week away from the laundry and you'll settle down."

"If you don't help I'll go over the wall on my own."

"And lose five years off for good conduct. You're stir happy. We all get it. You hop the twig and sleep rough for a week and they reach out and grab you."

"Not where I'm going."

"Where's that?"

"The other side of the Iron Curtain. And I haven't much time to make it."

"What's happened? Don't tell me—it's the girl who got you twenty years of porridge in the first place."

Lucas ran his fingers through his prison haircut and tugged at his earlobe. His broad face creased as he looked at Craig; he pulled out a packet of Player's, handed him one and lit it with a lighter.

Craig wondered how Lucas managed it. He always had fresh snout, extra sugar for his cocoa and a cache of canned meat which probably came from the truck drivers who brought in provisions and collected the mailbags. They had met four years ago when Craig first arrived at the Scrubs and Lucas was finishing a six-month spell for receiving stolen cars. Somehow, he had smuggled extra food and tobacco to Craig when he was an escape-listed prisoner on the top floor of the maximum-security wing. This time they had caught him with a load of whisky and transistor radios, which the magistrates refused to believe had fallen off a truck. He had served two of his six months and would do only another two if he kept a clean nose. Craig not only wondered how a man as intelligent and well-read as Lucas mixed with criminals, but also how he came to be caught. "The salt of the earth some of these geezers, Matt," he would say. "All right, they don't live by the rules, but who wants to when the rules are bent. Stir's not bad. It's the only society most of these poor sods know. Look at Mickey Parker. Did his last job so that the bogies would nab him and he'd be back with his mates. A lot like that."

While they dragged on their cigarettes, Lucas kept a watch for screws and was muttering out of the side of his mouth, half to himself, half to Craig. "You go over the dike and the bell goes in half an hour and you're back in the poky hole. You'll need to be crocked. You'll need a car. A nicked one. New togs. Papers." He paused for a minute. "You'll need a passport," he said.

"An old one would do," said Craig.

"That's all right. I've got a penman who can doctor it. Where did you get your last pictures taken?" With an effort Craig remembered the name of the studio in Chelsea. "Fine, I'll get somebody to buy a couple." Lucas was thinking aloud again. "You flash it at London or Dover and they bag you. So you go through Dublin, or . . . I'll look at the timetables." Suddenly, he rounded on Craig.

"You owe the state twenty, so they'll do all they can to collect."

"What are you getting at?"

"If you show signs of really croaking with that phony ulcer they'll hustle you across the road to Hammersmith Hospital and give you the treatment. The quack here's an old codger who won't take chances and won't latch on. Let's see—we had an ulcer last week and they kept him only an hour. But that diabetic the week before stayed a couple of days. If you had a bit of both . . . ."

"I hope you know what you're doing, Frank," Craig commented, half alarmed and half admiring at the way Lucas was planning his breakout.

"Got much blood? Not much, by the look of you." Lucas had taken a disposable syringe needle and was already rolling up Craig's sleeve. "Half a pint should do it." He grunted, stabbing the needle into a vein in the crook of the arm and connecting the end to a plastic tube; a few minutes later he had half a bottle of blood, which he hid under the table. Disappearing, he soon returned with some vinegar into which he poured a spoonful of sugar. This he heated over a spirit lamp to dissolve the sugar before drawing off the liquid into a syringe.

"An old lag's trick," he commented. "You inject it into a muscle and it boosts the blood sugar for a couple of hours so they think you've got diabetes." He broke off, cocking an ear at the car coming through the main gate. "That's the sawbones. Now you've got an ulcer. . . . You know where the pain is. When he's swallowed that tell him you've no appetite, you're drinking and pissing all night and you get dizzy spells. He'll think you're having him on, he always does. You'll get some stomach powder with belladonna in it and a couple of days away from the scrubbing board."

Lucas had uncanny insight into the doctor's mind; the prison physician huffed and puffed around Craig, finally giving him a tin of stomach powder and several days' rest. Lucas marched back with him to his cell. There, he slipped him the syringe and the bottle of blood.

"Now, here's the drill. Give us a couple of days to fix the passport, car and tickets. After nosh on the third night empty the blood into your slop pail, inject this stuff and take a couple of spoonfuls of this stomach powder. Don't get the breeze up when the belladonna sets your ticker going quick. You'll look so bad they'll have to carry

you over there on a stretcher. I'll tell you the rest then." Lucas
gripped him by the arm. "Matt, you still sure you want to do it?"

"If it kills me," Craig replied.

3 Three nights later, as he locked the cell doors, Jacko
the Screw found Craig lying unconscious, apparently bleeding to
death. The prison doctor did what Lucas had predicted: diagnosed a
burst ulcer and immediately transferred him to Hammersmith Hospital. The prison officer and Lucas carried him over to the casualty
ward, where an Indian medical officer examined him. "This man we
are being obliged to detain for two, maybe four, days of observation
while ascertaining if he necessitates operative surgery for his ab-
dominal condition," the doctor announced. "He also has positive
symptoms of diabetes mellitus."

"No prisoner stays here without the governor's permission," said
Jacko.

The Indian smiled. "Of this man's escaping there is absolutely no
danger whatever."

"The doctor can phone the governor," Lucas put in.

"I'll do that myself," Jacko snapped.

The moment he had gone, Lucas slipped into the casualty ward.
Craig lay, breathing deeply, his face flushed. "Matt, you all right?"
he hissed. Craig opened his eyes and nodded slowly. "You haven't
overdone it?" Craig shook his head.

"Listen," Lucas went on. "Everything's fixed for tonight.
They'll put you in a surgical ward over by the skyscraper. They think
you're too far gone to walk. Wait till the night screw comes on duty
at ten o'clock and the staff have made their rounds. It's an easy drop
to the parking lot, about eight feet. Head away from Du Cane Road,
through the wire and across the Scrubs. Look for a green Mini, SGO
36F. Say you're from Frank. The driver'll know the rest. Best of
British luck."

From casualty they wheeled him over a courtyard into a low red-
brick ward. He felt the stab of a needle. "Sedative?" he heard a girl
query. "No, sister, he may be in a hypoglycemic coma and we may
exacerbate his condition," the Indian said in his sol-fa voice.

99

When the door had closed, Craig opened his eyes to glance around. Jacko's shape hovered outside. He looked for a bedside clock and blinked; the drug bottles and the buttery light swam before his eyes. Everything had acquired a halo. The belladonna! Lucas had forgotten that the drug temporarily immobilized and expanded the eye pupils. So much the worse. If he had to use a white stick, he'd make that drop and stagger across the Common.

The staff changed shifts; the new guard appeared and Jacko barked out his instructions. Craig shut his eyes and let his head loll as both men entered. "So this is the bloke what sold us out to the Commies," the new man said. "Looks bad enough to get an early parole by the back gate." He snickered. "Too good for the bleedin' traitor," Jacko replied. The door opened and the ward sister said sharply: "Didn't the doctor instruct you that this man must not be disturbed? He's very ill."

"All right, sister," Jacko grunted. "Keep an eye on him from the door," he said to his relief as he left the ward.

Craig heard the young screw call to the nurses, "When's the tea coming up?" His footsteps receded toward the staff room. This was the moment. Craig pulled the transfusion tube from his arm, tying it in a knot. He stuffed two pillows under his sheets and pulled on his denims. No boots. He'd have to make it barefooted. Easing up the window, he climbed out, wedging himself against the surround while he closed the window and dropped to the ground. He skirted the skyscraper, squirmed through the barbed wire and sprinted across the Common. The green Mini sat by the curbside; the driver flicked open the door and was moving before Craig had settled in the back seat.

"The guv'nor cut it a bit fine," the driver shouted. "You've got forty minutes to catch your plane." Only on the motorway did he bawl instructions to Craig. "In the suitcase you've got new duds. Leave the stir kit. I drop that at Harwich so they'll think you took the Dutch boat." Craig opened the suitcase and wriggled into the shirt and lightweight suit. "There's a titfer on the rack," said the driver, pointing to a felt hat. "And 'ere's two hundred nicker." He handed over a bundle of English money. "Frank says you can pay him back when you're flush. No hurry."

"He's thought of everything," Craig commented.

"Frank's done too much bird to know that lags coming out can't

100

think for themselves,'' the driver said. He passed over a bunch of keys. "They're for VW's with the edges fined down. If you're nicking cars, pinch another set of plates and change them over to give you another couple of days.''

In the airport parking lot, Craig looked at Frank's henchman. In his twenties, with long hair, an anorak blouse and bell-bottom trousers. He felt suddenly old in his summer suit with a felt hat and a coat over one arm. As they walked to the terminal, the young man briefed him. He handed him two passports and a plane ticket. "You're on the Aer Lingus flight to Dublin so you won't need the passport. You're listed as William Vane, the name on one of the passports. He was a car salesman and the address is good. Make up the rest. Frank says you can buy your ticket for abroad in Dublin with this other passport. The name's Edward Clough and he's in Kensal Green cemetery so you can say what you like about him. Got it?''

Craig nodded. Two identities to throw off the pursuit. Frank had figured it out as he himself might have done had he not spent four years out of the game. They went up the escalator into the lounge. "Frank said to buy you coffee and a sandwich and see you onto the plane,'' said his companion.

Only an old prison hand would have thought of that, Craig told himself. His ordeal in the hospital, his vision still blurred, his escape—all this had unnerved him, though not as much as the noise and hustle of the airport lounge. The vast hall seemed to wobble and gyrate around him. After the drab and solitary prison routine, neither his mind nor his senses could accept the bright lights, the color, the clamoring crowd in summer clothing. He might have bolted had Frank's mate not stayed by his side. Now he realized why old lags broke *back* into prison. For four years he had ceased to think for himself; he had just obeyed, walked the well-worn prison tracks, kept his mouth shut. He'd have to learn once again to walk and talk and act like a human being. He would not feel safe from the impulse to run back and bury himself in the Scrubs until he was abroad. He had to start making his own decisions again.

"You needn't stay,'' he muttered to the youth. "You've got a long way to drive.''

"Sure you're okay then?'' Craig nodded and shook hands with the young man, who took his leave.

He ran an eye down the flight board. Lufthansa had a flight to

101

Frankfurt in an hour. Better than sweating a whole night in Dublin and finding that the morning papers had broken his escape story. He bought a ticket and waited until the last minute before sauntering to the passport control. The official gazed for several seconds at the picture, then turned his eyes to Craig.

"You all right, Mr. Vane?" he said.

Craig hesitated, bewildered by the question and his new name. "Er . . . yes . . . of course." He took the passport and stumbled on.

In the departure lounge he bought himself a bottle of whisky and two hundred cigarettes before going to the toilets. No wonder the passport officer had stared; the blurred face reflected in the mirror shocked Craig himself. He looked bleached and bloodless, with sunken cheeks and remote eyes; he had a dried-blood smear around his mouth. He reckoned twenty minutes till boarding time and quickly stripped to wash and shave. He could count his ribs, which stretched the waxy skin. No fat men in the Scrubs! Porridge, prison mash and cocoa. When he had finished, he went into the lavatory, locked the door and sat down to wait for the boarding call. Here, he did not need to confront his own spooky image or the crowds in the waiting room. Secret service men, he reflected, could do worse than set up a monument to the extracurricular uses of the public lavatory. He took out the two passports. He was now Bill Vane, a secondhand car dealer with a semidetached in Greenham Park Crescent, a wife who had two perms a year and two boys at the local Secondary Modern. In a couple of hours, if he were lucky, he would be sitting in Frankfurt as Ted Clough, born in Sheffield forty years ago, a traveler in spinning yarns with contacts in Frankfurt, Basel and Stuttgart; a bachelor with an aged father living in Leeds and a couple of aunts who had defected across the border to Manchester.

If anything, those two characters seemed more probable than Matthew Craig, age thirty-eight, former SIS officer, former double agent and presently British traitor and prisoner-on-the-run; he could no longer believe his own *curriculum vitae,* no more than he could credit the fact that the weedy figure with egg-cup eyes and milk-bottle face had decided to take on both British intelligence and the KGB for the love of a woman.

Lufthansa Flight 202 boarding now. The airport loudspeaker cut

102

across his thoughts. He picked up his suitcase and coat, walked out and joined the line hurrying toward the aircraft. Once installed in his seat, weariness overcame him; he fell asleep before the wheels were up and did not open his eyes until the plane thudded on the runway at Frankfurt-Main airport.

No one gave him a second glance as he passed through customs and immigration, then booked a flight to Berlin. He had nearly seven hours to wait for the first plane along the Corridor. Time to reflect, to make a plan. He bought himself coffee and a sandwich and found a corner seat in the lounge, deserted at that hour except for several American Army personnel waiting for a night flight.

When would the screw discover the empty bed and raise the alarm? In time for the morning papers to carry the story, and for Ross, the Yard man, to alert Interpol? He figured that he was leading the posse by two or three hours at the most. Long enough, maybe, to jump the Wall and start searching for Lora.

Where was she? What did her cryptogram mean? When Standish had palmed it from his pocket he had reacted genuinely. Beyond the fact that it was an obvious code, he had no idea what it signified. But he knew Lora and her fascination for puzzles; he had assumed that, given time and freedom, he could crack that message. Thank God she had kept it short enough for him to memorize. On the margin of a newspaper, he jotted down the dates she had written: July 28, his birthday; August 6, 14 and 24. They added up to something—a map reference, a street number, a phone number. But she had also scribbled the sentence that would baffle anyone but him. "I hope you remembered our anniversary." The day they had first met, the second day of the Penkovsky trial in Moscow: May 9, 1963. He added that to the list and juggled again with the figures. But the more he stared at them, the more bewildering they seemed.

4   The 707 banked to find its line into Tempelhof. Craig watched the boundaries of West Berlin tilt beneath him; the ragged shores of the Wannsee cut into the green carpet of the Grunewald like a cue rip in a billiard table; the jet effluent sent ripples through the smog. As they lost height, he glanced over the Wall at the towering Soviet War Memorial, capped by the bronze Red Army giant. That figure recalled somebody too well for him to put a face to it.

Passing through the airport, he bought the morning papers. Nothing in *Bild-Zeitung* or the *Morgenpost*. Nothing? Hadn't the Home Office released the news of his escape? He felt relieved, but he still sensed the hand of Standish somewhere. Maybe the SIS had decided against alerting everyone, including the Russians, until their own men had traced him. He waved away the taxi drivers (they remembered) and took the bus to the Zoo terminus. From the crippled black spire of the Gedächtniskirche the ten o'clock carillon rang out. He stepped into the Kurfürstendamm.

Immediately, that anonymous panic he had experienced at London Airport gripped him again. What did they call it? Agoraphobia. Fear of open spaces after the cozy claustrophobia of the Scrubs. Everything fused or fragmented around him: the stampede of traffic lapping the curbside; the crush of humanity strangling his movements on the pavement; the dazzle of the sunlight, the gaudy, eye-searing signs and awnings. Above, the mammoth buildings swayed against the sky as if about to topple over on him; the shrill racket of cars and horns drilled into his brain like some surgical instrument.

And he remembered mocking Lora for her confusion and bewilderment the first time she crossed the Wall into West Berlin!

No man-on-the-run lingered long on the Ku'dam. Not when half a hundred Allied officials took coffee at Kranzlers or the Kempinski. Somebody from the old SIS office in the Olympic Stadium might pop up and say, "Why, Matt, old fellow. What the hell are you doing here?"

"Nothing much, old boy. I've just hopped the dike at the Scrubs and I'm collecting fire, flood and suicide policies for a trip over that wall up there."

In a quiet side street he found a café with a phone and ordered a beer and bockwurst. Mottram would be arriving at the Allied Press Club; he gave him a quarter of an hour before ringing. "Johnny," he whispered. "It's Matt Craig."

"Matt! But you're . . ."

"Not since yesterday. You still in Charlottenburg?"

"Yes. Lisa will let you in. I have to put a couple of pieces on the London wire. See you later."

He took the U-Bahn to Steuben Platz and walked up Westend Allee to the block of flats. Lisa hustled him into the elevator and up to the fourth floor. Briefly, he explained what had happened. "Has Johnny still got a tape machine and a spare banger?" he asked. She brought him the Ufer and a portable typewriter and left him among her husband's books and papers in the study. Lisa asked no questions and did not seem surprised to see Craig, whom she had known when he worked in Berlin. Perhaps living through the airlift, the invasion from East Berlin, the Wall, the daily escape dramas had blunted her faculty for surprise.

He had typed two lists and a letter and was just finishing dictating when Mottram arrived. Was it nature's abhorrence for straight lines or Lisa's cooking? He had ballooned into the proportions of a Japanese wrestler. Craig's bones cracked under his bear hug. He had met Mottram on one of his first visits to Berlin when the journalist was finishing his stint with army intelligence. Now he was back freelancing for British and American newspapers. "I waited to see if there was anything on the afternoon tapes about your breakout," he said. "Not a line. I can't understand it."

"Some of our old friends in the Olympic Stadium buildings across the road might enlighten us," Craig replied.

He outlined his scheme while Mottram listened. "You'll never get away with it," he commented. "And anyway, is she worth it? You know, the SIS boys here claim that you confessed and took twenty years' stick to save her. Is that true?"

Craig shrugged. "Half and half. At least I knew they wouldn't chop me but I couldn't be sure of what the KGB would do if they suspected her. She took the biggest risk." He looked at Mottram. "I don't like involving you, but can you run me through the Wall tonight?"

Mottram poured two drinks and lit their cigarettes. "Why don't you put up here for a day or two? You look as though you could use some of Lisa's cooking."

Craig waved the idea aside. "If I get stuck this side I'll find myself back in the Scrubs. I only came through Berlin because I had a story to give you."

"Your story?"

"The stuff I didn't tell them at the Old Bailey trial. It's all on these tapes and I've made you copies of these two letters." Mottram took the letters. One was marked *For the attention of Vernon Standish.* Craig pointed to it. "You can hand that one in at the Olympic Stadium. The other you'll have to post from East Berlin or anywhere in East Germany." Mottram looked at the name and the Lubyanka address. "Flying way up there, aren't you?"

"It's an all-risks policy for an all-risks job."

"Who collects?"

"You—when you know for certain that I'm dead." He picked up the tapes. "A lot of it's covered by the Official Secrets Act, but that doesn't worry them in Europe or the States and you can flog the expurgated text in Britain."

"When I know you're dead. . . . Matt, you can't do it."

"It's either this or being buried alive for another ten years."

Mottram left the room. Craig heard the toilet flush. The big man returned with a package, wrapped in plastic which still dripped water.

"So Dick Middleton sent it," Craig cried.

"He did better. He came out of his way to bring it. He's a CIA man, isn't he?"

"Not that you would notice," said Craig. "He's honest."

"I met him a couple of times since and he thinks they handed you a rough old deal."

Craig took the package, which contained a crumpled envelope wrapped around some documents and a film in a cigarette packet. Four years in Mottram's cistern had done them no harm. The sight of them made Craig feel better.

Lisa entered to set before them two steaks like boxing gloves. "Yours is underdone, Matt. You look as though you need the blood," she commented. They had finished and were drinking coffee when the phone rang. Mottram picked it up, jotted down a few shorthand squiggles and turned to Craig.

"Reuter has it on the tapes from London. Reported missing at six o'clock this morning. A stolen car located midmorning in Harwich with your prison clothes in it. They think you took the boat to the Hook of Holland."

"When did the last evening editions go to press?"

"Half an hour ago. They can't do a thing with it." He thought for a moment. "But RIAS and the other German stations will lead their six o'clock roundup with it."

106

"But no pictures," said Craig thoughtfully.

"We'd better get you through the Wall," Mottram muttered, pulling on his jacket. "Better use Charlie. The Americans won't be bothered and the Grepos have to wait for the official word."

Mottram drove a VW because he crossed into East Berlin three times a week and the car attracted no attention. He chose the back streets, turning and running beside the Landwehr Canal until he hit Friedrichstrasse. "Don't say a word, Matt," he whispered as they reached the Checkpoint Charlie barrier. He flashed both passports at the American sergeant and the West German policeman who lifted the pole separating East from West.

On the other side of Zimmerstrasse, a young Grepo halted them. "How long do you intend to spend in East Berlin, Mr. Vane?" he asked.

"He's crossing to Schönefeld to catch the Warsaw plane," Mottram replied in German. The policeman saluted and handed back Craig's passport. As the pole dropped behind them, Craig let out his breath in a long sigh. The Scrubs lay several light years in his wake, he thought.

Mottram turned at Unter den Linden and went east. "There's a friend of mine who rents rooms in Grunbergerstrasse. I'll drop you at the end or they'll see the West Berlin car plates. Walk around for a quarter of an hour and give me time to phone. He won't ask questions."

Craig followed the instructions. The German who opened the door had a fresh complexion and white hair; his right sleeve was pinned to his shirt front. He showed Craig his room, where his wife was turning down the bed. *"Sie sind Engländer,"* he said, pointing to the collar and tie. Craig took the hint, producing a turtle-neck pullover. The German handed Craig the front-door key and slowly enunciated the telephone number. "If you ring I can get a message through to Herr Mottram."

Where are you, Lora? Somewhere in this cobwebbed, Kafka country, this gloomy metropolis of democratic centralism? You said you'd see the Lighthills (is that Lichtenberg?) on August 6. Tomorrow. But we knew only the Weichmanns in Lichtenberg and you would never trust them. So where? Not *our* flat in case they'd rum-

107

bled that. Maybe I should let you find me. But do you know I'm here? How do I tell you? Through *them,* of course. And, at the same time, warn you about the Weichmanns.

He walked to the nearest Europa, where a sullen waiter banged down a pair of perspiring frankfurters and sauerkraut that had been washed in Brand X. "You have West Deutsche Marks?" he hissed. Craig pulled out several pound notes, which the man changed at twice the going rate. East Berlin had not changed; still the old black-money market.

He took a tram to Lichtenberg and walked to the nondescript detached house overlooking the park. Scaling the garden wall, he crept up to the house. The Weichmanns were at their usual pastime—playing bezique. But upstairs, in a back room, a light filtered through the blind. They had company.

This time, he took the underground to Karl-Marx Allee. There, the Warschau glittered like a candle in a doss house. He chose a table on the pavement and ordered a beer. The Wall had certainly eaten into their trade. A handful of Russian and German soldiers were eyeing the merchandise, tarts wearing leather jack boots and carrying parasols like party badges. In the late fifties, when Standish had introduced him to the Warschau, it had style. It hummed with a polyglot army of spies and informers: Russian, Polish, Czech, Hungarian agents in one corner; American, British, French in the other corner; between them, West and East Germans shuffled to swap dubious secrets for a carton of Player's or papirosa cigarettes. The flea market of the spy trade, where the hundred-mark boys would sell you the Moscow addresses of Burgess and Maclean, whisper the name of the Smersh agent who pushed Jan Masaryk out of the Czech foreign-ministry window, give you the line-up of the new Politburo when they had kicked out Khrushchev.

Craig picked up *Neues Deutschland.* As faceless as the blocks of flats around him. But comforting, somehow. Curious, the moment he had ducked under the pole at Zimmerstrasse, his state of mind had changed. The prison atmosphere? The plunge from Technicolor to monochrome? That, and the fact that everyone in the West who looked at the box or read a paper might end his run. Here, people did not enter into the hide-and-seek game. Only his own kind, the devious underworld of spies who held the middle ground between criminals like himself on one hand, and the police. His world, the one he had chosen and in which he felt most at home.

He dallied over his beer, wondering how long it would take them to pick up his trail. He cast an eye at the girls around the bar. One satisfied his requirements; he nodded and she minced over to his table. *"Wieviel?"* he queried before her leather-sheathed legs had squeaked into position.

"You don't waste much time, *Liebchen,"* she said, simpering. "One hundred D Marks—West."

He ordered her sticky concoction of brandy and crème de menthe. "It's not for tonight," he said. "Two or three of my pals are having a party in Lichtenberg tomorrow night at ten o'clock."

"It's off my beat," she said, helping herself to several cigarettes from his packet. "It will cost two hundred D Marks."

He pushed fifty marks at her. "You can take a taxi there. I'll run you back in the morning."

"You're not German," she said, suddenly suspicious.

"I'm from Prague. We're here for the Eastern-bloc trade talks. We had to leave our wives at home. Security reasons." The irony escaped her; she seemed satisfied with the explanation. He gave her the address and emphasized that she must not be late.

He left money for another drink and walked on until he came to Alexander Platz. The fire buckets still sat in the entrance to the office block. He cached a cigarette package with a short message in the nozzle of the second hose. At Marx-Engels Platz, he gazed at Marx's bearded bust. No, they had not yet patched that crack in the plinth. He screwed another message into the hole. He placed three more notes before making his way back to the rooming house and going to bed.

The German's wife brought him the papers with his morning coffee. Not even a squib on his escape, though it must have made headlines the other side of the Wall. He dressed and walked to Warsaw Street and found a cab. As they cruised around Marx-Engels Platz, he noticed two men, sweating under felt hats and overcoats, squinting at the bronze whiskers with more than ideological interest. The new breed from Lubyanka? Outside the office block he spotted a couple of Aryans from the Staatsicherheitdienst in a car. Another one of his dead-drops was staffed. It said something for Russian thoroughness that they were watching three out of five dead-drops that Lora and he had not used for more than four years. He prayed that Lora would keep clear of them until tonight.

He lay low that afternoon, then gave himself three hours to reach the villa in Lichtenberg. On his previous visit he had noticed a school with a flat roof farther along the street on the opposite side. He leapt over the wall and clambered up the fire escape onto the roof; from here he could survey the street and the house entrance.

At nine o'clock, two cars appeared and stationed themselves facing each other fifty yards away on either side of Weichmann's gate. Two men from one car entered the house. Not long after ten o'clock, the taxi drew up. In the dusk, Craig could almost have sworn himself that it was Lora who paid the driver and opened the gate.

She had no sooner closed the gate than the two men burst from the house while the others closed in from the rear. Craig heard her screaming and cursing as they hustled her into a car which sped along the street.

He would have liked to witness the expressions all around when these agents confronted their Russian and East German bosses with that pro from the Warschau Restaurant. But that mattered nothing compared with the facts he could deduce from setting and springing the trap.

Lora was still free. She was still fooling them. Only . . . what did her cryptic bit of paper really mean?

5   He sat up into the small hours wrestling with Lora's conundrum, twisting its words and figures one way and another until his mind went dead on him and he threw himself on the bed to fall asleep instantly. At four o'clock, as though a light had snapped on in his brain, he awoke and cursed himself for having missed the obvious point of her code. Leuchtenburg-gasse, of course. The flat above the Seilers'. No, they would never betray them. Now the figures tumbled into place. May 9, July 28, August 6. Separately, the months and days added up to 20:43. The Seilers' old phone number, which he had forgotten because they so rarely used it.

Lora was no more than a mile away.

She had taken a risk, choosing the old flat. He quashed the impulse to run there. Too dangerous an hour before dawn. Too few people and too many Vopos. Nor could he move in daylight since everyone knew he had crossed the Wall. He would have to fret it out until evening.

Dusk was settling over the city as he slipped out. In dimly lit Weserstrasse, he found a parked VW. Its handle yielded to the fourth key and he slid behind the wheel and drove north. He would pick up Lora and bring her back to the room. They had a lot of decisions to make. Both had put most of the world out of bounds, she the East and he the West. Where could they go?

Leuchtenburg-gasse. The two familiar terraces of sleazy, red-brick houses still showing the bomb holes. He crawled past No. 17 in second gear. No black cars in sight. At an upper window, a hand drew back the curtain; he glimpsed the face. Lora! Even in the half-shadow, he recognized her. He still moved warily, parking the car a couple of hundred yards along the road and walking back. He gave their knock—three long and three short taps.

Before the door opened, something warned him that he had walked into a trap. He was stepping back when four hands reached out, grabbed him and pulled him inside. He felt his body rattle against the wooden floorboards and the partition, then he lunged out and heard a grunt as his foot thudded against a shin. He tried to claw upward, out of the tangle of arms and legs, but at that moment pain exploded in his neck and head as the edge of a hand chopped at him like a guillotine.

He came to, his ears racketing, his body vibrating. Two pairs of heavy shoes pressed on his chest, holding him down on the floor of the car. They had thrust a gag into his mouth and blindfolded him with his own scarf. The sound of traffic told him they were still in East Berlin. Heading where? Schönefeld Airport and Moscow? "By the back door," he heard somebody say in German. Not Moscow for the moment. The car halted. Expert hands bundled him out, thrust him forward over a polished floor and into an elevator. *The elevators in Moscow University go up at 3.2 meters a second,* his brain repeated. Eleven seconds. The fifth or sixth floor. Another fifty yards of skating rink. Through a door. A fist thudded into his chest and he collapsed in a chair. Someone ripped the sticking plaster off his mouth while other fingers wrenched away the scarf.

Craig blinked in the strip light, which threw a figure into silhouette. He had no need to see the square face, the wire-brush hair, the steel-tipped teeth. The iron man from the war memorial in Treptower Park.

"Greetings, comrade," Kudriatov grated, leaning heavily on the words.

"Hail and farewell," Craig replied, matching the sarcasm.

"For you this time it is good-bye," the KGB man said. "So your masters thought they'd let you find Comrade Trusova for them."

"They weren't wrong, were they?" Craig shot back. Let Kudriatov go on thinking that Standish had made a bargain with Lora and him.

"Only we found her first." Kudriatov grinned. Crimping the end of a papirosa between his hairy fingers, he lit it and blew the smoke into Craig's face. "Now, this message she passed to you?"

"Haven't you found that, too," said Craig, nodding at his jacket. The Germans had ripped away the lapels and torn the pockets and linings. "Don't say they've even stolen my cyanide capsule."

"That will be superfluous where you're going," the Russian commented.

"May I ask where?"

"You may," said Kudriatov with another grin. They must have given him top marks in English humor at the KGB Institute. "Now, this message?"

"What's it worth now that you have Lora?"

"It is evidence of her collusion with the British intelligence service and its hired lackey, Mr. Matthew Craig."

"Four years ago, the British said I was one of your agents and you didn't deny it. I'm a bit confused. What am I?"

"Fortunate to have lived for those four years. You have five minutes to write down that message. After that, I cannot vouch for your continued existence."

"You'd better start now, Sergei Antonovich, because if there were such a message I wouldn't remember it."

112

"You remembered enough to get to No. 17 Leuchtenburg-gasse," Kudriatov snapped. "Maybe we can jog your memory a bit more." He nodded to the three men standing around Craig. They moved slowly, purposefully. Carrying him into another room they stripped him, bound his hands and hung him to a hook on the wall. He had once watched two prison officers giving an old lag a going-over with wet towels knotted in the right places. Crude, effective and no marks. Kudriatov's henchmen, no doubt graduates from the Karlshorst school of thuggery, had updated the method by stuffing nylon sheaths with wet cotton wool. They had style, too. They aimed at the nerve plexus in his stomach, not forcibly enough to stun him, merely to send the pain throbbing through his whole body. With each blow Craig screamed to deaden the agony and distract his mind. Abruptly, the pain ceased; the screams decayed in his throat; his head sagged.

The shock brought him around; he was spluttering and struggling against hands which were forcing his head into a bath of crushed ice and water. Again, they suspended him from the hook. They pried open his legs and he felt the terminals brush against the soft flesh. "Where did she pass the message? What did it say? What were your orders?" To each of Kudriatov's questions he shook his head. His body twitched and jerked and jackknifed as they switched the current on and off. With each burst of pain he bellowed until his tongue seemed to swell in his mouth and choke off the sound.

When they revived him for the third time he was whimpering for them to stop. He had the bittersweet tang of blood in his mouth and one of the Germans was holding his head above the water to save him from drowning. Kudriatov was smiling grimly.

"Well, Mr. Craig, you seem to be losing your English sense of humor," he said. "Now, this message?"

"She only said to meet her at 17 Leuchtenburg-gasse on August 6."

"Yesterday?"

"I was a day late."

"Whom did she tell?"

"One of our embassy men."

"Name?"

"They didn't tell me. It wasn't important."

"Where was the message passed?"

"At the embassy in Warsaw."

"Well, your little game is over, Mr. Craig. You will sign a deposition." Within a few minutes he brought a typewritten document on which Craig scrawled his signature. Kudriatov studied it, clicked his tongue. "I won't be seeing you again," he said. "That pleases me." He turned to go, but Craig called him.

"Sergei Antonovich . . . look, we used to be friends."

"Friends! No friends of mine betray their ideals for money."

"You forced me to take it. Anyway, I'm not pleading for my own life but for Lora's. You could let her go."

"Never," Kudriatov shouted. "She's a worse traitor than you because she's Russian, of a good revolutionary family."

"It wasn't only politics that made her flee. You know that."

"I know swine like you corrupted her and this time she has to pay."

"And I thought you were fond of her, Sergei Antonovich," Craig said.

Kudriatov's mouth twitched with fury; his big hands were working violently as he advanced on Craig. "Get this . . . scum . . . out of here," he bellowed. The last thing Craig saw was the heel of that huge fist chopping down on his throat.

6 Somehow he would find a chink in that barrier between him and Lora. He was groping blindly, through murky water, his lungs bursting with the effort of staying under. Those steel bars across the Spree must have a flaw or a hole somewhere. Did they think they could end his home run by putting this steel gate across the river? He grasped the grid and shook it, but he could not budge it. He suddenly felt exhausted, drained of strength and will. Three thousand miles he had swum, from the icy Arctic waters, and no bars would stop him reaching his spawning ground! Frantically, he probed and tested each bar. Tap . . . tap . . . tap . . .

Craig broke surface slowly. A window swam into focus; against its rain-streaked panes the branches of an ash tree were tapping. Through the misty green fringe he could discern the Europa-Center. Painfully, he rotated his head. On a chair beside his bed, Standish was sitting; his dark, well-greased hair appeared over a copy of *The Times*. Craig read the date: August 9. He stirred and the paper was folded.

"Matt, dear boy, you've made it. I thought we'd lost you for good. You gave us a good run, by God. A good run." His salmon-pink features contorted with pleasure; Craig fancied he saw the gills quivering beneath his jawbone. "Whom did you meet, Matt?"

"Just a friend."

"Old friends are best, you know," Standish murmured.

"He was an old friend. Sergei Antonovich."

"I thought as much. He must have brought you across himself with CD plates on his car. They stole a Merc and dumped you in it, then one of them phoned the police post on Bismarckstrasse. Another half an hour and you wouldn't be here. They'd filled you with Pentothal. The quacks in this place had to use a dialyzer for two days."

Craig looked at the syringe plugged into his right arm and the bottle above his head. "Why did you bother?" he asked. "Did you want me to do the rest of my time?"

"How could I let you die, Matt?" Standish looked hurt. "And there's no hurry to get you back. Relax here for a couple of days and Ross will come and take you home." Standish produced the two passports which Kudriatov had left in his pocket. "Use one of these. We've made no press announcement so there'll be no fuss. Fleet Street is still scouring Amsterdam and the Rhineland."

"So he gaffed me and threw me back," Craig muttered, half to himself.

"A very foolhardy thing to do, my dear fellow. Magnificent, but hardly the ticket." Standish fished a bottle of Scotch from the bedside table and poured three fingers into two tumblers. He fed Craig sips from the glass, then he inserted a cigarette between Craig's lips and lit it. He walked to the window, wiped away the condensation with his hand and looked east to the broken shard of the Gedächtniskirche. "You didn't talk to her, did you?" he asked.

"No, and nobody else will. I saw her in a house we used years ago. Then I walked right into it."

"I suppose your friend Kudriatov was concerned about his *zapiski*."

"His *zapiski*?"

115

"The file she stole."

"Why should he be? He's got it back."

Standish stepped over to the bed, drew up a chair and whispered, "Matt, maybe I shouldn't tell you this, but he's like us—still hunting."

"So Lora has hidden it."

"Why else would they rip apart that house where they ambushed you?"

"She might as well confess now. Kudriatov and his ex-Nazis, Herr Belsen, Herr Buchenwald and Herr Dachau, will tear it out of her."

"What if it wasn't her you saw, but somebody playing the part?"

"No, it was Lora all right."

Standish shrugged. "You merely wanted to think it was. She was too clever. She did what you'd have done in the old days—waited and watched. She knew the house was blown."

"How do you know?"

"Oh, you weren't followed. We'd lost you. But only one in four East Berliners are Communists. Somebody saw the scuffle and the girl rode away in style afterward."

"It was Lora," Craig insisted, as though to torture himself.

"We didn't dismiss the possibility either. She might have been setting a trap for you—or us. We ruled that one out when we picked you up."

"They wouldn't have chucked me back, you mean?"

Standish nodded. "We wondered why they did that."

"I told them nothing they didn't already know, if that's what you're getting at."

"I didn't doubt that, Matt. But why not keep and use you? They could have boasted springing another of their men and given you a steady job in Moscow."

"Maybe Philby, Maclean and Blake didn't want a fourth for bridge."

"Maybe Kudriatov merely wanted you to die this side of the Wall—maybe he wanted to see you do your full time." Standish stiffened both glasses with Scotch. "No," he said. "Your girl friend has given them the slip once again."

"I don't believe it."

116

"I couldn't credit it either. But she rang the Arena yesterday. She remembered the old drill and called our Leipzig man, who gave her the private number. We told her we'd picked you up but didn't know whether you'd pull through."

"Standish, you've got to send somebody over there to bring her out."

"Who, for instance? And where do they start hunting? She'll only settle for you."

"Then turn your back and let me go. I know every house and every dead-drop we've ever used. I know the KGB and SSD men in East Berlin."

"You really do ask for a kicking, Matt. We can't take the chance of picking you out of the Spree next time."

"Let me worry about that. Give me a week and I'll find Lora and your file."

"And I'll join you in the mailbag shop at Wormwood Scrubs. No, it's just not on. Anyway, you're all in." He came over and held out his hand. Craig let it dangle. "I'll leave you the bottle. If you need another one there are two of our chaps within spitting distance. Have a nice trip back." With his hand on the doorknob he turned. "Don't worry about the loss of remission. I'll put in a word with the prison magistrates. . . . Oh, and Matt, I realize you've no reason to believe this, but I have been working on the Home Office to grant you a parole."

"Standish, wait! Wait, you bastard! You owe me a week. You got me into it in the first place." But his weak voice only echoed back from the empty room.

7   Craig had to make an effort to place the face with its red network of capillaries, the jutting jaw and blue eyes. "Remember me, son?" Craig nodded. The hat had tricked him. Ross had not worn it on his visit to the Scrubs. The Special Branch man settled into a chair, his waistcoat sliding up to ride high over his paunch; he stuffed his pipe and lit it. "We gave you three extra days to lie up," he said. "Do you reckon you can walk now?"

"Where to?"

"I don't have to spell it out, son. Fifty yards to the car here, a couple of hundred at Tempelhof and London Airport. They're getting your cell ready."

"You can carry me back." Craig disliked paternalistic detectives.

Ross shook his head. "You don't want any fuss and neither do we. No TV and reporters. Stretchers attract them."

"All right, I'll walk."

"That's better. We're booked on the night flight at eleven o'clock. You can use one of the passports you came in with. Clough will do." He looked at the picture. "Hmm. Wonder where Lucas got hold of them."

"Lucas?"

"You must remember him, son. The man that sprung you. We're not that dim. The prison beaks sent him to the Moor to break rocks for the rest of his time."

So Frank Lucas had paid for helping him. The visiting magistrates would lean pretty heavily on him when he got back. Loss of three years' remission at least. What did it matter?

"I've checked your gear," the detective was saying. "A hundred and fifty pounds, two passports and your clothing. I don't know if they'll let you keep it." He grinned at his own joke, then ran over the arrangements. He would drive them to the airport in a plain car. No passport control and no customs at either end. Just a couple of VIP's coming back from a trip to West Berlin. "No monkey business, son," he said as he left the room. He was the sort of copper who drove good men to crime, Craig thought.

Should he make an attempt to phone Mottram and tell him to recover the suitcase? He decided against involving the newspaperman any further. If Kudriatov found the file and papers it would amount to no more than a rough sort of justice. Instead, he sat up and finished the last of Standish's whisky.

Ross arrived early and searched Craig before escorting him to the Opel Rekord. "Sorry, son," he said as he took Craig's left wrist, handcuffed it, then clipped the other bracelet on the safety handle. Now he could only move his free arm by rotating his whole body, and Ross knew it.

They drove south, crossed the Ku'dam into the side streets and turned east. A light drizzle had begun to fall. At Hauptstrasse, they halted at the lights and were just pulling away when it happened. Craig first noticed the car headlights, which partly dazzled him. As the big Ford bore down on them he braced himself for the shock. He caught sight of the face, blurred, and its outline fractured every second by the windshield wipers. Somehow, it stamped itself on his mind, even though it looked like the last thing he would ever witness.

The car hit them behind Ross's door, slewing them around on the greasy surface. Craig heard the thud of the burly body against the paneling; his own handcuffed arm tightened like a fiddle string and pain shot through his shoulder as he whiplashed into Ross's body. His reflex caused him to twist around in the seat to save his arm. Now, as he lay over Ross, his right arm was free. The key? Ross had thrust it into his waistcoat pocket. He groped for it and had just time to unlock the handcuffs and push them into Ross's pocket before the door opened.

"Jemand zu Schaden bekommen?"

"Yes, my friend's hurt," Craig gasped. "Get an ambulance." Two policemen shouldered through the crowd. Let Ross open his eyes and squeak and he'd make a run for it. But the Special Branch man did not stir as they levered open the door on his side and freed him. An ambulance arrived quickly—a converted Ford station wagon. Craig helped the driver to hump Ross onto a stretcher and into the car. He rifled his pockets, finding his passports, the money and even the keys Lucas had procured. The driver was now heading north, across the Ku'dam.

"East Berlin," Craig shouted.

"Nicht möglich."

"East Berlin," Craig repeated. He had found the Yard man's revolver; he now dug it into the driver's back. "Which hospital are you from?" he asked.

"The Bethesda Krankenhaus."

"Now listen and remember this. This man's a tourist. He was knocked down in Hauptstrasse and treated for bruises and shock at the Bethesda Krankenhaus. He's staying in East Berlin with friends in Leipzigerstrasse, No. 75. Their name is Schenkendorff. Just tell them that at Checkpoint Charlie and nothing will happen to you. All right?" The ambulance bore half right toward Friedrichstrasse.

119

Ross's eyes opened and he groaned. "What happened?" he gasped.

"Just lie where you are, mate, and don't ask any questions. If you as much as utter when we're going through the Wall, I'll kill you."

The superintendent glanced at the gun in Craig's hand. "You'll never get away with it, son," he said, as though quoting from a TV script.

"If I don't, what's the odds? Fifteen years or life? It doesn't matter to me."

He squirmed under the second stretcher and pulled a blanket down to cover himself as the ambulance drew up at the West German barrier; the pole rose quickly and they bounced over the tramlines until a Vopo stopped them. The driver lied well, better than he did. The Vopo flashed his torch on Ross's face, muttering something to his comrade about a drunken English tourist. The ambulance lurched forward into East Berlin.

Along Leipzigerstrasse, Craig signaled to the driver to halt. "Take him to the nearest hospital and leave him there," he shouted as he leapt out.

He was free. For the second time in a week he felt grateful to the Russians for building that Wall. He began walking. Eleven o'clock struck from a church tower. An hour after the socialist curfew. For him a dangerous hour. As he marched down Warsaw Street, two policemen halted him. *"Ausweis, bitte,"* one said. Craig flashed Clough's passport at him. *"Wo gehen sie hin?"*

"I'm lost," he slurred. "I'm looking for my hotel—the Europa."

"Second on the right and four streets farther on," one of them said.

At least they had told him something. No general alert had gone out for Clough. Or perhaps for Vane and Craig. Yet, as he stepped through the drizzle, keeping to side streets, he had the strange notion that someone was following him. Imagination, or the apprehension that clings to every hunted man?

None the less, he watched the entrance to the rooming house for an hour before daring to let himself into the dark hallway. He slipped upstairs to his room.

His case and coat, his microfilm and papers—they had all disappeared!

He slipped downstairs to wake the landlord, who followed him into the living room. "You are not staying here," the German said. From his stony gaze Craig guessed something had happened.

"I only came for my things—where are they?"

"I burned them."

"Burned them! Not the papers and the film, too?"

"Those she took . . . the girl who came the night after you left. She had this address from Herr Mottram."

So Lora had risked phoning Mottram. "Did she give you any message?"

The man took a small medallion from the mantelpiece and tossed it to Craig. "She dropped this from her bangle. You keep it. I have no use for it." As Craig fingered the small silver disk, the landlord moved to the door. He held it open. "Now get out," he said.

"But why?"

The German glowered. "Because I don't hide traitors. If I had known you were Craig, the man who betrayed good Germans, you would not have spent one second in my house."

The door slammed behind Craig. Where now? He must change money and then think how to cross the next two frontiers. He walked south, aimlessly. The German's words still rang in his ears. Craig, the traitor. He saw an open café with only a few people inside. He bought a beer and made a hushed bargain with the waiter to change £20. Even this man seemed to flick his eyes suspiciously on him. He was sipping the drink when he suddenly caught sight of his own name; it flared at him from the corner of a folded newspaper in the corner seat. He went over to pick it up and stuff it in his pocket. Quickly, he paid and left the café.

Following his feet blindly, he stumbled into Ostkreuz station and glanced at the departure board. In fifteen minutes, the last train went to Erkner. Didn't that lie near the south motorway? He bought a ticket but waited until the last minute before walking through the barrier. He found an empty compartment where no good party member would spot him reading a smuggled copy of *Bild-Zeitung* about a double traitor.

He expected them to have uncovered the story of his arrest in West Berlin. But there the police had obviously not connected his two false passports with Craig. The paper was running a double-feature on his escape from England. It had recapitulated the whole story, condemning him for everything: the deaths of dozens of agents, the killing of Strutchkov, the betrayal of the Berlin Tunnel. Curiously, he felt no resentment, no indignation. Those accusations had burned so deeply into his mind that now they almost rang true. It seemed as though his own kernel of guilt about those years had swollen to embrace and sanctify even these lies.

8 He screwed up the clandestine newspaper and tossed it out of the window, fearing that they might check the train at Wilhelmshagen, the frontier post between East Berlin and East Germany. On that murky night, however, no one bothered. Another border behind him. Could he brazen or bluff his way across the next one? As the train ran through the forest, he fingered the silver disk Lora had let drop in the rooming house in case he returned for his papers. Good King Wenceslas. He had bought it for her four years before outside Hradčany Castle. He wondered if she had managed to slip through Kudriatov's net and reach Prague.

At Erkner, he crossed the bridge and strode down the main street. The fine rain had penetrated his lightweight suit and his left shoulder throbbed as though he had dislocated something when that car hit them. The pain did not worry him as much as another much stronger sensation. That someone was trailing him. His logic dismissed the suggestion as absurd. Who could have picked up his trail from the moment he crossed Checkpoint Charlie? Yet the impression persisted. He took several steps along a side street and waited. No one. He must be getting jittery.

Why did every car in these back streets have to be a Wartburg or a Skoda? He marched half a mile and was dripping wet before finding a parked VW. His fifth key turned the lock; he muttered a benediction for Frank Lucas, breaking rocks in Dartmoor for putting him over the wall. He drove east for several miles before hitting the motorway, which he followed westward until he spotted the southern spur for Dresden. Now he could check if he had company. After an hour, he drew into an all-night station to fill the tank and have coffee and a sandwich. For a quarter of an hour he watched the parking lot and the café, but no one pulled in. Two motorcycle policemen gave him a glance before speeding north. His stolen VW would not show in their diaries until tomorrow. At last he had shaken them off. Running an eye over the road map in the garage, he reckoned ninety minutes to Dresden and half an hour to the Czech frontier. He'd have to ditch the car and walk across. That hurdle he'd jump when he met it. As they said in the Scrubs, he'd busk this one.

Just after three o'clock, the lights of Dresden receded in his mirror as he left the autobahn and forked left. The moon was rising as he crossed the Elbe into Pirna and began to climb into the Erzgebirge range. Switchbacking and bending on itself, the road plunged through deep gorges and wooded valleys. Saxon Switzerland, they called it. What an hour to take in its sights and risk your neck! Below him and to his left, the Elbe appeared from time to time, glittering like frosted glass. He calculated five minutes to Bad Schandau, the East German frontier, and wondered when he should get rid of the car.

He was descending to cross the river once again when he caught sight of something that lifted his heart. Barges! Going back empty to Děčín and Ústí and even as far as Prague. He found a track leading through the woods to the river and drove down it; he got out, released the brake and pushed the VW until it slid over the bank and out of view under the water.

As he made his way along the riverbank to the line of barges, he saw a swath of light. A car at that hour on the road he had just left! Turning, he scrambled up the bank and lay in the undergrowth. The Wartburg went past, gunning its engine, too quickly for him to get the number. But he noted only one figure silhouetted against the glare of its headlights. Had they picked him up, after all?

At the river frontier, the bargemasters stood in a huddle, waiting for their customs and police clearance and drinking schnapps. Craig chose his moment to leap and grasp the rail of a barge; he hauled himself up, opened the hatch and dropped into the hold. In five minutes, he heard the bargemaster return; he was chortling with his mate. "What did you think of that crazy Englishman who'd lost his pal? Says they had a wild night in Dresden and the last he knew of him he was making for the frontier."

"Serves them right for running after those bits of Dresden lace."

Perhaps he had underestimated the Special Branch. Had Ross been shamming? Had he jumped out of the ambulance after him, then tailed him all the way? Someone had passed this frontier and was chasing him.

His barge inched forward; the master bawled farewell to the Germans. They halted again at the Czech post, then picked up some speed and headed for Děčín. He was on the way. When the barge tied up, he lay on the straw bales and waited until the master had left and he heard no other sounds. It was nearly dawn. In the half light, he slipped over the gangway onto the quay.

To get to Prague he needed money and he had only West and East German marks, plus his pounds. At that hour only the waterfront cafés catering for Czech and German barge crews showed a light. He would have to risk it. He entered the first and largest café and ordered ham and eggs, bread and coffee. When he came to pay, the proprietor waved aside his East Deutsche Marks. "I can give you these," he said, producing his English money.

"You English?" the man said. Craig nodded. "All right, I change these for you," he went on, indicating the marks. He had gone to the till when the car drew up; two men in black hats and mackintoshes got out. The proprietor hurried over to clear his table. "The back room," he hissed. Craig rose and walked slowly to the kitchen. The hum of voices ceased as the door banged; he heard the café owner's guttural tones. "No, they're all my regulars, as you see." The door closed and he bustled through. "You in police trouble?" he asked.

Craig shrugged. "They just want to throw me back over the frontier. I got drunk and hit a copper in Dresden. I crossed the frontier in a truck."

The man swallowed that one; in Děčín they did not esteem Germans highly. "Not mixed up in politics?" he queried. "Those weren't local cops. Slovaks, I think."

Craig shook his head. "I helped a few Czechs across the Austrian border in 1968, but that can't interest them."

"My brother has a son who went over. He's studying in England now." He paused and looked hard at Craig. "Where are you heading for?"

"Prague."

124

"All right, there's a beer truck leaving in half an hour. It loads up in the yard. Got somewhere to go?" Craig gestured that he hadn't. "There's a café on the left bank, off Neruda Street. A man called Jiri Bykov runs it. He's had trouble and doesn't like the security police. Just mention Děčín and Vačlac."

Just before midday, the truck dropped him on the Vltava embankment at Letna. For a moment, he stood gazing at the castle and cathedral, at the receding line of bridges over the river, at the Gothic spires and cupolas traced against the puffy clouds. He had first "collected" Prague as a city when he was attached to the embassy in 1962 as a junior attaché, so-called. For six months he had wandered its splendid avenues and its narrow, drunken alleys and had spent hours contemplating the blend of Gothic, Slav and Italian architecture, admiring the arcaded squares and wobbly red roofs. He liked the Czechs, too. In 1968 he had watched them bend though not break, using their wit and sense of the ridiculous, their courage and inborn culture to combat tanks and guns. A city for him full of remembered things that never palled.

He strolled around to Charles Bridge and turned to climb the medieval canyon of Neruda Street. Embassy country. British to the right, American to the left, with several others in between. Tourist country as well. The pile of Hradčany Castle and the spires of St. Vitus's Cathedral lay in front of him.

Bykov's café sat on the corner of a small square where a cupid fountain played and pigeons slow-stepped over the cobbles. Except for several sight-seers sitting over beers at a pavement table it was empty. That gave him pause, but he pushed open the door and entered. "Jiri Bykov?" The woman behind the counter led him through the kitchen into a sitting room where a man lounged, buried behind the morning paper. Through steel-rimmed glasses, he scrutinized Craig. "What do you want?" he said.

"Vačlac at Děčín said you might help."

"So you'd like to stay."

"Only for two or three days."

"Have you got papers?"

"I won't need them."

"What about the police, eh?"

"I hope I won't meet them."

"All right, I'll put you up here—for Vačlac's sake." Craig followed him upstairs to a bare room opening onto a courtyard surrounded by old apartments and overlooking the castle. Neither Bykov nor his dialogue impressed him. He could not trust this man. No one could. His café was well-positioned but empty, which meant that the folk in those apartments shared his suspicions. He had talked about everything but money, and people with crow faces, snake eyes and thin lips broke the law for nothing else. He had walked into a trap.

"I've seen you somewhere before," Craig said.

"Such as where?"

"Wenceslas Square when the tanks came in?"

Bykov shook his head; he removed his spectacles and polished them with a corner of the newspaper. "Maybe," he admitted. "I was driving a truck full of hot newspapers. I had some fun, I can tell you—until the Russians, God damn them, picked us up."

"They must have given you a hard time."

"I'll say. I had it for two months, but I kept my mouth shut." (Yes, Craig reflected, you yelled like a banshee when they put a finger on you.)

"I'm sorry," he said.

"What were you doing?"

"I took a few people out to save them from what you got."

"Ah, I know. The Mělník road. Maček's farm. I ran a few out there myself. Pity it had to end the way it did."

So Bykov was a nark. They had released him and set him up in this café which no Czech worthy of the name would patronize. Here, he could listen and relate what embassy men, tourists and anybody else were saying. Maček's farm. He must remember that one. If Bykov mentioned it, the Russian and Czech security men had it under surveillance.

Bykov had put on his glasses. His reptile eyes flickered over Craig's face. "I could buy you an identity card—an East German one."

"I won't need it. I'll be out of here in a couple of days."

"Oh, just a bit of business?" He dwelt on the last word.

"I have to meet somebody and take them out, that's all."

"I wouldn't mind slipping over the border with this one," Bykov said. He smirked, unfolded the paper and stabbed a finger at a picture on an inside page. Craig stared at it.

He was looking at a police identikit portrait of Lora!

"She's not bad," he muttered, taking the paper and peering closer.

She was no longer Lora Trusova, but Maria Zolòtka. The story, boxed in a black line, described her as a Czech girl who had absconded with the funds of the Prague bank where she worked, committing the most heinous of bourgeois crimes by stealing the hard-earned savings of her comrades. It was every citizen's duty to report to the police if they caught sight of such a miscreant.

He studied the picture again. No mistaking the face and the slight, upward tilt of the eyes. But what did it mean on an inside page of *Rude Pravo,* the Party organ? They had obviously lost Lora's trace in the four days he reckoned she had been in Prague. They could hardly admit she was Russian and had fled with a state secret. So they had given her another identity, which would enable them to conjure her out of the country without Prague, London or even the man-in-the-Moscow-street being any the wiser.

"If you need anything, call me," Bykov said.

Craig knew that he would go downstairs and ring the Czech security police, who would alert the KGB. In half an hour, perhaps, Kudriatov would knock on that door. Only this time they would not string him up on a hook, torture him and heave him back. He locked the door and took Ross's revolver out of his pocket. High-velocity Smith and Wesson 357. The Special Branch man evidently meant business. This would stop even a charging bull like Kudriatov and several more of his kind. He snapped open the chamber and counted the six shots.

It seemed as though history—his own personal history—would repeat itself here in Prague. On an August night four years ago, Kudriatov had caught up with him. How many times had he played that scene back? How often had he heard Lora's scream? Why had she now chosen this city, which she must know housed a dozen offices of the KGB? And where had she hidden for the past four days?

To ease his body and let his mind relax, he lay down. Lora's mnemonic he knew by heart; he cast up the figures she had jotted down, separating days and months, as he had in East Berlin. He made them 81:36. A phone number? A street number? A tryst or a cache? How many steps in front of the National Museum? How many chapels in St. Vitus's Cathedral? No, as a reference point it didn't make sense. Yet that number must belong to someone or something they had seen or done together four years before.

The hand on the gun loosened; the eye on the door blurred; the weariness and strain of the past week overtook him and he drowsed.

9 It was no more than the rasp of a floor board, but it alerted him immediately. Creeping to the blind side of the door, he tensed and waited. Twice, the handle rotated slowly. "Englishman, are you there?" So they had told Bykov he was English. Craig answered and asked what he wanted. "I forgot to give you the front-door key," the Czech shouted. "Open the door." He inched the door open and Bykov passed him the key, saying that it would save him waiting up if the Englishman were late.

That spindle of metal in his hand meant a great deal. Now he understood why Kudriatov had not come barging through that door with his heavy men. Bykov obviously expected him to return to the room that night, even though his Russian allies had flushed him. This time, Sergei Antonovich was going to let him run, was going to point him like an infrared missile toward Lora and his precious file. He'd try to make it interesting for them.

He waited half an hour before strolling downstairs, past Bykov, who sat by the phone ready to warn them. He had no illusions about the eight men in the Skoda and Tatra by the curbside, or the woman who walked her dachshund at his pace. Using dogs in a dirty racket like this! Down the twisting street he ambled toward Little Town Square. To give the impression of wariness, he paused now and again to use the odd shop window as a mirror, or to glance over his shoulder.

In the square he took a café seat on the arcaded pavement and ordered a coffee. The Skoda parked while the Tatra disappeared toward Charles Bridge; the dachshund was running dry of messages to squirt on the lamppost and the side of St. Nicholas's Cathedral.

128

Craig wondered idly about the two men in open-necked shirts discussing photography two tables away. A man could go round the twist suspecting everybody. From here he could spit on the British Embassy. What were they doing? Did Moonface still lighten its darkness?

His waiter flat-footed to the table. "Your name Craig?" he asked. The sound of that name startled him, but he nodded. "Somebody wants you—inside, on the phone." He wandered in to pick up the receiver at the bar.

"Craig?"

"Who is it?"

"Never mind. And don't talk. Just listen, hard. You're towing every CTK and KGB man behind you from here to the Russian Embassy. You're the ferret. If you know where she is, don't, repeat don't, make a single move to contact her if you want to get out of here alive. . . . I think I can help you. . . ."

"How?"

"For God's sake, shut up." The voice had a remote echo as though the caller had gagged the mouthpiece with a handkerchief. "You know Maček's farm? Kilometer post 9 on Route 9 to Mělník. Turn left two hundred yards beyond it. The farm's about one thousand yards up. Be there in two hours—ten o'clock. It's seven minutes past eight exactly now. Listen and don't make notes. In New World Street you'll find a blue Skoda, 9436 PX. The keys are in the Café Gottwald, in the cistern. Don't bring any of your present friends with you." Before Craig could utter a word he had hung up.

It had not been Ross last night at the frontier post. Who was it? That voice intrigued him; the man had disguised the timbre but not the intonation; though he had barked out the instructions he still had a whisper of an accent. He gave up the guessing game. It could have been any one of a dozen newcomers recruited by Standish in the past four years. All the same, he should have credited even a blown agent with more know-how than to lead the hunt to the quarry. Had he not banged down the receiver, he might have heard that they had their eye on Maček's farm. Maček's farm! Lora had mentioned it in almost her last words to him. Route 9, kilometer post 9. Lora's code: 81:36. Was she there, too?

He paid for the coffee and sauntered on, repressing the impulse to

129

pick up the Skoda now and head for Mělník. The dachshund had emptied and gone, its mistress replaced by a student carrying a load of brand-new textbooks. The Skoda crawled behind him. He made it too easy for those rubber-heeling him by dawdling down Národni, stopping every yard or so. At the lights before Wenceslas Square a trolley bus slowed; he leapt for the platform, ignoring the conductor's curses. Two stops later he jumped off. The Skoda still sat at the lights; the student was nowhere. He hailed a cab. "Trziste 15—the American Embassy," he ordered. He had to risk being remembered by the two Czech policemen at the gate. Inside, he asked for the air attaché and got just what he wanted—a young man straight out of the CIA's Area G who introduced himself as Laurence G. Mercer. "You had a man called Middleton here four years ago," Craig said.

"Yessir, that's correct. Richard F. Middleton. Now second secretary at the Warsaw Embassy."

"Can you reach him at home and tell him that Matt Craig needs that help he promised?"

"It's strictly irregular, sir."

"I'd let him decide that. Tell him I have a package for him—the one he handled for me."

"I'll call him." Mercer glanced at Craig as though he ticked or carried plutonium.

"I know this is irregular but it's a matter of life and death. Can you drive me to the Café Gottwald up the hill in New World Street?" The attaché nodded. Craig hid himself on the floor of the car until they reached the café, then leapt out.

He found the keys. (What would secret service men do without gents' toilets?) The blue Skoda sat a hundred yards along the narrow street. He drove through the park and alongside Letna Gardens. He had twenty minutes to make the rendezvous but lost ten of those in back streets and waiting for a train. If he remembered rightly, Route 9 forked north from the main Dresden road several kilometers above Prague. Did the voice mean the ninth post from there? Stopping to verify this lost him more time. He'd be late at the farm, but they'd wait. Of that he was certain.

He had reached wine country, rolling vineyards left and right, when his headlights picked up the kilometer stone. Two hundred yards beyond he spotted the track and edged slowly along it, relying on the rising moon now for light. He left himself five hundred yards to walk and backed the car into a clump of birch and oak trees and concealed it with branches.

This time he took no chances. If they were keeping surveillance they would have men outside and inside. He had guessed right. As he crept through the trees he heard rooks squawking and saw them trundling above the trees. Something had disturbed them. He crawled forward until he saw the farm, a low, half-timbered building with pitching roof and too much open ground at the front for his liking. He maneuvered around to the back, where he had some cover from the undergrowth and trees. Inching on, he reached the door, lifted the latch and nudged it open. He gave whoever was inside five minutes to react before he felt safe enough to squirm through the door. The large room led off to a kitchen and open stairs ran up to the attic rooms. No one appeared to have lived here for some time, yet he smelled the ash from a wood fire.

First, he explored the kitchen. Empty. He tiptoed upstairs. From the landing, a single partition divided the attic. In one room, moonlight spilling through the dormer window made it easy to confirm that it, too, lay empty.

The second room was in darkness. He entered cannily and struck a match. In the center he noticed a bed and one chair. And something glinting on the floor. A gun! The same type of high-powered Smith and Wesson 357 that he had taken from Ross. He struck another match and moved around the bed; his foot stubbed against something soft lying behind it.

It was a body!

The man crouched on his side in his own blood. Craig rolled him over on his back. He was not quite cold. He struck another match and used a blanket from the bed to wipe the man's face. In the spurt of light, the gray eyes seemed to flicker at him; the jaw had clenched firm. He had died hard.

He could stop racking his memory for that face and voice.

It was the face of the man he had spotted the night before, fractured into several pieces by a windshield wiper at a West Berlin crossroads.

He had heard the voice, too. Long before it had reeled out instructions to bring him here.

The body had once belonged to the man he had known in Wormwood Scrubs as Frank Lucas.

No wonder Lucas had sprung him so painlessly; he had then followed him across half a continent, even arranging his second escape. Craig had no time to ponder why. As his match burned down, the flame twitched slightly; the tattered curtain at the window shivered.

Someone had just opened the back or the front door of the farm.

He crushed the flame between his fingers, slid to the floor and edged behind the bed to a position from which he could observe the landing. Whoever had entered took his time. Five eternal minutes elapsed before he heard the stairs creak. As he levered the safety catch of Ross's revolver free, a shadow crossed the landing and vanished into the first room. At that instant, Craig caught another sound from downstairs. How many of them? The stairs creaked once more. The first shadow was flitting back across the landing; now it was a silhouette, groping toward him. He could smell the black Russian tobacco from the man's clothes as he shuffled into the room. No need to guess who they were: the *istrebeteli,* the KGB executioners who had stage-managed so many killings. The man had snapped on a pencil torch; its beam traveled over and behind Craig to fix on Lucas's body. He took the first pressure on the trigger. The light swung around toward the landing.

"Nobody here," he heard the shadowy figure shout in heavily accented Czech.

"I'll come up and give a hand with him," the voice called from downstairs. The man mounted the steps quickly, the beam of his more powerful torch wavering in front of him. In a moment, Craig realized he would be caught in that circle of light. To prevent himself from being dazzled, he shut his right eye and waited until the beam had traversed the landing and was sweeping toward him. He opened his eye, aimed a foot above and to the left of the torch and fired; he tracked the figure who sprang for the door with the gun and fired again. The bullet spun the man around and sent him sprawling face down on the floor.

Craig pounced on the torch. "Don't shoot," he heard the second man moaning. He shone the light on the face of the first man. He was dead.

"How many of you outside?" he asked the wounded man.

"We're the only two."

"What are you—Czech or Russian?"

"Czech," the man grunted.

"Your reliefs? When do they arrive?"

"At midnight."

Craig looked at the watch on the dead man's wrist. Ten-fifty. In the torchlight, he examined the other Czech's wound. He had hit high up on the left shoulder. Messy, but his reliefs could cope. He tore the blanket into strips and bound the man's hands and feet. Searching the dead man, he discovered a Czech police identity card bearing the name Josef Petrik. He took the few hundred crowns from the pockets. This was no time for abject men to grow sentimental. He moved over to Lucas. Poor sod. As the whisky-faced brigadier had remarked, you wind up with a bullet and no thanks. Which cabinet minister had read Lucas's reports? He flipped open the passport he had carried. Frank Stafford, aged thirty-three, born London. Diplomat. No special peculiarities. No, Frank Lucas had lived and died a faceless man. What was his real name? Was he married? Did he have a wife and kids? A mother or father, or both? Did it matter? Just another expendable agent, they'd say in London, then forget him.

So Vernon Alveston Standish had cast Lucas at him and he had swallowed him, hook and all! He remembered how Lucas had shown him the wrinkles in his first months at the Scrubs. He'd pretended to have done two months with another two to go. They had ended that assignment when he refused to confide in Lucas or anybody else. He'd materialized again when Standish got wind from somewhere that Lora might try to escape. But Lucas hadn't pumped him, so they must have guessed he'd jump the wall. And, of course, willing Frank stepped in to give him a shove. He'd finished up on his face, here, after trailing him through four countries, waiting for the moment he'd found the file to lead him quietly back to Standish and his cell in the Scrubs. He and Standish must have had a shock when Kudriatov lobbed him back over the Wall. But they had another ace up their sleeves: the car crash. Was Ross in the act? Hardly probable, since he had taken a bad knock.

Standish, you bastard! You've killed a man and you've forced me to kill a man.

He climbed to the dormer window and drew back the curtain.

133

Moonlight silvered the courtyard. Lucas's car had not moved; the *istrebeteli* had hidden theirs somewhere. Could he trust the wounded man's word? The moment he stepped outside, he might meet other executioners.

As cautiously as he had entered, he left the farm by the back door. Only when he had reached the wood did he dare walk.

He had marched less than a hundred yards when he picked up the whisper of a foot on dry bracken. He halted and listened. The sound ceased. He repeated the drill. Someone was walking in his footsteps.

His clothes clammed to his body with the sweat of fear; the night breeze shivered through him. This time he might run out of luck. He broke into a trot, then a run, then a dash; he crashed, gasping, through branches and bushes until he blundered against his car. He had his hand on the door handle when something between a sob and a shout went up behind him. He whirled around, revolver in hand. "Matt, *dushka,* darling. It's me. Lora."

Craig collapsed over the bonnet of the car, sick with the shock and the relief at seeing her. Lora fell over on him, laughing and crying. "I knew you would come. . . . I even prayed for it. . . . I knew that if you got my message nobody could keep us apart."

Craig lifted his head. "Lora . . . is it you?" he mumbled. "You gave me a hell of a scare."

They were hugging and fondling each other as though neither could believe in the reality of the other's flesh.

"Did you see what happened?" he asked.

"They were watching the house and I have been watching them for four days," she whispered. "I didn't know who had gone into the farm, then I heard the shots. I knew that it wasn't you. I would have felt it here." She pointed to her heart. "They killed that first man, did they not?" Craig nodded. "Was he a friend of yours?"

"I thought he was."

"I was afraid he might be meeting you, so I came down the track to warn you. I saw this car hidden but empty. They must have heard it, the policemen. They came to look and then went back. I waited until I heard the two shots, then returned to the farm."

"They were *istrebeteli*—the Czech version. I had to kill one of them and tie the other up."

134

Lora began to pour out her story: how she had stolen the file and managed to join a Russian trade delegation to Warsaw as an interpreter; how she had flown to East Berlin and hidden there in a small pension run by a German couple; how she had watched them trap him at their old flat, which she had thought still a secret between them; how she had stolen a car and driven to the Czech frontier and walked across it.

Craig hushed her. "Tell me one thing—when did your father die?"

"Six weeks ago. Did they tell you that he died?"

He shook his head. Six weeks ago, somebody must have read and relayed that *Pravda* obituary notice on General Trusov, prompted, no doubt, by Standish. Six weeks ago, Lucas had made his second appearance at the Scrubs. He had to admire Standish's prescience. It paid, as the great man had remarked, to have a hobby. Such as the spawning habits of salmon.

"Matt, we must go. Kudriatov's men will be here in less than an hour." She directed him along the main road for two kilometers and up a farm track to a building like Maček's. She explained that it belonged to Stefan Rovnak, who was married to Maček's sister. Both hated the present Czech government and the Russians for torturing and killing Maček when they discovered that he was hiding Dubček supporters and helping them escape in 1968. Maček's sister, Ludmilla, had installed her in the barn four days ago. From here, she could watch Maček's farm and reach it in a quarter of an hour through the woods and fields. They did not wake the farmer and his wife. Lora opened the massive pine door and Craig drove the Skoda inside.

Sadness settled over her face as she gazed at him in the dashboard light; she ran both hands over his face and through his hair. "Forgive me, Matt," she whispered. "I was so selfish, talking about myself when you have suffered so much for me."

"We're both still alive. And I only suffered because I didn't know what had happened to you."

She kissed him. "Was it hard in prison?"

"I can't say I feel homesick for it."

"And for me you escaped from there and from Kudriatov. How did you succeed in doing this?"

"It's too long a story, sweetheart. Let's say it was a combination of brilliant and ingenious planning and native bloody-mindedness."

"I know you are brilliant, Matt. But I wondered if you would break that stupid code I had to write."

"All those nines—how could I go wrong? The ninth kilometer post on Route Nine at nine o'clock on August 14. I'm sorry I was an hour late."

Lora laughed. "I would have waited," she said. Lighting a hurricane lamp, she led him up a ladder to a rickety wooden loft covered with straw. For the first time in four years he could study her face; in the guttering light, he perceived that she had lost weight; her face appeared drawn, the skin taut over the prominent cheekbones and around the eyes. She was burrowing a hole for them in the straw. And he thought: maybe, after all, there is some crazy analogy between those silvery fish in Standish's hatchery and us human beings.

When she had finished she turned and raised the lamp so that its weak, wavering beam fell on his face. *"Dushka,* you look exhausted," she murmured.

"It was a hard swim," he said. He caught her puzzled frown but did not enlighten her. That would have taken too long.

Yet, what happened to a couple of salmon in love once they had made it to the parent stream? They have a fine-drawn, half-dead appearance. But they have already triumphed; they have accomplished their greatest journey; they are together! Drained of will by their life obsession and their immense effort, they fall prey to the angler, the Standishes and the Jameson Garvies. Even that doesn't matter to them. With her fins and snout, the female gouges a niche in the riverbed with the male looking on. There, she spawns with the male hovering behind her, quivering with sexual pleasure, waiting to void his milt on her eggs. And after that? They die, don't they? Or aren't some of the rare ones given a second chance to coast downstream to the open sea, where they thrive again? Now dying! Not a bad idea at that! He must remember it. Tomorrow. At the moment, he didn't much care what happened.

Lora had lain down and was contemplating him as though she, too, felt that life and death hardly counted now that they had found each other. He crept in beside her and they made love gently and slept like two people who had an eternity of moments before them.

136

10 Some instinct aroused Craig. Distant voices reached him and, with them, the smell of smoke. Lora lay on her side, her body pressed against his, an arm thrown around his neck. He levered her gently away and looked at the watch on her wrist. Half past one. Groping toward the skylight window he thrust it open. To the south he spotted the glow and gouts of flame shooting into the smoke pall. So Kudriatov had decided to cremate Lucas and the Czech agent where he discovered them, to destroy the evidence in Maček's farm.

"Lora." She stirred, rubbed her eyes, then put out a hand to grasp his as though to reassure herself she was not dreaming. "They've set Maček's farm on fire. They'll search every farm for miles around now they've found the bodies. I'll have to get rid of the car."

"I'll come with you."

Craig rejected the suggestion. "You'll be much safer here. Kudriatov doesn't know we've met and Rovnak can hide you somewhere else until they've gone. Do you know of another hiding place?"

She thought for a moment. "There's another farm on the road to . . ."

"Don't tell me," he cut in. "I don't want to know."

"But why?" He did not answer even when she repeated the question. "I know," she said. "If they catch and torture you then you can't tell them. Is that it?"

"We can't take that chance," he whispered, remembering that he had almost betrayed her a week before in East Berlin. "If anything happens to me you can make it on your own."

"No, Matt. Now that we have come all this way we're not parting." She threw her arms around him and he felt her breast heave. "If anything happened to you I wouldn't want to live." He listened to the jumbled sentences. "Matt, don't go alone. . . . We have the car. . . . I can get us across the frontier. . . . You said once we could find somewhere that nobody would ever know us."

He put his hand over her mouth. "Lora, whatever frontier we crossed now they'd catch up with us, sooner or later. But we have something that Kudriatov and Standish want desperately and we can make a bargain with them. I've got to do that alone, and in Prague."

137

Lora was delving into the straw pile to emerge with a handbag in which she rummaged. He recognized his own package. She handed him a typed list. "These are the names of Russian agents in Western Europe. I was going to sell those to the British as well in exchange for your freedom." She had produced two small steel cylinders, which she passed to him. "These," she said, "are the Cassius files—the only two copies in the ministry archives."

"Cassius?" Craig vaguely recalled her first mention of that name in Berlin. "Cassius? Who is this character?"

"I met him many years ago when he came to Moscow. His name is Patrick Holder and he was a member of parliament with a trade mission."

"Holder?" He tried, vainly, to place the name while Lora was explaining how she had inveigled him into the flat where Kudriatov had compromised him by taking homosexual pictures. The old trick, he thought. So it was this Holder who had pulled the strings in those spy barters in the sixties. He wondered if the same man had dropped a hint in the ear of the judge who had put him out of commission for twenty years. Whatever else, he must rank high to have influenced the British government and to have inspired Standish to plot his own escape from Wormwood Scrubs. Running over the catalog of Standish's friends in government circles, he still drew a blank. With a cuckoo like Holder in the nest, no wonder Vernon Alveston considered the file vital to British security. Now he understood why the man himself had popped up at the Scrubs and again at his bedside in Berlin.

He pointed to the file Lora had recovered in his room. "Strutchkov mentioned the cover name, but no identity."

"But Strutchkov must have known," she said. "He worked for a year in London and would have connected the code name with Holder."

"And Strutchkov died before he could cross the Wall and tell anybody," Craig mused. "I wonder who really tipped off your people that day they shot him."

"You do not mean that somebody on the British side betrayed him?"

"I mean that Standish, my revered boss, was ready to let me rot for twenty years for some of his own mistakes. But, no, it wasn't him. London knew, and I'd say the anonymous call came from somebody there. Holder himself, perhaps.''

He felt her body stiffen against him. ''Matt,'' she pleaded, ''don't go back to Prague. We have enough to ask the French or the Germans for asylum.''

''And they'd either hand us back for diplomatic reasons or someone would blab and we'd be run over by a car. We don't chance anything until we've taken out some more life policies.''

''Then you're not going back without me.''

''No,'' he said. But she insisted. She would give herself up at the Russian Embassy if he left without her. He realized that she meant it. ''All right, let's get going,'' he said. She went to say good-bye to the Rovnaks while he maneuvered the Skoda out of the barn.

They headed north, away from the glow of the blazing farmhouse. At Mělník he bore left, swinging in a circle until he hit the road running into Prague above the Vltava. At that hour he met nothing and he drove very fast. They would dump the car in Prague and call at the American Embassy to wait for Middleton. Only when he had briefed the CIA man would he consider his next move.

They had breasted the last rise and spotted the lights of Prague when he heard the siren behind him. In his rear mirror he saw the police car, growing in size, gaining on him. Should he stop and try to brazen it out? With a phony passport. No car papers. A girl whose picture they'd have in their notebooks. He urged the car forward, watching the clock pass the 130-kilometer mark as his lights ricocheted off the new apartment blocks in Letna. But even with his foot on the boards the siren was dinning in his ear. At the Vltava embankment he turned and sped along the river to the Smernov Bridge. He might lose them by dodging into the maze of Old Town streets. No, he'd never make it. The black Skoda behind had veered left to pass him and block the way. He saw the crossroads and braked suddenly to mount the pavement. The police car shot past. Craig spun the wheel so viciously that Lora was hurled against him as the car slewed around, into the side street. At most he had stolen half a mile.

''Now listen,'' he shouted. ''Beyond the Old Town Square I'll stop and let you out.''

''No.''

''Shut up and do what I say. It's our only chance. Take these''—

139

he thrust one of the Cassius files, his own package and a revolver into her hand. "You know where the American Embassy is. Ask for a man named Middleton—Richard Middleton. If he's not there, wait for him. He'll remember you from 1968 and you can trust him. Tell him I'm in the police station and can he bail me out. Understand?"

Above the racket of the car in the narrow streets he heard her cry, "I'm not getting out, Matt."

Abruptly, they left the houses behind. Old Town Square. He flashed past the Kynsky Palace and the Hus monument. Beyond the town hall he jammed down on the brake, throwing Lora forward so violently that she put out her hands to protect herself. At that moment Craig snapped open the door and bundled her out. He swung around and headed back into the square and along Tynska Street. There they caught him.

In the lamplight he watched the two policemen approach, their faces grim between their cap peaks and button-up tunics. "Get out," one shouted, brandishing a revolver. Craig sat still. He would play the dumb Englishman. He spread his hands to prove that he would not resist. The door was wrenched open; a hand grabbed him and jerked him out of the car. They handcuffed him and pushed him into the police car. He noticed the blue Skoda behind when they got out at Celetná Street police station.

They hustled him through an outer office. "We found him and the stolen car," he heard one officer say to the desk sergeant. So the Skoda had given him away. They thrust him into a bare room with no windows and lit by fluorescent light. One man barked at him: "Papers!"

Craig hesitated, pretending not to understand. He had one of the Cassius files with him, and the envelope he had recovered from Johnny Mottram. If they found those he would be finished.

"You'd better search him," the police sergeant ordered.

As they went to carry out the order, Craig produced the passport he had taken from Lucas's body. "I am a diplomat," he said, handing it to one of the policemen. "I wish you to contact my embassy in Prague."

The sergeant glanced at the passport, then walked to the door and called in a young officer. Craig heard him say that they had arrested an Englishman who spoke no Czech. "What do you say?" the young man asked in guttural English. Craig repeated his request.

140

"The British Embassy, eh!" The sergeant snickered. "That's a laugh. Go on, search him."

They made him strip to his underpants and began to go through his jacket and trousers.

"What's this?" the sergeant snapped, pointing to the cylinder of microfilm.

"I don't know," Craig replied. "I found it in the car."

"You stole it," said the sergeant. He turned to the envelope. "And this?" Craig shrugged his shoulders. "You stole that, too."

Craig drew a deep breath. In a minute, the sergeant would pry open the tube and find the microfilm, would see the name on that dossier he had compiled all those years ago. But instead, the man merely cataloged them and lifted the passport once more. Thank God Lucas had gone through customs and immigration at Děčín! The sergeant looked at the photograph, then at Craig. "I suppose if we cleaned him up . . ." he muttered almost to himself. "Ask when he entered the CSSR."

"Yesterday, at Děčín," Craig told the interpreter.

"With this car?"

"No, I borrowed it from a friend in the British Embassy, where I work. You can confirm that by phoning them."

"You stole the car," the sergeant bellowed. When Craig reiterated his denial, he said: "Then why didn't you stop when we ordered you? Why did you nearly kill two policemen? You have committed serious breaches of the law."

"I am a diplomat and I claim immunity from Czech law."

"We'll see about that," the sergeant said. "Take him downstairs."

Still handcuffed, still in his underpants, Craig was marched down to a row of cells, each with a massive pine door and a small peephole. The policeman thrust him inside and switched on the blue night light. Craig sat on the iron bed, wrapping the single blanket around him against the damp, musty air which seeped from the underground walls.

You crossed four frontiers. You had a beautiful plan for crossing the fifth and last. You made an elementary mistake by not foreseeing that Lucas had pinched that car and you paid for it with everything. Of course they would call the SNB counterespionage section; they would screw open the file, would read the name on his papers. They would, they must, call the KGB office in Prague. And Sergei Antonovich would come running to shatter his beautiful little ploy in those muzhik hands of his. And Lora? She might cross one frontier or two with Middleton's help; but they'd eventually lay their great paws on her, too. What had he hoped—to beat the KGB and the SIS with two bits of film and a flimsy, forged document? Better not to think about it, to switch his mind to anything but the next meeting with Kudriatov. He stretched himself on the wire trellis and shut his eyes to blot out that craggy face.

"Naw, laddie! Naw! You canna hope to grip them like that. You need to be ga'e canny to get spring saumon to rise to the bait even in water like the Spey." Jameson Garvie turned his eyes reproachfully on him. "You dae it like this, see." Seizing the split-cane rod and flicking his wrist, he sent the silk line in a hissing arc downstream to land the bait lightly on the broken water and make it twitch like a live fly. Craig stood in his rubber waders, his feet awkward and unsure in the pluck of the current and the shift of the pebbly bottom. He tried once again to cast but sent the bait no more than twenty feet.

"You're a Lowlander, son, are you no'?" asked Garvie, a disparaging edge to his voice. "Aye, I thocht as much," the gillie went on. "Weel, weel, there's no saying you'll no' learn. Now, yon boss o' yours, Mr. Standish—he micht ha'e been born up there by Aviemore. I've never seen a Sassenach with his hand for saumon fishing."

Stung to the quick, Craig cast again, flying the bait fifty feet and setting it down gently in the rock pool. He felt the line go taut; his instinct shouted, "Pull," but he remembered Garvie's advice. "Let 'im swallow the lot, then reel in." The line tensed; he reeled frantically. "Steady, laddie. He's a big wan. Play him a bit." Craig reeled in and out like a Yo-Yo, keeping his eye on the threshing water and the desperate leaps of the fish, attempting to disgorge the hook. "Mair line, or you'll lose him." Even in the breeze from the Cairngorms he sweated as he stumbled after the fish, chest high in water but still holding on. It seemed no longer than two minutes, but he played that fish for half an hour. He felt as slack as the line as he saw Garvie pounce with the net. "He's in the net, laddie. In the net. And all o' thirrty pounds. No' bad for a Lowlander." The salmon

142

still bucketed in the net, still gasped and fought. Garvie made to grasp it and squeeze the life out of it; the vicious hands were around the gills. "No," Craig shouted. "Let him go." He grabbed the net and tossed the fish back into the river. Garvie gazed at him, thunderstruck. "Aye, laddie, there must be other things you can do besides fishing." Craig walked away, thinking: where had he seen that fish face before that he could not kill it?

11

He was still on Speyside when the guard prodded him and jerked him off the bed. Up the steps, along the corridor and back into the barred room. The file and envelope still lay there with his clothes. "You have a visitor," the interpreter said with a cold smile. Craig glanced at the wall clock. Ten past three. They had not wasted time. His stomach and spine tensed as he heard the footfall outside the door. The sergeant thrust the door open to admit a burly figure. For a moment, Craig imagined himself still dreaming in the cell below.

Vernon Alveston Standish stood before him, grinning, his jowly features as pink as the rose in his buttonhole.

Craig could not move. His mind refused to transpose his confused thoughts and almost refuted his senses. He had expected and dreaded the arrival of Kudriatov and felt relieved. But how far could he trust Standish?

"Stafford, my dear boy, I had no idea you were the culprit," he said, holding out his hand. Craig took it mechanically. The SIS man turned to the Czech sergeant. "I'm awfully sorry, officer, there appears to have been a fearful misunderstanding. This man works at the embassy and, of course, he had a perfect right to borrow the car. It's our stupid fault." He paused for the translation, then looked at Craig. "Naughty, old man. You ought to have informed us. I'm afraid I've put the police here to a great deal of trouble for nothing. But I was worried about those embassy documents in the dashboard locker." Gloom spread over the sergeant's face as his interpreter repeated Standish's remarks.

He had never admired Standish more as he watched him handle

these policemen; a polished performance, combining offhand authority and British phlegm. Standish flourished the car papers, then pointed to the revolver they had taken from Craig. "I do have the permit if you would care to see it." The sergeant shrugged. "I know it was found on Mr. Stafford, but we can overlook that, can't we?"

"You mean, you don't want to prefer any charges against this man?" the sergeant asked.

"Oh, I know I should—to teach him a salutary lesson. But then he would plead that he's a member of Her Majesty's diplomatic service on attachment in Prague and we'd all look a bit foolish, don't you think?" Standish bared his teeth at the policeman. "I was merely worried about the firearm and the papers in the car."

"You mean these," said the sergeant, pointing to the envelope and the microfilm.

"Ah, yes. I'm certainly relieved to see this," Standish said, picking up Craig's documents. "Oh, and my cassette of films. I'd forgotten about that." He pocketed both, proffered his hand to the sergeant and the two other policemen, thanked them and then had an afterthought. "Ah, hmm, I realize this is slightly unorthodox, but I'd like to make some amends for the trouble I've caused. Perhaps a small contribution to a police charity if that exists?"

"We have a fund for police orphans," said the sergeant, suddenly amiable.

Standish pulled out a wad of notes and counted out five hundred crowns. His expression stiffened slightly as he paid them into the sergeant's hand. No expenses, these, Craig said to himself. But the SIS man could afford some magnanimity now that he had his precious file.

They handed Craig back his clothes. When he had dressed, he followed Standish out of the station to the Skoda, still parked in the street.

"You drive, Matt," Standish said. "Over Charles Bridge and into Letna. I'll tell you where."

In his rear mirror, Craig noticed that a car was tailing them. Not an official police car. He said nothing but followed the instructions, which took them along the river and through Letna Gardens to a villa with a long drive, flanked by firs and limes. They seemed to have lost the car behind them. "Here it is," Standish said as they reached the front door. "Just climb out slowly, Matt, and don't do anything rash." Craig saw that the SIS man was pointing a small Webley automatic at his face.

"What's the idea, Standish?"

"Just get out," Standish said, following him out the left-hand door and pushing him toward the villa. "I've got to be careful, Matt. You've nothing to lose and nobody takes chances with a man like that." Craig opened the door, revealing a large hall and a living room. "We can have a quiet chat here with nobody to bother us. I think the embassy counsellor who normally stays here has even left us some of his whisky."

He indicated a chair for Craig and sat down himself in front of a small table which had a whisky bottle, a pitcher of water and several glasses on it. "I don't want to tie you up, Matt. I do have your word, don't I?"

"You have my word."

"Straight?" Craig nodded, and Standish poured two sizable whiskies, pushing one across the table but still keeping the gun pointed at him.

"What's this—the final drink before the execution?"

A pained look creased Standish's face. "Who said anything about execution. I have to remember that you're a criminal on the run, that's all."

"I'm wondering what that makes you, for aiding and abetting my escape."

"In the line of duty, I assure you."

"Whose duty—Her Majesty's or your own?"

"What do you think?"

Craig regarded the puffy features, the pink jowls, the marbled eyes. Was Vernon Alveston going to kill him after playing him like a salmon? A pound a minute, wasn't that the time they took to land? He might not last that long unless he talked a good line.

"What do I think? That you'd have already used that gun on me if you knew where the other Cassius file was. You guessed there were two copies, didn't you?" Standish showed no surprise, merely nodding as though aware of the existence of the second file. "I supposed you'd want both," Craig went on.

145

"Why would you suppose that?"

"You've always craved one thing—C's job, the top SIS job. So you get the unfortunate Mr. Holder off the Russian hook and he fixes it for you just as he fixed all those spy swaps."

"Interesting thought."

"Or, if you're blackmailing Holder for some reason, you'll still need both files. You can't have a competitor like Kudriatov hovering in the background."

"Then shall we say you get the second file for me and we strike a bargain?"

"I wouldn't give twopennyworth of prison snout for my chances once you had that other microfilm."

"Am I that bad, Matt?"

"Oh, no. You fixed me—one of your own boys—for twenty years."

"That was Kudriatov and you know it."

"And you marked poor Strutchkov's card, too."

"Kudriatov again," said Standish. "The leak came from London."

"What about Lucas or Stafford, the man who sprung me on your orders? You reckoned he was expendable, like me. After all, who would bother about a lag from the Scrubs if they fished him out of the Spree or the Vltava? You thought you had the right. You created me, you ran me as a spy and you could stop me in my tracks when you wanted."

"You still have a lively imagination," Standish drawled. "But you've been too long in jail to think straight."

"Maybe. But there's somebody in Berlin sitting on the story I gave him a week ago, waiting for that file. The moment he hears I'm dead, he'll blow the lot."

"We'd simply deny the whole thing."

"You might. But think of poor Holder. A man weak enough to have his trousers taken down in Moscow would either break down or eat a fistful of barbiturate to prove the truth of the story. I can see those two male nudes in a KGB love nest going down big on world TV."

"You're a despicable fellow, Matt."

"An abject man, remember? You can't trust us abject men."

"What do you really want for the other file?"

"I thought I'd strike a bargain with you and Kudriatov to call off the hunt."

"An excellent thought. I've heard so much about that gentleman that I'd like to meet him. But"—Standish sipped his whisky—"the trouble is you haven't got much of a case and now you know too much."

"Dead or alive?" Craig said. But the words were gluing in his dry mouth; he was running out of time.

"Dead would be better," Standish replied. "Who'd question it if I killed you now? You've already escaped twice and threatened a member of the Special Branch. Who's to say that I didn't catch up with you and you shot first? You'll have the satisfaction of knowing that you did your old employers one last service by taking the file home."

"In my shroud pocket?" Craig muttered. How would Standish finish him off? With a bullet, obviously. But not in the house. Too messy. Standish liked things tidy. As though reading his thoughts, Standish began to screw a silencer tube into the barrel of his pistol.

"Don't they give the condemned man a last cigarette?" Craig said.

"Of course." Standish fished for his gold case, flicked it open and proffered his handmade brand; he lit it with his gold lighter. "Out of interest," he said, "how did you intend to convince Kudriatov to escort you over the border?"

"By giving him back his money," Craig replied, indicating the file he had carried from Berlin.

Standish guffawed, but picked up the envelope and spilled out its papers. He skimmed over them and lifted his eyes to give Craig an admiring look. "Clever, old boy. Damnably clever. It might have come off at that." His eye ranged over the columns. "A tidy sum. They do pay well."

Over Standish's inclined head Craig made out a shadow on the wall. He kept talking, commenting on the documents, watching the shadow grow longer. A hand reached for the switch. Craig tensed. With a gun no more than six feet away how should he jump?

The finger snapped off the switch. Craig was already diving sideways to roll over on the floor and lie still. A slapping sound filled the room, then the wrench of a bullet in the wall behind him. He could discern Standish's moving toward the door and the light switch; he

147

was about to spring when he heard a grunt and a thud. The light flashed on.

Lora stood over the fallen figure. Craig ran to pick up the pistol and noticed the heavy wrench in her hand. "I think I hurt him," she said.

"Why didn't you use the revolver?"

"I was afraid I might hit you," she said.

"And you didn't go to the embassy?"

She shrugged. She had learned to distrust embassies and she could not leave him in the hands of the police. So she had followed him to the police station, where she noticed Standish arrive. She had stolen a car and followed them to the end of the drive, dumped the car and walked up. Craig picked up the metal tube that Standish had dropped; he must find out what it contained to make the SIS man want to do him in.

But as he rolled the slack body over and bound the hands he began to wonder if Standish had really meant to kill him. He would have surely done it more subtly and more quickly, without the cross-examination for answers he already had. Craig looked at the bullet hole—high up on the paneling. Standish shot better than that. That scrambled, encoded dialogue of his was leading somewhere else. But where? What did Standish really want?

He explored the villa, which had two upstairs bedrooms and a cellar and garage under concrete stilts. He hid the Skoda in the garage. When he re-entered the house, Standish was sitting up and Lora was bathing his bruised head with water. "Matt, dear boy," he groaned. "You don't think I was trying . . ."

"Oh, no. It went off in your hand."

"I've always been a bit six-fingered with firearms."

"All right," said Craig. "Now, tell me how long this embassy man's on leave for."

"Another fortnight, at least. I've got free run, so if there's anything you need, help yourself." He looked at Lora. "I wouldn't mind a cup of coffee, Miss Trusova." She looked at Matt, who nodded, and she disappeared into the kitchen.

"Who is this man Holder?" Craig asked.

"Cross my heart, I know nobody of that name."

148

"I can always get the American Embassy to develop the film."

"I wouldn't do that if you want to leave here alive, Matt." He uttered the statement so quietly that Craig had no doubt that he meant it.

"Who'll do the killing?"

"Your friend Kudriatov. If he discovered that the CIA had that dossier, both our lives wouldn't amount to much."

"What would you do?"

"If I were you? Get Kudriatov up here somehow and let your old boss handle him."

There was a hook in that one somewhere, though he could not feel it. Maybe Standish was right and he could act as his go-between.

"I don't trust you, Standish," he said.

"You've no alternative and neither have I. We've got to trust each other. Anyway, you hang on to the files and you've got . . ." He stopped.

"I've got what?"

"Your documents—your bit of penmanship."

A smell of frying eggs and sausages drifted through from the kitchen. Several minutes later, Lora appeared with a tray. She set the table for three people and put down the plates of sausage and egg, toast and coffee. Craig freed Standish's hands and he sat down and began to stuff himself as though nothing had happened. Craig marveled at the man's impudence and impenitence as he watched him smack his fleshy lips and pay Lora outrageous compliments. "You're a fortunate man, Matt, to find a girl who's both beautiful and practical. Handy with a monkey wrench, good at first aid and a cordon bleu to boot."

"What's a cordon bleu?" Lora asked.

"An English title they confer on anybody who can do a three-minute egg," Craig replied.

"Anyway, I feel a lot better," said Standish, swilling down the last of his coffee. He turned to Craig. "Well, Matt, is it a bargain, what we were discussing?"

"I'll think about it."

"You know, Matt, it was the most vexing day of my life when I lost you . . . through your own stupidity, you must admit. I feel it's just like old times working with you again."

149

"The only difference is that I'm deciding the moves," Craig said. "And you're moving downstairs." He hustled Standish into the cellar and tied him to a chair.

"I'm not sure, dear boy," he protested, "that this is in accordance with the UN convention on the treatment of hostages."

Hostages! The word rang in Craig's head as he mounted the stairs. Was Standish casting another baited hook at him? Hadn't he sprung him and set him running with a bit of paper and a few loose hints? He had done much the same in Berlin last week. Who was planning the moves? Himself, or that overblown gargoyle he had strapped to the chair?

And yet, he did need that other hostage.

12 That embassy phone was a direct line to Czech counterespionage through the tap at the exchange. From them to Kudriatov, too. But they'd have to wait until eight o'clock for the playback and translation. It gave him at least three hours. He dialed the number. He heard the click and hiss as the receiver was lifted at the other end. "Yes?" said the voice, hazy with sleep. "Aren't you awake, Larry?" he shouted. "You forget we're going fishing this morning with Dick?"

"Is this some sort of a joke?" Mercer mumbled.

"But we arranged it yesterday, remember?" (The CIA would have to buff the corners off Laurence G. Mercer and put a finer sheen on him.) "With Richard F."

"Richard F? Yes . . . ugh . . . now I get you."

"We're a bit late. Pick me up in ten minutes at Letna Square."

He collected the three lots of microfilm and his documents. Lora was elbow deep in the kitchen sink, washing the dishes. "Look after Standish," he said. "I'll be back in a couple of hours."

"Where are you going?" she asked anxiously.

"To have a peep at what you saw in the flesh—Mr. Holder, alias Cassius."

Mercer was waiting at the square. Yes, he had rung Mr. Middleton, who had instructed him to give Mr. Craig any help he needed. He would fly down that afternoon.

150

"Has the embassy got a darkroom, a projector, a good camera and a photocopying machine?" Craig asked. Mercer nodded. Craig crouched down on the floor of the car as they went past the two Czech policemen guarding the embassy gates. Within minutes, he had started work in a basement room.

He projected the Strutchkov film first, to refresh his memory and search for the names of Cassius and Holder. As each image appeared on the six by six screen, he photographed it. What a legacy the dead defector had left! Even after four years such revelations could turn the KGB inside out and fetch a hijacker's ransom from half a dozen other intelligence agencies. Craig finished with a casebook of Russian and East German spying activities stretching from 1962 to 1967; with a list of dozens of agents probably still operating in the West; with the full story of Alfred Frenzel, the Soviet spy in the Bonn parliament, and Hans Felfe, the double agent who planted himself on General Gehlen; with the authentic Kremlin reaction to the Berlin tunnel-tapping coup.

Finally, he located the name he sought, scrawled in Strutchkov's stiff Russian. "British politician, compromised Moscow in late fifties, working for KGB in London. Many contacts among ruling circles. Name not known but code-named Cassius. Might have assisted in release of Karl, Juno and Graham." These were presumably cover names for trapped Soviet-bloc spies. Craig pinned several sheets of paper over that entry before snapping the microfilm. No need to give everything away. He quickly copied his own file of documents and Lora's list of Russian agents.

Now for Holder. He unscrewed the cassette ends and shook out the tiny negatives and the roll of film that had converted a weak man into a high-class traitor.

As he blew up each document, he had to admire KGB thoroughness. Everything carried the date and some comment. Cassius had launched the idea of spy exchanges, for trade concessions at first, then for other spies. He had pulled strings in the Wynne-Lonsdale swap. In the middle sixties he had acted as a quiet mouthpiece for Soviet policy in the Eastern bloc, the Middle and Far East. What would he, Craig, have given to read the Hansard reports on some of those parliamentary speeches? Scattered through the Cassius time-and-motion sheets were names from *Burke's Peerage* and *Who's Who,* proving that Mr. Holder was biting the right ears. But why, he

151

wondered, did the entries stop in the autumn of 1968 as Cassius-Holder was negotiating quietly for the barter of Gerald Brooke, the London lecturer imprisoned in Russia, for the Krogers, two master spies?

Lora must surely have made a mistake. There must be a third file! And if that existed, they had come all this way for nothing.

A second blow. Nothing identified Cassius. The KGB had taken good care of that. Had Lora not participated in trapping Holder, had she not remembered the code name, those files would have revealed nothing.

But he still had the films they had snooped. Feverishly, he thumbed them into the projector. So Holder was a homo. Obscene acrobatics, or the obvious artistry of the KGB camera crew, did not interest him. Only the decadent, doped face of Mr. Patrick Holder, which he studied from every angle. He tried to imagine it five or ten years older; he fitted it to politicians he had met or seen on TV; he tracked his mind over Standish's friends in the higher Civil Service. Those pictures evoked nothing. Somewhere he had met something like those fine-boned features, but he might as well have tried to picture a lost sculpture from one fragmentary chip. At last he gave up and sat down to smoke a cigarette while the negatives dried and he could print them.

Where had they hidden this man? Why did the KGB dossier stop in 1968? Who was Holder? If he could unravel that puzzle he would know why Standish had manipulated him out of prison and what the SIS chief was doing in Prague. Full of gloom, he packed up the originals of the microfilm and his own documents but kept the prints. He handed the cassettes and documents to Mercer. "Put them in your safe," he said. Mercer drove him back to the villa. Middleton, he said, would arrive that afternoon. Craig crossed his fingers that he would get here. He needed at least one honest man around him.

Lora recognized Holder but dismissed the suggestion of a third file; she had carefully checked the whole Central Index. But she had no idea why the dossier stopped in 1968. Craig untied Standish and brought him up. He tossed the pictures at him. "Do you know him?" he asked. Standish merely smiled and murmured, "I fancy the other chap more." But the copies evidently worried him. "How many sets have you made?" he asked.

152

"Only this one."

"And the originals?"

"In a safe place."

"Ah, with your CIA friend, Middleton. Another honest man." This with a sneer.

"You're well briefed, Standish."

"I've got to know whether you're worth the trouble of saving, Matt."

"You're in no position to save anybody."

Standish took out a cigarette, lit it and puffed out his cheeks. "All right, try selling these stolen goods back to your friend Kudriatov. See how far you get on your own."

"Of course, you could persuade him."

"With these snapshots of yours I think I can promise results." He paused and looked at Lora. "Oh, I'm not only doing it for you, Matt. I've rather taken to your Miss Trusova."

"I have a better idea," said Craig. "Why don't I invite Kudriatov up here where we can keep an eye on you?"

"No," Lora exclaimed.

"The KGB gives them good training, Matt. Miss Trusova is right. He arrives with half a hundred men and we all find ourselves in Moscow by sunup. I shall be arraigned for possessing vital Soviet secrets, you'll be shot and the charming Miss Trusova will spend her life filling the nation's saltcellars."

"I can get him up here alone," Craig said. He turned to Lora. "Who's the KGB chief in Prague?"

"Vladimir Semeonov," she said. At Craig's insistence she looked up his private embassy number. "But what do you want with him? He is scared of Kudriatov."

Craig dialed the number. He explained who he was and told Semeonov that he had some documents and a proposition that might interest him and the KGB. Could they meet? Semeonov suggested the Russian Embassy, but Craig said quickly, "No, I don't want to meet tovarish Kudriatov or want him to know I'm meeting you. I shall be in the Wenceslas Chapel of the cathedral at six o'clock this evening."

"You're mad," said Lora. "He will tell Kudriatov."

"He knows that, Miss Trusova."

153

"But he doesn't understand. Kudriatov will kill him. I don't know why he didn't kill him after Berlin."

"He won't kill him in a cathedral, Miss Trusova," Standish drawled. "That is, not quite."

"You shut up," Craig snapped. It irked him that his old boss seemed to foresee every step of the complicated scheme he had evolved, as though he were masterminding it. Moreover, he did not relish meeting Kudriatov and taking another hammering; he merely felt it essential.

He bound Standish's feet and thrust him into a chair. Despite the protests, he tied his hands, then wrapped several lengths of blind cord around him and the chair back. That way, Lora could easily and safely free him. He outlined his plan. If he could lure Kudriatov to the villa, Lora would release Standish the moment she heard them arrive. But she must keep the KGB man and Standish covered. If either made a false move, she was to shoot.

"Do you think it will work?" Lora asked. To his chagrin, Craig noticed that she looked to Standish for the answer.

"It's a long shot, my dear, but maybe one or two of us will survive," he intoned.

"You know that if we don't, the CIA will have the full copyright of those blue films on Cassius," Craig said. "So you'd better put on your best act, whatever that is."

He gave himself a couple of hours to walk to the rendezvous and call on the American Embassy. As he turned into the courtyard, he spotted Middleton's fullback figure running out to greet him. Rapidly, he gave the CIA man a censored version of his escape and Lora's flight as they went inside. He left the two Cassius films in the safe, but handed Middleton the other cylinder. "Remember the package you took out for me in sixty-eight? It's yours, if you want it."

Middleton looked at the copies Craig had made of the Strutchkov data. "This is fissionable material." He whistled. "They'd give you both a Park Avenue flat and a life pension for this. But I don't know that I can accept it."

"You mean you couldn't be sure of getting us out." Middleton nodded, but Craig shrugged his shoulders. "We don't want asylum.

154

At the most, a couple of days' lodgings in the embassy and one other favor.''

"What's that?''

"Ask your people in London to background a certain Patrick Holder for me.'' Craig furnished him the details he had. They would have to use the diplomatic bag, he suggested. Finally, he handed Middleton the phone number of the villa and asked him to ring in a couple of hours. "If I don't reply you can hang on to the other two files in your safe.'' he said.

13 He climbed the steps to Hradčany Hill, turning there to gaze at the city. Some inspired action painter might have thrown the sky together in stark white and lowering grays, in blues and sun-flushed orange and pink. Oblique shafts of sunlight transfixed Prague's spires and domes, its terra-cotta roofs and bridges, like the etchings in an old book. Craig hesitated. The castle behind him looked more and more like the Kremlin; the two giants locked in mortal combat at its gates appeared symbolic, ominous. He could still take Lora's advice. Backtrack and run for the frontier, then consider Middleton's offer. Instead, he drew a deep breath and stepped through the two narrow arches leading to St. Vitus's Cathedral.

The last of that day's tourists were leaving, walking through puddles of prismatic light from the stained-glass windows. The place smelled musty, and spiders were busy on the Gothic arches. Czech democratic centralism did not have much room in its five-year plans for St. Vitus's. He followed the sign to the Wenceslas Chapel, halfway down on the right. It lay empty. The Good King stood on a dusty ledge, sword and scepter in his hands; semiprecious stones threw back the half-light from the walls. Craig heard the echoing voices recede, then another sound: the clicking of the heavy door behind him. He whirled around.

Before him stood Kudriatov with something between a sneer and a scowl on his face. "So they gave you another week,'' he said softly.

"But,'' Craig stuttered, "I arranged to meet someone else here.''

"Semeonov, you mean. He is most sorry he could not keep the appointment. He pleaded with me to replace him."

"I have no authority to deal with you," Craig exclaimed, putting more conviction into his voice.

"Then I shall have to use my charm to persuade you." Before Craig could ride the blow, a hairy fist banged into his face, sending him spinning against the guardrail surrounding the ikons and the statue of Wenceslas. As the Russian pounced, Craig seized an ankle and twisted viciously. Kudriatov howled as he somersaulted over Craig's head and smashed into a wall. (Before capitulating, he would inflict some pain.) Craig rose slowly, giving Kudriatov time to advance. He parried the fists thudding at his face and body, then suddenly chopped back to catch Kudriatov on the neck, on the jugular. The KGB man gasped, then shook his head as though he had water in his ears. (A pity! He could have taken this man out had it been in the script.) Kudriatov was now pounding at him; he took the sting out of the punches by bending and riding with them. He pushed his chin at one that looked good and sank slowly to the floor, pleading with the Russian to stop. Puffing hard, Kudriatov grasped him by the hair and yanked him to his feet.

"Who sent you?"

"You know who."

"Your friend Standish, eh!" He grabbed Craig by the lapels and shook him. "What did he want with Semeonov?"

"Go and ask him yourself."

"I'm asking you." Craig's mouth filled with blood as a fist battened on his cheekbone. He tore free and seized an ikon to use as a weapon. Kudriatov sprang at him and felled him with a blow on the side of the head.

He lay there feigning unconsciousness as the Russian ransacked his pockets; he heard him cursing as he looked through the envelope containing his own documents and at the Strutchkov photographs. Kudriatov was murmuring to himself, "Does that English idiot think he'll frighten me with all this rubbish?" He pulled Craig to his feet and slapped his face until he opened his eyes. "This is what I think of your master's stupid little bourgeois plot," he snarled. He ripped the files into shreds, which he tossed into Craig's face.

"He has the originals."

"And what does he think, that he can destroy me by selling this trash to my good friend Semeonov? What else has he got?"

"I don't know."

Kudriatov drove his fist into Craig's stomach, doubling him up. "You know and you will talk."

"He has the Cassius files," Craig gasped.

That had struck home; he noticed Kudriatov flinch, his face flush. "So he found her," he got out. He grabbed Craig by the chin and banged his head against the wall. "Where is Lora Ekaterina?" he asked very quietly.

"How should I know?"

Kudriatov now had him by the throat, his thick fingers bunching around his neck, thumbs on the windpipe; he squeezed slowly until Craig felt the blood racketing in his head and ears, his face and eyes swelling, his legs ceding beneath him.

"Where is Lora Ekaterina?" He relaxed the pressure to allow Craig to speak.

"She's with him . . . Standish. . . . He planned to buy Semeonov's co-operation . . . then he'll take her out to London. . . ."

"When?"

"Tonight . . . by car."

Kudriatov cracked him across the face. "Nobody is taking her anywhere," he whispered hoarsely, as though to himself. "Where are they?" He increased the pressure again until Craig's head felt as if somebody were pumping it full of air. He signaled weakly with a hand. Kudriatov removed his thumbs.

"A house in Letna. . . . I don't know the street."

"But you can find it?" Craig nodded. "Pick up those papers," the Russian ordered. As Craig stooped to retrieve the shredded documents, Kudriatov said sneeringly, "What did she ever see in a pimp like you?"

The truth suddenly hit Craig. Kudriatov was not chasing his KGB files; he was chasing Lora. Of course, he should have picked up the hints that Standish and Lora had dropped about this meeting. He should have tumbled to it years ago when the Russian betrayed him to let him rot in prison, when he chucked him over the Berlin Wall to finish his term.

Kudriatov, this pig-iron monument to KGB and party conditioning, this desiccated set of Marxist-Leninist principles—Kudriatov was in love with Lora! He would never again shave death that close.

"On your feet and walk straight out without turning," the Russian ordered. He wheeled him left out of the chapel and left again through the southern entrance to where a black Skoda stood. "Just sit there and don't move, for if I have to kill you now, I will." He drove fast through the light evening traffic until they entered the driveway of the villa. A few hundred yards up, he stopped. "We leave the car here and walk," he said.

With a gun prodding him, Craig staggered painfully toward the villa, praying that Lora would spot them. But something had gone wrong; the front door was ajar and the garage door swung on its hinges. Kudriatov halted him twenty yards from the house. He bellowed, "Standish—come out and bring Miss Trusova with you or I shoot your boy." Nothing moved. He pushed Craig forward, up to the open door. "If you are playing tricks . . ." he growled. "They were here when I left," Craig answered.

The house was empty; they searched the attic, the bedrooms, the bathroom, the kitchen and every cupboard.

"I give you two minutes to find Lora Ekaterina," Kudriatov said.

Craig felt his legs go weak. He stared at the pistol a few feet from his chest and his thoughts gyrated. Somehow, Standish had overpowered Lora. What had happened to her? Were they really on the way out of the country?

"You have one minute," said Kudriatov.

"You might as well shoot now," he said. "Standish has taken her away." His mind had gone numb, conscious only of the seconds he had left and the hairy finger tensing on the trigger.

"Sergei Antonovich!" Lora's voice rang out from the hall. Instinctively, Kudriatov spun around, and, at that moment, Craig leapt, chopping at the hand holding the pistol, then scrambling after the weapon.

"Good boy, Matt." Standish made it sound as though he had just done something splendid in the Eton Wall Game. He had slipped through the hall and stood, negligently, pointing a revolver at Kudriatov.

"It seems these days that you two can never meet without a physical quarrel," he murmured.

"Where is Lora Ekaterina?" Kudriatov roared.

Standish ignored him. "Matt, off you go and clean yourself up while I show our Russian friend our snap album."

14 Craig ran to the cellar from which Standish had made his entrance. It was empty. And the blue Skoda still sat in the garage. How then had he spirited her away? He returned to the living room in time to see Kudriatov throw the Cassius pictures angrily on the table while Standish smirked at him.

"Where's Lora?" he demanded.

"She's quite safe, my boy. She merely decided that she had no desire to meet her old boss." He turned to Kudriatov. "You know, some people just don't like our kind."

"You took her by force," said Kudriatov.

"I'll come to that in a minute." His bantering tone changed. "Go through his pockets, Matt. And don't miss anything."

Craig searched the Russian meticulously, placing everything on the table: the personal and KGB passes, a small pistol hidden in an inside pocket, which Standish pocketed along with a crude papirosa cigarette case, his money and the papers he had torn up in the cathedral. When he had finished, Standish motioned them both to sit down; he gestured toward the scraps of paper. "Is that all he thought of your proposition?" he said.

"You mean your blackmailing plot," Kudriatov interjected.

Standish shook his head. "No, not mine. I wish I had thought it up. Quite brilliant. But it was Craig, here. One of my best men he was, as you know."

"Those papers are false." Kudriatov sneered. "He used the money I paid him like every traitor I have ever known."

"You and I have been too long in the game, Kudriatov. We've grown cynical about human nature. We don't recognize honesty when we see it. . . ."

"You mean treachery."

"Don't interrupt, there's a good chap. We both used Matt and Miss Trusova for our own dubious purposes. They owed us nothing, and still don't. From our viewpoint, it's a pity they turned out to be two honest people who fell in love with each other. And, as you know, honesty and love are the things that cynical characters in our racket fear most—because there's nothing we can do about them.''

Craig listened, astonished. He did not know *this* Standish who was defending so eloquently the power of good over evil, of love over corruption. No one could carry the art of lying that far! He could have sworn that, for the first time, the urbane mask had dropped and something of the real Standish was showing through.

Standish had picked up the frayed scraps of the file. "Craig banked that money week by week—but in the name of Sergei Antonovich Kudriatov. An honest thing to do, since it was your money. A practical thing to do, because if your KGB chiefs checked the numbered account there would be no doubt that the papers were genuine."

"Genuine! When he forged my signature and made false statements?"

"If the end is good, so are the means. We're both on the hook, Kudriatov."

"You and your bright boy are on the hook, not me."

"Let's say we kill Craig. Somebody in Berlin will post the original of this file to Moscow, to Kyril Levovich Gregoriev, a good friend but jealous of your job. The KGB will have to investigate the allegation that one of its eminent officials has a lot of money in a numbered account in a Zurich bank. In the Marxist code you'd be found guilty of the most despicable crime—abusing state funds. The KGB would throw its whole rule book at you for malfeasance, for exploiting an agent, then breaking faith with him. They tell me that Lubyanka is built on the bodies of KGB men who've done far less."

"They would accept my word."

"Every spy knows what the word of a spy is worth."

"I will run that risk," said Kudriatov, though now his voice had lost its snap.

"But there are the files. You can't go back without those, can you?" Standish hefted the Cassius photographs in his hand. "These copies will do me—and I'm certain that Matt will surrender the originals to you."

"I am also taking Miss Trusova back with me."

"Yes, I forgot. You need her, don't you?" Kudriatov glowered as Standish shuffled the pictures and grinned. "Didn't you ask your-

160

self, Matt, how your girl friend managed to cross all those frontiers without the *istrebeteli* or some keen KGB man laying a hand on her? I began to wonder about that before the answer hit me. Know what I think?''

Craig reflected for a moment: Kudriatov had used Germans in East Berlin and Czechs at Maček's farm; the identikit picture of Lora had appeared in an inside page of *Rude Pravo* under a different name. And they had burned the farm!

"Kudriatov did not report her as missing," he replied.

"Nor the files. What did you say, Sergei Antonovich? That she was on special leave or a special assignment?"

"She's sick," Kudriatov muttered. "She needs treatment and somebody to look after her."

"You, of course. You're in love with her, aren't you? Or maybe you just confuse love with that special relationship that the spy master has with his agent."

"She is ill in her mind," Kudriatov said. "Give me half an hour to talk to her and she will see reason." He was pleading now.

"She has already said all she wants to say to you," Standish drawled. He walked to the door and returned with the tape recorder, which he placed on the table. "You'd better listen to the whole message," he said, running back the tape and setting it. He switched it forward.

"Sergei Antonovich," Lora's voice said. "I am recording this statement without any compulsion from anyone. When my father died and you could no longer threaten him or me, I fled from Russia because for several years—from August the twenty-first, 1968, to be precise—I ceased to have loyalty to its principles and I wished to be free to live my own life with someone I love. I have no intention of defecting or betraying more of your precious secrets than I need to ensure my freedom. I have, equally, no intention of returning with you or anyone else to the Soviet Union. You can kill me if you wish. But if you or anyone else tries to take me back by force, I will kill myself."

Kudriatov listened in silence, his jaw and his hands working. Finally he said, "You held a gun to her head."

Standish switched off the machine. "How could I? It's in Russian and my languages are Greek, Latin and a little German. She

161

could have fooled me and said anything, but I knew what she wanted to say and do. If I were you, Kudriatov, I'd cut my losses, take the microfilm and catch the first Aeroflot back to the Kremlin.''

"I will not be blackmailed," Kudriatov shouted.

Standish held the Cassius pictures aloft. ''You don't like being caught in your own net, I know. But you've spent long enough blackmailing poor devils like this man to realize that blackmail exists only in the mind of the victim. We're only asking you to be reasonable.''

Kudriatov fell pensive for a moment. ''You say this traitor will hand over the files?'' Standish nodded. ''And if I choose to release them and reveal everything?''

''What! Tell the whole world how the dirty division of the KGB operates!'' Standish shrugged his broad shoulders. ''As I told you at the beginning, the only man who can make use of these is our honest friend, Craig. He can land us both in it up to the neck. We have to listen to him, Kudriatov.''

''What does he want?'' They both turned to Craig, who had been enthralled by the verbal fencing and the way that Standish had handled the situation.

''What do I want? Two death certificates, two obituary notices, two new passports and a safe passage across the Austrian frontier.''

Now, they stared at him. ''I think we need some enlightenment, Matt.''

''Well, you both know spies don't resign. They die or they're found dead. You know I'm officially a criminal on the run. So I need my own death certificate and Miss Trusova's, one obituary notice published in *Pravda* or *Izvestia* and the full story of my own death carried by a reputable agency.''

''So that as far as the KGB and Her Majesty's government are concerned, the cases of Miss Trusova and Matthew Craig are closed,'' said Standish. Craig nodded.

''And this man in Berlin who has the original of your piece of blackmail?'' Kudriatov asked.

''He'll be warned to ignore the news of my death—this time.'' Craig saw from the fraction of a second that Kudriatov's gaze crossed his own that the Russian was weighing the implications of such a maneuver; he could almost follow the chess moves he was making to checkmate him and Lora. ''But we don't move from here,

162

or hand over the Cassius film until we've read the obits in the Russian papers and the press accounts in Britain," he said.

Kudriatov picked up his cigarette package, took a papirosa, crimped the cardboard holder and lit it. He studied Standish for a moment through the smoke, then muttered, "There must be an easier way than this." In his turn, Standish fixed his fishy blue eyes on Craig. "What the comrade means, Matt, is why don't he and I just shoot you, bury you in the garden, where you have a wonderful view of Prague, and forget to mention it to anybody at all. Is that it, Sergei Antonovich?" Kudriatov's silence said nothing, yet everything; his eyes flicked toward Standish's revolver.

"What do you say to that idea, Matt?"

Craig glanced at Standish's watch. Five to eight. "In five minutes, the man who has those files will ring. That's your answer."

At eight o'clock, the phone rang. Craig handed the earpiece attachment to Kudriatov. They heard Middleton's voice. "Matt—you okay?"

"Fine," Craig said. "If I'm not with you in half an hour you can hang on to that material in your safe." He hung up.

Standish beamed at him. "I really must take my hat off to you, Matt. You've thought of everything. He's a credit to both of us, Kudriatov, don't you think?" The Russian scowled.

"Well, Kudriatov, what have you decided?" Craig asked.

"I shall write and send an official report tonight and talk to the *Pravda* correspondent in Prague."

"And you, Standish?"

The SIS chief reflected for a moment. "You died in that fire this morning. I'll issue a statement through the embassy early tomorrow. We can alter Stafford's passport, driving license and other papers for you and fabricate a birth certificate. What about Comrade Trusova? Will you do them, Sergei Antonovich?"

Kudriatov sat with his head hunched forward. He did not answer.

"The same papers," Craig put in. "Under the name of Laura Catherine Truman."

Standish nodded. Keeping an eye on Kudriatov, he beckoned Craig to one side. "Your charming fiancée is in our embassy with Ross, who's really not a bad chap. He came to find out what had happened to me and the girl didn't have a chance to shoot, thank God.

163

Anyway, it was too risky for her to play a part in this little drama, don't you think?'' He placed a hand on Craig's shoulder. ''You can both put up at the embassy for a day or two until we equip you and get you out.''

''Where to—the Scrubs?'' Craig said dryly. ''You can deliver our death notices and new identities to the embassy just around the corner—the American.''

As he left, he threw a final glance over his shoulder at the two improbable collaborators—or plotters. He knew that during all the time the Russian and British secret services had functioned, no one could recall a single instance of co-operation between them. He was aware that, even in the blackest days of the war, they had viewed each other with the deepest distrust, spurning all offers of mutual aid. No one would ever discover that he had broken that record by forcing two sworn enemies to work together for their own ends. And his salvation. Yet Craig had no faith in either man. Given the chance, they would destroy each other. Him too, if he faltered. At the moment, he held the cards. For how long? As he drove the blue Skoda toward the Vltava and the American Embassy, he wondered.

15 He thought it prudent to let Middleton fetch Lora in an embassy car. She wept with relief on seeing him, then looked at his battered face and raged about Kudriatov. She listened to his explanation of what had happened at the villa, shaking her head. ''I know Kudriatov too well, and he would never have agreed to such an arrangement unless he were sure of one thing—that we will never get out of here alive.''

''How long did Cardinal Mindszenty stick it out in your Budapest embassy?'' Craig asked Middleton. ''Sixteen years?'' The CIA man did not share the joke.

Lora brought one snippet of information that fitted his theory about Standish's blackmailing motives. Ross was packing his things and catching the London plane that evening. Now that Vernon Alveston had his dirty pictures he had no further use for the Special Branch

164

man. Poor Holder! He would soon realize that he had two albatrosses around his neck—the KGB and Standish. That was his worry. The embassy had still received no background on Holder from London. Middleton reckoned that it might take another day or more.

He showed Craig the guest flat and introduced him to the man who would look after them, Bill Knox, a former Marine sergeant and now head of the security corps. "You know, that girl of yours is right," Middleton said. "When those obituary notices appear and you're officially listed as dead, the KGB can erase both of you without anyone stirring a finger."

"They'll try," Craig admitted. "But they can only kill us this side of the Iron Curtain where they can cover it up. On the other side, there'd be an inquiry and they can't take a chance on the news leaking out. Both Kudriatov and Standish know that I'm just as dangerous for them physically dead as I am living."

"How do you get out? Have you figured that one?"

Craig shrugged. He did not even know where he would attempt the crossing, let alone how. He did not dispute that those hundred-odd miles would be their most hazardous.

"I can get a couple of people and come along as an escort."

"That wouldn't stop them, Dick. I'll think of a way."

He still ached in every limb and his head throbbed too much to think about anything. He felt better when Lora came in with water to bathe his face. He teased her. "You didn't tell me you had a lover," he said.

"A lover! You mean that bear. How could I let somebody like that touch me?"

"Even Standish guessed that he didn't give a damn about these—" He pointed to the two Cassius films. "He wanted you."

"Can you imagine me . . . ?"

"As Madame Kudriatov Mark II handing around caviar slices in the Kremlin? Yes, I think you'd do it brilliantly. After all, what can I promise you?"

She kissed his battered face. "I would like to tell you," she whispered, "but you need to rest now." She went to turn down both beds, but he stopped her.

"We only need one."

"Tomorrow," she said.

"Tomorrow," he repeated. "Tomorrow we won't exist and I want us to remember our last night as Comrade Trusova and 23201 Craig late of Wormwood Scrubs."

The pain had left him and the troubled expression no longer haunted Lora's eyes. For four years they had despaired, hardly daring to dream of moments like this. How many dubious ideals had they betrayed? How many barriers had they crashed, how many still lay ahead of them? "Does it matter, Matt, what happens to us?" Lora sobbed. No, it did not matter. Only their love mattered, and that dissolved their doubts and fears and every other emotion, except itself.

Knox, the Marine sergeant, woke them late with a breakfast of fruit juice, ham and eggs, toast and coffee. Half an hour later, as he carried out the tray, he thumbed toward the street outside. "We haven't been as popular since the fall of sixty-eight."

They looked out. Two men were plodding up and down Trziste Street with such disinterest as to make their role obvious. "I'd feel lost without them," Craig said. "What would you say they are— Czechs or Russians?"

"How can anyone tell?"

"Sherlock Holmes would look first at their shoes. Bata? No. The Komsomol Footwear plant in Volgograd, he'd say. Square toes and too many eyeholes. And the wide lapels and flapping pants. Special issue to lieutenants and under. The Czechs are too snappy in their dress to be seen dead in ties and hats like those. Sherlock would say that your erstwhile chief has enlisted some of Semeonov's men to keep an eye on us."

"So we're prisoners here," Lora said.

"Only you. They can't touch me until I'm officially dead. I'll prove it to you. How much money have you got?"

She counted out nearly a thousand crowns. Craig pocketed them and sauntered out the gate; the two men fell into step behind him. He crossed Charles Bridge and walked down Národni Street. He made several purchases while they paraded up and down outside shops. However, they made no attempt to approach him as he made his way back to the embassy. He unloaded his haul in front of Lora: two bottles of champagne to celebrate their departure, two tins of beluga caviar to prevent her growing homesick on the trip and a bottle of French perfume.

To take Lora's mind off the KGB patrol, he sat her down in front of several maps he had borrowed and asked her to look for a point where they might cross the Austro-Czech frontier on foot west of the main Budějovice-Linz road. He had ruled out planes and trains and plumped for a dash by car. He checked the Skoda, filling its tanks and putting five extra gallons in the trunk.

"But they'll follow us or ambush us," Lora protested.

"We'll save them the bother by taking them with us," Craig answered. "We still have these." He pointed to the metal capsules containing the Cassius dossier.

He still did not know who Cassius was. He wondered if it really mattered. Middleton regretted, but his London contact was having difficulty digging out information about Holder.

What worried him more was the fact that the BBC World Service broadcasts had made no mention of him. All that day he tuned in to the short-wave bulletins. He was beginning to wonder if Standish had double-crossed him again when suddenly he heard his name on the nine o'clock broadcast. It gave him an eerie, spine-tingling feeling to listen to the report of his own death; he noticed that Lora, too, looked pensive. "Turn it a bit lower, Matt," she said, as the announcer went over that day's headlines and came back to him:

Matthew Craig, the former Foreign Office official who was serving a twenty-year sentence for spying on behalf of the Soviet Union, has been found dead in a burned-out farmhouse several miles north of Prague.

Craig's charred body was identified this morning by British Embassy officials in Prague and by experts who carried out fingerprint tests.

The thirty-eight-year-old double agent, who betrayed many of Britain's vital defense secrets and dozens of Western agents in the sixties, escaped twelve days ago from Wormwood Scrubs prison in London.

Police followed his trail to West Berlin, where he is thought to have crossed the Berlin Wall into the Soviet sector. From there he traveled through East Germany to Czechoslovakia.

Embassy officials in Prague do not know why Craig made for Czechoslovakia, but point out that he had many Eastern-bloc contacts with whom he worked during the Dubček crisis in 1968.

A correspondent in a dispatch to the BBC says that Craig appears to have died accidentally when fire gutted a deserted farm building near Mělník, some twenty miles north of Prague.

The correspondent suggests that, like other Soviet agents who have escaped, Craig might have been hidden in one of the satellite countries until Moscow considered that the right diplomatic moment had come to reveal him and to grant him citizenship.

During his trial, much of which took place behind closed doors, Craig admitted to having spied for the Soviet Union. But, during his four years at Wormwood Scrubs, the Russians never acknowledged him as one of their agents, nor did they make any attempt to exchange him for any Western agent. There is no evidence to link Moscow with his escape.

"Lora, *dushka*, I'm dead." He seized and hugged her. "Think of it," he cried. "No more running, no more hiding." He broke open one of the bottles of champagne and filled two glasses. He clinked his with Lora's. "Here's to Matt Craig, the double agent who never was, and to Frank Stafford, the man who has just risen from the ashes." Lora drank, but she did not appear to share his elation.

"What's the matter?" he said. "It's something to celebrate."

"I was just thinking of a Russian saying that I've never understood until now. 'The dead have no need of us, but we shall need them forever.' "

"This isn't the night for Kirghiz old wives' tales."

"I have to get used to the idea, Matt. When I listened to that man, I almost believed you were dead."

"That's only because it was the BBC and not Tass." He grinned. "When we're over the frontier tomorrow, I'll remind you how morbid you were. Hasn't Standish carried out his part of the bargain?"

"Yes, but Standish is . . ."

"I know, a British gentleman."

"You don't understand Kudriatov."

"I don't understand either of them. But at least with Kudriatov I know roughly where I am. His psychology is based on the Pavlovian dog, while Standish draws his inspiration and insight from fish, a more obscure experimental species.''

"Then tell me, why are they working together?"

"Because I forced them to."

"Maybe you're right," she said dubiously.

"We'll get the proof tomorrow when we read *Pravda*," he said.

Of course, Lora had asked the vital question—the one that worried him. Had he found out who Holder-Cassius really was he might have had the answer. No word had arrived from London when they went to bed. He waited until Lora was sleeping, then fished out the negatives he had kept of the Cassius file. He played with the puzzle for an hour, until the effete face and those spaniel eyes waltzed around and around in his mind like a roulette ball that refused to drop into any slot. He lay down beside Lora and concentrated his brain on the face and the name Holder, thinking that his subconscious mind might resolve the problem while he slept. All he had was a bad dream.

16 It was the middle of the afternoon before Standish phoned. The British papers had arrived and he had a copy of *Pravda*. Should he pop around the corner with them? Ten minutes later Craig and Lora heard a row outside their door; several choice Marine epithets were colliding with the familiar Oxford drawl. Knox and the Marines had obviously triumphed, for they caught Standish's pained tones. "All right, search me, you idiot, if you really believe that a diplomat from a friendly nation would march into the American Embassy bearing side arms."

Standish entered, beaming. "Morning, Mr. Stafford . . . Miss Truman," he said. Breaking the clasp of his leather briefcase, he spilled a bundle of newspapers onto the table. "Splendid show, old fellow," he boomed at Craig. "The British press has done you proud. Not many of our breed get such a send-off." Craig looked at the papers. The headlines hardly surprised him; none the less, they gave him a prickly feeling, as though someone was walking over his grave. TRAITOR CRAIG FOUND DEAD. DOUBLE AGENT CRAIG DIES BEHIND CURTAIN. That was the usual pattern, and the stories echoed the agency messages and the BBC bulletin. A few, however, suggested that he had died at the hands of the Russians because he revealed too much about their operations during the closed-session part of his trial.

Standish was flicking through *Pravda* like a cashier counting bank notes. "Not anything like the same play, I'm sorry to say, Miss . . . Truman," he said, handing her the paper. They had tucked away the obituary notice near the back of *Pravda:* Comrade Lora Ekaterina Trusova, daughter of General Ivan Vasiliovich Trusov, hero of the Second Patriotic War, had died in a boating accident on Lipno Lake while on holiday in the Czechoslovak Socialist Republic. Comrade Trusova had been a loyal and dedicated Komsomol, later a trusted member of the party; she was a gifted linguist whose talents would be missed by her colleagues in the Ministry of Internal Affairs. "So that is what they would have said about me," Lora muttered.

Standish had produced two passports and several documents from his folder. Craig could see that he had done them impeccably. Their tourist visas showed they had entered the country two weeks before at Prague. Standish had even filled in their financial declaration and handed Craig several hundred crowns and £100 in English money. He seemed carefree about the money, which Craig presumed was coming out of his own pocket. But then, he had the Holder pictures, a good bargain.

"You see, Matt, old chum, we've kept faith. There are only a couple of minor points to settle. The first's a bit gruesome. Your . . . er . . . ashes? Where would you like them buried?"

"Do they have a Garden of Remembrance at the Scrubs?" Craig asked, with heavy irony.

"Leave that to me." Standish was eyeing the two Cassius cylinders, which lay on the bedside table. "Only those little trinkets now," he said, moving over to pick them up.

"Leave those alone," Craig snapped.

"But you promised our friend Kudriatov that he could have them," Standish protested.

"In return for the death notices, the documents—and safe passage. He'll have them the moment we cross the frontier."

"Ahhh," exclaimed Standish. "He won't care for that." He

170

paused. "But I see your point. You can't part with your life insurance that easily. Which frontier does he meet you at and when?"

"You'll both know when we get there."

"Both . . ." Standish stuttered. "But you're not seriously thinking of taking the two of us with you?"

"Why not? It's the only way for Kudriatov to recover his files and for me to keep an eye on you."

"Please, Matt, keep me out of this."

"And Kudriatov, too," Lora interjected. "How can you trust that man in the same car when he has already tried to kill you twice?"

"It's because I don't trust either of them that I'm taking Standish's tip and collecting hostages. But just until we get another stamp on these new passports."

"But I've booked my London flight," Standish complained, his face showing concern. "Look, take along the security man from our embassy as a hostage if Kudriatov scares you."

Craig shook his head. "It's got to be you, Standish, old chum. And in case you meant to try anything on the road, I've arranged to call Middleton from Austria. If he doesn't hear from me within twelve hours of leaving here he wires the release of all the Berlin material."

"You're a hard man, Matt."

"Not as hard as your friend Holder will find you."

A wintry smile played over Standish's flaccid cheeks. "All right, have it your way. What's the order of march?"

"We leave from here by car at nine o'clock precisely. Tell Kudriatov that if he does not come alone, or if any of his gorillas out there attempt to follow us, he'll never see his Cassius files. I'll hand over everything to the CIA and squat in this embassy until they get us out."

"You wouldn't do that, Matt—not after all we've been through together." Standish was pleading now, and, for the first time, Craig noticed the heavy flesh wilt on his face; he appeared more apprehensive about the Americans than about Kudriatov. "I'll see that he's here—alone," he muttered. But he had recovered his old poise and was chatting amiably as Craig walked downstairs to the front door with him.

171

The moment they had gone, Lora picked up the British newspapers and *Pravda* to read the accounts of their deaths again. Her intuition whispered that the whole operation was going too smoothly. Kudriatov, she knew, would never have agreed to insert that obituary notice unless he meant to do one thing: kill her. He would therefore have to kill Matt as well. Maybe Matt was right. Take them along as hostages. But he was too trusting.

The phone rang, cutting across her reflections. It was Middleton. "Is Matt there?" he queried.

"No, he's gone to the front door."

"Okay, I'll find him. We're just starting to decode the Holder material."

Lora replaced the receiver. Holder? That was where it had all begun. Or a few months before, at the spy-training school in Kuchino with Kudriatov, the chief instructor. She could see him, during those grisly lectures, passing round the glass phials, the capsules, the ampoules, which the members of the class handled like nitroglycerin. How would an old spy instructor kill someone who was holding a gun in his back in a closed car? Maybe that way. Matt would laugh at her if she suggested it, but she had thought seriously that Kudriatov would have murdered her had he caught up with her. And like this. Without leaving any trace.

Her gaze fell on the remaining bottle of champagne. They would have a farewell drink, Matt said. She rummaged in her handbag and produced the kit they had issued at the Kuchino school. She checked its plastic bottle of blue-and-white capsules and the dozen ampoules. They had survived the journey. But did they have an expiry date? They would have to take that risk.

Outside, feet racketed on the stairs. Lora only had time to stuff the drugs back into her handbag before Craig burst into the room waving a piece of paper, his eyes wild.

"Cassius is dead!" he shouted.

"Dead! But he cannot be dead."

"Have a look at this." He tossed her the message that Middleton had just decoded. She read:

Lord Drude, Third Baron, formerly the Hon. Robert Patrick Holder. Born 1917, educated Eton, Cambridge and the Sorbonne.

MP for Southwood 1955 to 1959, for Liverpool (Docks) 1959 to 1963. Inherited title 1963 and took his seat in House of Lords. Member of Defense Estimates and Science and Technology committees of House of Commons. Chairman of House of Lords disarmament committee. Appointed one of Her Majesty's Privy Councillors 1964. Died in September, 1968.

Note: Drude was an obscure, backstairs figure. Hansard parliamentary reports show that his favorite themes were improvement of East-West relations, mutual disarmament, better trade and cultural exchanges between the Soviet and Western blocs. He spoke out against provocative espionage during the U2 crisis (1960) but took a temporizing line in the Cuban missile crisis (1962). Some mystery surrounds his death. An inquest at Cheltenham brought in a verdict of death by misadventure when he was found to have taken an overdose of barbiturates. Several press reports suggested at the time that the overdose was not accidental.

"Lora, you're positive that Holder was Cassius?"

"Kudriatov said so and he would never make such an error."

Craig picked up the microfilm. "And these were in the 'live' section of the KGB Index?"

"Of course. Otherwise I would not have taken them."

"Then why the fuss? Why are Kudriatov and Standish so frantic to get hold of a dead man's dossier?"

"The KGB needs it because they fear the world will discover how vile they are to have blackmailed someone and driven him to commit suicide."

"But Standish?" Craig insisted. "I was convinced that he wanted these files either to get Holder, or Drude, out of the KGB net, or alternatively to blackmail him into pulling strings for him."

"He probably wants them for the same reason as Kudriatov," Lora suggested.

"Hmm. So that the British government can keep the fact secret that a prominent MP and member of the House of Lords had given everything to the Russians for nearly ten years, including some of their master spies."

She nodded agreement. However, something still niggled at Craig's mind.

"But why keep those files on your 'live' Index as though the KGB were using them?"

To that question, neither had a reasonable answer. What had Standish told him in the waiting room at the Scrubs? Cassius was a matter of state security of the highest importance. All right, he had to conclude that Vernon Alveston was acting officially with Special Branch help. Didn't that spawn another puzzle? Why travel this far to watch Kudriatov snatch those files from under his nose?

Again, he sat down to study the negatives of Holder. Somewhere in those lay the answer. He had died in September, some weeks after his own arrest and probably before the trial. Did that connect? He did not see how. Nor did Cheltenham signify anything. Only that effete, epicene face troubled him like some fragment of a half-remembered melody.

From the bathroom, he heard the hiccup of a champagne cork. Lora emerged with two brimming glasses of champagne. She had procured biscuits and layered them with butter and caviar. "We eat the caviar first and then drink the champagne straight down," she ordered.

"I'll have to get used to these Kirghiz customs." He grinned, but he complied.

"What do you say—down the hatch?" Lora asked, draining her glass at one gulp. As Craig swallowed his, he pulled a wry face and picked up the bottle.

"I must tell Moët or Chandon that this French stuff doesn't drink well in the Socialist East," he complained. "Let's have another taste."

She grabbed the bottle. "Not now," she said firmly. "In half an hour we leave. You can have one glass before we go."

He gave a glance at her watch. The time had gone quickly. Outside, shadows were beginning to invade the narrow canyon of Trziste Street; he could just discern the two silhouettes against the opposite wall. Still there, the murder squad. He began to gather his documents, his film and the two metal tubes containing the Cassius material. For his own peace of mind, he wished he had unteased the last part of their puzzle. Which of the two secret-service chiefs, Kudriatov or Standish, would finish up with these bits of smut? Whichever of them, Craig decided that it did not really matter to

174

him. He would heave them back over the frontier pole from Austria and let them squabble for them. Which would he bet to win? Standish, the highly buffed Saxon peasant? Or Kudriatov, the city-bred Slav who remained a muzhik at heart? He had to choose Standish.

17 At precisely nine o'clock a British Embassy car dropped Standish and Kudriatov at the gates of the embassy. From their window, Craig and Lora watched the Russian cross to have a word with the two KGB men, who shrugged, got into their car and drove off. Knox let them into the courtyard. They could hear Standish protesting again as the ex-Marine searched him, then covered both men with a pistol.

"Time to go, *dushka*," Craig said.

"You've forgotten something," she replied. Producing the champagne bottle, she filled the glasses once more and drank hers empty. Craig kissed her, then gulped his down, shuddering again at the curious tang it left on his palate. As they went downstairs Middleton joined them, coming as far as the main door. "If you ever need a job . . ." He grinned.

"Thanks, Dick, for everything. But this is our last run in your game." Craig wondered if his remark sounded as ominous to Lora.

Knox handed Craig his revolver. "The Russki had nothing on him, but the Englishman had this." He showed them a small automatic pistol. "It was only for my personal protection," Standish complained. As Knox brought the Skoda around, Craig searched both men once again. While he dealt with Kudriatov, Standish was lighting a cigarette. "You getting nervous, Matt?" he said as he spread his arms, still clutching his case and gold lighter.

Craig ignored the comment. "Which of you wants to drive?" he asked.

"Sergei Antonovich had better drive. I'm not much good at driving on the right," Standish said.

Kudriatov, who had remained strangely silent, got behind the wheel. Standish took the right-hand front seat and Lora and Craig climbed into the back.

175

"The first sign of trouble and I shoot both of you," Craig snapped.

"No need to fret, old chum. Our friend has warned off his mates. Nobody will bother us."

"You know the road to České Budějovice and Linz?"

"I know the road," Kudriatov said.

They turned right along Karmelitska Street and headed south, parallel with the Vltava. In the city streets, quiet at that hour, nothing followed them and, as far as Craig could tell, no one was tailing them when they joined the state road south to the frontier. If nothing happened, they would reach the Austrian border just before midnight.

It was Kudriatov who broke the silence, saying suddenly in Russian, "Why did you do this mad thing, Lora Ekaterina?"

"Did you not hear my message?" she answered.

"You were not free when you recorded that."

"I meant every word and I still do."

"Why then did you betray Russia?"

"I didn't betray it. You and your kind did."

"You can return with me," Kudriatov pleaded. "I will see that no harm comes to you." He jerked his thumb backward at Craig. "I will even forget about this . . . traitor."

"In your life you have only done one good thing for me—written my death notice," Lora cried. "I despise you."

Kudriatov half turned to make some new appeal, but Craig thrust the muzzle of his revolver at his face. "Now shut up, Kudriatov," he shouted.

"Don't shoot the driver, old man," Standish murmured.

They drove on in silence, the yellow headlights splintering against the birches and limes flanking the route. The moon was rising as they left the medieval city of Tábor behind and plunged into the forest beyond. Lora switched on the roof light to study the map. "Only another fifty miles, *dushka*," Craig whispered.

"They can't go too quickly for me," Standish said, turning to smile at them. "After this little game of *cache-cache*, I feel we're all due a holiday."

"I'll think of you, Standish, slaughtering salmon on the Spey with trusty old Jameson Garvie."

"Oh, I don't have to travel that far these days, Matt." His teeth glinted at Craig. "But, of course, you wouldn't have known, where you were, that I've been catching my own breed for the last three years." Standish chuckled. "Funny, only Marjory and . . ." he hesitated . . . "and one other friend believed we could do it."

"How is your wife?"

"Very well, Matt. She got over her bit of a breakdown several . . . several months ago." (What was happening? The Standish lying machine was short circuiting.)

"Give her my regards."

"I will, Matt. Pity you didn't meet her more often. She still talks about you. You must have made quite an impression that weekend you spent with us."

There it was—the lightning flash that forked across his whole mental landscape, illuminating even the darkest corners. Back and forth through Craig's mind the thoughts and images zithered. Tea, that genteel English ritual in the manor house overlooking the Severn. Vacillating, the other side of the Spode, that fine-boned, delicate face. That fluting, upper-crust accent to match. "Of course, Vernon, you'll manage to stock the river. And Bob is sure of it, too." The blue-veined hands with their crazed skin maneuvering the silver sugar tongs. "One lump or two, Mr. Craig?" They sipped gracefully. "I hope you'll come and see us again soon. These days, we meet so few people." They nibbled the cucumber sandwiches. "Next time, Vernon, you must run him over to see my brother. He has a farm just this side of Cheltenham, you know." Craig, you crack-headed idiot! She's the Hon. Marjory. And if you never heard her maiden name—Holder—you might have guessed from that etiolated, half-doped face you were carrying around in those metal phials! Robert Patrick Holder, alias Lord Drude, alias Cassius, alias Standish's brother-in-law.

"It's a pity the Right Hon. Bob didn't live long enough to see your smolts find their way back upriver to their spawning ground," he said without emphasis.

"Yes, Matt, a great pity," Standish murmured, equally casually.

"He knows, Standish. He knows everything." Kudriatov broke his silence to burble the remark as though he had just scored a vital point off his enemy.

"What can it matter now?" Standish replied. "What can anyone do about it?"

177

Craig was watching his old chief intently. He saw him fish in one of his pockets; he leaned forward to grab his arm and thrust the revolver into his back. "Keep still," he cried. Standish held up his cigarette case. "Do you mind?" he chortled. "I was merely looking for a light. You took my pistol, remember?" Calmly, he produced his gold lighter. In the spurt of flame, Craig noticed that the smile had left his face and his jaw had clenched.

"Not for the record books, of course, Matt, but as a matter of interest, how did you find out?"

"Don't you recall? You broke your own rule about keeping your private life private and introduced me to your little pals, *Salmo salar*."

Standish sighed. "So you've only just got there?" he said.

"Four years in a maximum-security cell doesn't exactly put a fine-honed edge on the mind," Craig replied. "But now I see the whole picture."

His attention was riveted on Standish, who had turned away to look at the road; his hard profile was lit by the glow from his cigarette, which was burning like a quick fuse. He wound down the window and threw the stub out. Within seconds, he had dipped into his pocket for his cigarette case and lighter and was smoking again.

"I had no choice, Matt. I had to shield him."

"Shield yourself, you mean. You always wanted only one thing, Standish—to be top dog in the SIS. If the scandal over Holder, or Drude, had broken it would have finished you, both in the service and with your precious court-and-county set. A secret-service boss with a traitor in the family, what!"

"It would have killed him, Matt."

"It did kill him when I went up for trial and you had to tell him you couldn't assure him that I would plead Not Guilty."

"He died long before that—killed by these men." He stabbed a thumb at Kudriatov.

"Ah, but by then Kudriatov was no longer interested in Cassius," Craig said. "When did you discover, Sergei Antonovich, that you had landed two big fish in your net? Don't tell me. Berlin, 1964, wasn't it?"

Kudriatov chuckled as though enjoying a huge joke. "You always said, Standish, that he was one of your best men."

"Just what you both needed," Craig went on. "It was an ingenious little ploy you both worked out. You'd use Lora to trap me so that I could act as your errand boy, carrying all those innocent secrets, those innocent names, between Mr. Standish and his spy master, tovarish Kudriatov."

Craig heard Lora gasp. "You mean Kudriatov was blackmailing this man as well?"

"That's why they kept the Cassius file in your current Index. That's why they had to put me away where I couldn't get any wild notions. Right, Standish?"

"Kudriatov forced my hand."

"He didn't have to twist hard. I wondered why C and the SIS found nothing in their records of the stuff I passed you from Kudriatov. You flushed it down the pan as soon as you got it, didn't you? And then bit the ears of your legal chums to have me sent down for twenty instead of five."

"Believe me, Matt, it was the worst day's work I ever had to do."

"I realize that, old bean. Thinking about me in the Scrubs must have upset your work on Speyside or the Severn with rod, line and gaff."

"I told Kudriatov to let you both make a run for it in Prague in sixty-eight. But no"—he swung around to the Russian—"you couldn't bear the thought of losing your pet pupil, could you, Sergei Antonovich?"

The car shimmied, its headlights glancing from the trees on both sides of the deserted road as Kudriatov looked around. "I did it for your own good, Lora Ekaterina," he said.

"And I hated you all the more for it," she snapped back.

"At least I gave you both a second chance," Standish put in.

"Oh, yes, I was forgetting," said Craig. "You gave me a leg up over the prison wall—but only to recover these and get yourself off the hook." He held up the two cassettes of microfilm. Standish half turned to look at them and Craig saw the flash of his teeth.

"No, Matt, you haven't got the whole story. . . . I wanted more than those," he murmured, almost inaudibly.

Craig watched him give another glance at the road. In five or ten minutes they would reach České; they were running along the Vltava valley, the moon tracking in the river below them. Standish rolled up the window against the night breeze. Fumbling in his pocket, he emerged with his cigarette case. Conditioned by twice witnessing the action, Craig gave the object only a glance.

Standish's next move alerted everybody.

Suddenly, he threw out a hand to jerk the ignition key from its socket. As the Skoda faltered, his hand rose with something glinting in it. At that moment, Craig heard Kudriatov bellow in Russian, "Standish, you dirty swine." He took one hand off the wheel, whipping it out to grab the SIS man by the wrist. Lora, too, had sprung to seize the object in Standish's hand. But now Kudriatov was wrestling desperately with Standish and the car was wobbling and swaying out of control. It lurched suddenly, heaving Lora against the door panel.

They had hit the edge, were slithering off the road and over the bank. Everything was happening too fast for Craig to react, to think of using his revolver or even of saving Lora and himself. The contorted shapes of Kudriatov and Standish shuttled from one side to another, banging against doors and windows, struggling and grunting. A voice bellowed desperately in Russian: "Get out, Lora Ekaterina. Get out. Save yourself." Lora was picking herself up, tugging at Craig and attempting to wrench open the door. Standish had finally torn his hand from Kudriatov's grip. Mesmerized, Craig watched the arm arc, almost in slow motion, toward the Russian. Two muffled detonations sounded, one a second after the other. Craig felt the pressure thud against his eardrums as though he were drowning in deep water. Suddenly, he was choking and gasping in the cloying yet acrid gas cloud that filled the car, enveloping them all.

They were rolling and pitching, but now his mind had throttled back on everything. His body seemed to float, suspended between the roof and floor of the car in a vortex of dinning sound and spinning movement. The crazy tilting of the car, the crunch of earth on the metal floor, the rattle of branches on the doors and roof—his mind filtered all these sensations as though he were watching a playback in slow motion of something happening light years away. As the Skoda teetered on its side a door swung open and Lora catapulted over his head. One last image registered: the bulky shadow of Standish planing over Kudriatov, now a tawdry bundle hanging over the steering wheel. Craig's consciousness had detached itself from the clamor

180

and the splintering images. The prism had darkened. "Lora," he cried. "Lora." But no echo came back. His own voice was suffocating him.

He surfaced slowly, spluttering and retching as though he had oil in his lungs. Someone was kneading his stomach and pressing a handkerchief against his nose and mouth. He caught the distant whisper. "Breathe in, Matt . . . *dushka* darling." He sucked air through the handkerchief and was racked with coughing. "Breathe, *dushka*, breathe," the faraway voice murmured. Gradually, pain began to break through his numb body; his chest and back were throbbing, his head felt twice its normal size and his eyes refused to focus. Though the pungent gas cut his respiration, he kept complying with the quiet voice until the pain ebbed and the blur before his eyes took shape. Lora was bending over him, holding his head and breathing into his mouth. She stopped to break an ampoule into her handkerchief and sniffed it herself before applying it to his face. Several times he made a great but vain effort to speak. Finally, he managed to utter the two syllables. "Lora," he said.

"Oh, Matt, darling." She turned her face away, burying it in her arm. He could hear her sobbing.

For half an hour she kept giving him artificial respiration until he was breathing regularly and the pain in his head had subsided.

"What happened?" he asked.

"I cannot believe it, but Standish tried to kill us all," she said. "He had a gas pistol—this." She held up the metal cigarette case he had seen in Standish's hand.

Yes, he could piece it all together slowly: the fight in the car. The blast of sweet-sour fumes. Bitter almonds. So that was a prussic-acid pistol. Something he should have twigged when he rifled Kudriatov's pockets in the villa and found the cigarette case. It had not escaped Standish. He had pocketed it. Clever Vernon Alveston! He had manipulated him, had manipulated them all like marionettes. He was chasing the Cassius files, yes. But also his blackmailer, Kudriatov. And Matt, old chum, would lead him to Lora, and she would lead him to Kudriatov. If he got all three with one whiff of cyanide gas he would clear every obstacle to the top job. Why hadn't it worked? Why hadn't he killed them all?

"Lora. How did we get away with it?"

181

"I thought Kudriatov would attempt to kill us with cyanide gas because it leaves no trace. They trained us to use it and issued safety kits. I brought mine along just in case."

"That foul champagne," he whispered.

Lora nodded. "I put crystals of sodium thiosulphate in it." She broke another ampoule and made him inhale. "The crystals are an antidote and this amyl nitrite will bring down your blood pressure."

"Where are the others?"

"Kudriatov is dead. I think he was dead before the car crashed. He could not have taken the antidote."

"But Standish must have taken it. Where's he?"

Before Lora could reply, he caught a weak voice calling his name. It came from behind the black shadow of the car which lay, mangled, on its side ten yards up the slope. "Matt, are you there?" the voice repeated. Still too dizzy to walk, he crawled up the bank to the car. Moonlight spangled from the ragged edges of the windshield, blanching the twisted, agonized face of Kudriatov, murdered by his own murder weapon. He inched forward until he located Standish, who was pinned between the front fender and the tree that had helped to arrest the plunging car.

"Matt, my dear boy," he gasped. "Give me your hand." Craig stretched out a hand and Standish closed his big fist around it. "Can you wipe my face?" He ran the sleeve of his jacket over Standish's face, cleaning off the blood and grime.

"You have to hang on until Lora gets help," he said.

"Don't let her go. . . . You'll lose her. . . . They'll find us." The hand tightened on his. "It's no good anyway. . . . I'm kaput . . . kaput. . . . Just stay with me." The strangled whisper no longer sounded like Standish. Nor the words. He had finished playing his game with life. Curious, Craig thought, how closely they had collaborated over all those years and how little real communion or understanding they had had. He saw that Standish could move only his right arm; the rest of his body and his legs lay wedged and crushed between the crumpled fender and the tree.

"You know Kudriatov is dead?" he said.

"Too late, son. Ten years too late for me."

Ten years! They had blackmailed him all that time. A year before that lunch in St. James's. Standish had used him as his pawn since then, had fixed the Moscow trip to set him up for Kudriatov. No doubt they had, between them, arranged his first meeting with Lora, the other pawn.

Standish was speaking again. "Matt, my boy . . . say you forgive me."

"What's to forgive between abject men?"

"Abject men, eh. . . . My mistake, thinking you were one of us . . . too honest . . . always said that face of yours would get us into trouble." He coughed for several minutes, then tugged on Craig's hand to signal that he had something to say. Craig bent his head to catch the croaking voice. "You'll square things away? . . . We like everything tidy . . . in the service." He appeared to drowse for several minutes, then mumbled, "She mustn't know. . . . Marjory must never know. . . ."

"I'll fix everything," Craig said. He wondered if Standish could hear him now. The hand had slackened.

The moon rode high. Through the trees, the Vltava shone like a sheet of foil; the fields and woods beyond seemed petrified in the yellow light. Down the hill, Lora was searching the bushes with a flashlight. He was glad that she had left him alone with Standish. What was the bond between them? Two men of confused and conflicting loyalties, of disparate character. He did not know.

Standish's hand now lay flaccid in his. Once or twice the head stirred and the body jerked. Finally the head lolled, the fingers tensed, then went limp in his hand.

Vernon Alveston Standish, the traitor who had betrayed himself and his country, who had betrayed and twice tried to kill him, was dead. And Craig would never understand why, at that moment, he could not prevent himself from weeping.

He sat there, silent, until Lora ran up the hill. She had discovered what she had been seeking and held up the twin cassettes of microfilm which had rolled out of the Skoda with him. She pried his hand loose from the dead fingers that he still gripped and helped him to his feet. "Can you walk, *dushka*?" she asked.

"Just about," he muttered. He pointed to Standish and Kudriatov. "How do we cover this up?"

Lora wiped the two microfilm tubes with her handkerchief and slipped them into Standish's inside pocket, pulling out the envelope which Craig recognized as the one containing Kudriatov's forged bank account. "We can use this money," she said practically. She searched Standish's other pockets, emerging with the Russian's passport and KGB papers. That explained Kudriatov's quaint behavior. Standish had held him hostage in the villa for the last two days. Lora slipped the documents into Kudriatov's pocket with her own Russian passport and KGB pass, her driver's license and other papers. Her own list of Russian agents she placed in Standish's pocket. "There is only the car," she said. "They will trace that."

"No, that's all right. It belongs to the British Embassy."

They had no need to spell out each other's reasoning. Someone would spot the skid marks, the car and the bodies, and report the accident to the Czech police. They would give one look, inform their secret police, who would call in the KGB. Lora's papers would confirm her reported death. The list of KGB agents in Standish's pocket would convince the Russians that Colonel Sergei Antonovich Kudriatov had sold out to the SIS and was defecting to the West. The Cassius files would prove that, as part of the pact, he had handed his blackmail material over to the victim. They would remove the KGB chief, strip Standish clean before informing the British Embassy that one of their citizens had died in a car crash.

Lora and Craig knew that they could rely on the British and Russian secret services to keep their own secrets. The Cassius file was closed. So were the cases of Matthew Templeton Craig and Lora Ekaterina Trusova.

Lora put the gas pistol in her pocket; she scoured the ground and the car to make sure they had left no clues for the police.

"I was thinking," she said.

"You're doing brilliantly."

"There is an old foot trail south of Vyšší Brod where we can cross the frontier into Austria."

"Thirty miles? A bit far the way my legs feel."

"But it is only two kilometers along the Vltava to České Budějovice. If I walk there and steal a car and return for you . . ."

"We stay together, *dushka*," Craig cut in.

"But . . ."

"No buts. Do you think I've waited four years and traveled all this way to risk losing a sad-faced, old-fashioned girl with KGB training who has saved my life twice in as many days and dopes my champagne with sodium-what's-its-name?''

Lora laughed. She slung Matt's arm around her shoulder to support him and they began to pick their way, gently, down to the river.